ROUNDABOUT

Also by Rhiannon Lassiter

Waking Dream

ROUNDABOUT

Rhiannon
Lassiter

YOUNG PICADOR

First published 2006 by Young Picador
an imprint of Pan Macmillan Limited
20 New Wharf Road, London N1 9RR
Basingstoke and Oxford
www.panmacmillan.com

Associated companies throughout the world

ISBN-13: 978-0-333-99736-9
ISBN-10: 0-333-99736-0

1 3 5 7 9 8 6 4 2

A CIP catalogue record for this book is available from
the British Library.

Typeset by Intype Libra Ltd
Printed and bound in Great Britain by
Mackays of Chatham plc, Kent

Dedicated to Pat White with many thanks for all her unfailing support. Also to Deirdre Ruane, Elizabeth Lovegrove and Jo Smith, without whom this novel could never have been completed.

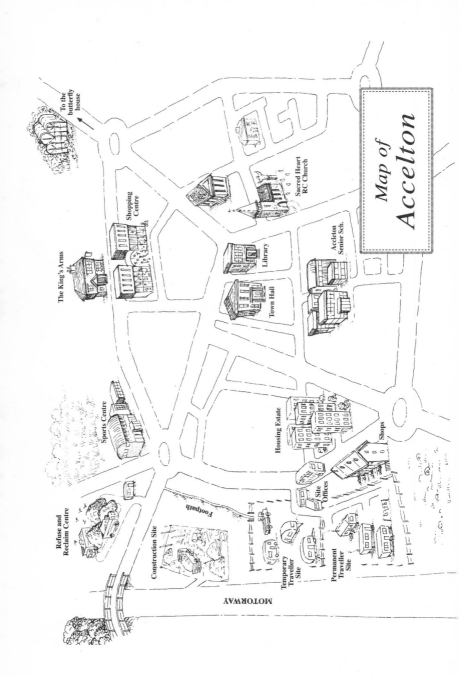

Map of
Accelton

To the
butterfly
house

The King's Arms

Shopping
Centre

Sports Centre

Refuse and
Reclaim Centre

Footpath

Construction Site

MOTORWAY

Temporary
Traveller
Site

Permanent
Traveller
Site

Site
Offices

Shops

Housing Estate

Town Hall

Library

Sacred Heart
RC Church

Accelton
Senior Sch.

CONTENTS

PRELUDE

Accleton is one of the many towns that the grey ribbon of the M1 snakes its way past, even as its tendrils reach out to tangle the surrounding countryside in a spiderweb of junctions, flyovers and roundabouts.

In January the weather is bleak and the sky a dirty white from horizon to horizon. The driver of a haulage truck swears when a flashy red Lexus that has zoomed past in the fast lane suddenly signals left and shifts into the lane ahead of him. He has to brake to slow down and as he does so two black saloons, a BMW and a Merc, pass him and signal left as well.

Ahead, the Lexus, still indicating left, pulls over on to the hard shoulder. The two black cars follow it and the trucker shifts gear again, sparing a curious glance for the group of cars now parked by the verge before shifting his attention back to the radio.

At the side of the road several men in suits have left their cars and are walking single file up a narrow track that leads though the underbrush. The owner of the sports car is the first to reach the top of the track, where it opens out into a rough clearing. He stops. He, alone of the party, is not carrying a briefcase but a brightly coloured rucksack. From it he takes a pair of expensive binoculars and raises them to his eyes.

'I think you'll agree with me that this land is the ideal site for the development,' he says, turning to address his companions. 'It's not green belt. It's not anything – just dead land between the designated clearance zones of the motorway and Accleton ring road.'

'So, we've already discussed the advantages of a direct link to the motorway,' another man chimes in, rubbing his hands together and wishing he'd remembered to bring his gloves. 'We have all the relevant plans, gentlemen. But I thought you should see the site for yourselves.'

'Yes, yes.' A third man takes the binoculars. 'The council can hasten it through at the next meeting. Imagine the jobs it'll bring into the area.'

'Well, there's champagne chilling back at my offices,' the man with the rucksack says. 'If you'd care to adjourn there, gentlemen?'

'You're sure there's no problem with proximity to a built-up area?' another man asks, still shading his eyes as he looks towards town. 'I seem to remember . . .'

'No problem at all,' the second man, still chafing his cold hands, insists. 'The relevant points are all addressed in section three b of the briefing material.'

The wind chases them back down the slope. Hands go simultaneously to pockets and produce key rings and there are clicks and whirrs from the waiting cars as doors unlock.

2

The sports car is the first to pull back on to the motorway and quickly outdistances the others as it accelerates to twenty miles over the speed limit.

Twenty minutes later the driver of the heavy haulage truck swears as for the second time that day a red sports car flashes by in the fast lane and then signals left, cutting him up. His annoyance is fleeting; the sports car swings off at the next exit, signposted Accleton.

ON THE VERGE

The cars on the motorway zipped past in smears of colour. The girl standing on the sloped scrubby verge of the southbound carriageway lifted her head to stare at them as each mosquito whine built to a roar. Standing still, it was impossible to see the people inside the cars, but she knew that they would be able to see her and she imagined their eyes drawn up from the grey ribbon of tarmac to glance at her, before being forced back to the road.

She'd travelled enough herself to know that any driver couldn't help but notice her. The verges were owned by the council or the Highways Agency. The only people supposed to be here came to strim the long grass or plant hundreds of miniature trees, each a regulation distance away from its neighbour. Sometimes a car might park briefly on the hard shoulder and a man get out to piss in the bushes, turning his back to the passing traffic. But really this was wasted land; the only reason it existed was to cushion the motorway and block the sight and sound of it from the town.

Tess laughed when the next passing car changed lanes, moving from the outside to the median. She wondered if the driver thought she was going to step out on to the motorway in some crazy stunt. She wasn't that stupid. Even if you managed to duck the cars all right, the drivers all had mobile phones and police didn't appreciate being called out for a silly game. Instead she started to walk against the flow of traffic, making her way though the tangle of furze that dotted the verge. On the other side of the motorway there were fields behind the light screen of trees, but here the scrubland went back much further before coming up against the borders of Accleton.

There wasn't any place Tess had lived where she hadn't learned the roads and the short cuts between them. She knew the blank spaces on the maps that meant green belt or brownfield sections of land, the dotted lines of footpaths and rights of way, the snaking ladders of the railway lines and the crinkled edges of river courses and estuaries. To anyone else this was a bit of motorway like any other. But Tess had it marked and this stretch of verge, between the 'in case of emergency' telephone box to the south and the grey concrete bridge of the overpass to the north, was her territory. Not all the time, of course. She had other places up and down the country, little bits of wasted land that no one thought about. Not parks or recs, although she hung out in them too, but places that nobody came to at all. She was drawn to them precisely for that reason.

Tess stopped walking for a moment and hunkered down between the bushes, hiding herself from the road and the wind that whipped past with the speeding cars, digging out the baccy packet from the pocket of her jeans. Even here the wind made rolling up difficult and she fumbled with the Rizla for a moment before sticking it down. Cupping her hand around the cigarette in her mouth, she had to spark her disposable lighter three times before it would catch, and then inhale quickly so as not to waste the flame. Standing up again, she took another deep drag on her roll-up and looked down at the cars. Her eyes watered as the wind whipped the smoke from her cigarette into her face and she blinked, looked away – and saw a flash of orange on the roadside.

It was a cone. As Tess wandered over to it she saw that it was the start of a line of cones that straggled along the hard shoulder, tied together with red and white tape. It wasn't much of a line and a couple of the cones had fallen over, but Tess eyed it suspiciously before dropping off the grass and on to the edge of the tarmac to follow it. The motorway curved slightly just before heading under the overpass, so it was a minute before she saw where the cones were leading. A yellow 'men at work' sign stood forlornly by the edge of an unexpected spur of fresh black tarmac that cut through the bushy wasteland, heading back in the direction of town.

Tess broke into a jog as she took the turn-off. Last time she was here, six months ago, there had been nothing, just more bushes and long grass. Another sign stood just round the corner. This one read 'WORKS ACCESS ONLY' in capital letters and Tess ignored it as she jogged past, following the road up to where it spilt suddenly into an open circle of raw earth surrounded by piles of grit and sand. Heavy yellow earth-movers and bulldozers stood parked around the area, looking like kids' toys in a giant sandpit.

Tess stared, coming to a halt at the end of the access road and trying to orient herself. There was only about a mile of verge between the motorway and the town; if it wasn't for the piles of earth she would probably be able to see Accleton. There simply wasn't space to build anything here, not without it intruding on the edge of the town. And Tess knew exactly what was on that edge. What on earth did the council think they were doing, building here of all places? Dropping back into the scrubland, she started to circle round, heading in the direction of Accleton.

The sky clouded over as Tess made her way through the scrub and she glared up at the grey threat of rain. The first pricks of it stung her face and arms with the feeling of pins and needles. She hunched her shoulders defensively, ducking her head so her long dark hair shielded her. It was stupid not to have brought a jacket, but she'd only intended to wander about for a while – having got into Accleton last night, she'd wanted to reacquaint herself with the place.

She came out of the scrub up by the side of the overpass. There was a small edge of pavement next to the verge where Tess stepped over the crash barrier. Her jeans were already sodden at the bottom and the crack in the sole of one of her boots was starting to let in the wet. She walked fast along the roadside, not looking at the cars, but when one of them hooted as it passed her she glanced up to swear viciously at its tail lights as it sped away.

The pavement was more wet than dry now and the roads shone silver with the drizzle of rain. Tess's mood lightened when a shaft of dirty yellow sunlight pierced the clouds ahead for a moment: a spotlight on the junction with the ring road. Tess followed the pavement round to the right before turning aside where a gate appeared suddenly in a gap in the hedge. She let herself through it. Here in the passage between two tall hedges the rain was blocked out and Tess slowed her pace as she wondered for the first time what she was going to say when she got back.

Ahead of her the Traveller site shone wetly through the last of the rain, trailers and caravans damp and gleaming in reflected shafts of sunshine. The washing lines strung between caravans were still empty, but a group of little kids had started up a football game over at the edge of the site and their voices rang out shrilly as they quarrelled over the ball.

Tess thought back to what she'd seen on the side of the motorway. Whatever it was, it meant trouble. Tess and trouble were old acquaintances and she knew how to recognize it when she saw it. The construction site was close enough that other Travellers would have noticed it if it had been there for long, but no one had said anything about it last night. It wasn't normal to come in with bulldozers that fast unless there was some kind of emergency, but if there was an emergency there would have been men at work there today, Sunday or not.

Tess frowned, her dark eyes reflecting the storm clouds

above as she headed across the field to a battered trailer parked beside a brown van. The trailer door was open and Reenie was coming out with a collection of washing tubs.

'It'll be raining again in ten minutes,' Tess said as she came over and Reenie glanced up at the sky before looking at her.

'I know, but I have to get this wash on. You can take it to the launderette to dry later.' Her eyes focused properly on Tess then and her face got a pinched look of annoyance. 'What have you been up to anyway? Your jeans are all over with mud.'

'I went out to the motorway . . .' Tess began but Reenie was already shaking her head.

'Some day you're going to get yourself killed, hanging around the roads like that,' she said, bumping and banging the laundry tubs as she set them out. She shot Tess another pinched look. 'I expect you went out there to smoke, didn't you?'

'No,' Tess said and Reenie's mouth curled.

'Don't lie to me,' she snapped, twisting round to pick up a load of clothes from the doorway. 'You're just like your dad, you are.'

Tess turned away angrily. Another couple of people were out on the site now and she saw a neighbour glance over at the sound of Reenie's voice before returning to her own work.

'Are you listening to me at all, madam?' Reenie's face was red with exasperation and Tess took a step away. 'Don't walk off when I'm talking to you!'

'Why not?' Tess glared at her. 'You only ever listen to

your own voice anyway. I don't care; you can find out yourself if you're not going to listen to me. Probably when they evict you.'

Reenie had been talking over Tess's words, voice rising as she tried to drown her out, but now she came to sudden halt and Tess waited.

'What do you mean, "evict"?' Reenie's eyes narrowed suspiciously and Tess laughed at her sudden change of tone.

'The council are messing with the empty land down by the verge,' she said, 'not far from here.' She could see from the corner of her eye that the neighbour was no longer pretending not to listen and a couple of men had stopped unloading bags from the back of a car and turned to look at her.

'What's that got to do with anything?' Reenie was winding herself back up again but Tess wasn't having any of it.

'There's a big works site been set up,' she said. 'Bulldozers and earth-movers all over. The council's building something.' She waved her arm vaguely towards the hedge at the edge of the site. 'And keeping it secret too. There's hardly any signs or anything. Just bloody big piles of earth.'

Reenie opened her mouth to speak, but noticed their audience just as one of the men by the car made up his mind and came over.

'You saw this?' he asked Tess and she nodded.

'Just now,' she said. 'You can't miss it.'

'So they're building something,' Reenie said, her

washing abandoned as she looked from the man to Tess. 'It doesn't mean anything.'

'Want to bet?' Tess asked and the man nodded.

'Let's go and take a look, shall we?' He turned to look back at his mate and waved him over before fixing Tess with a dark look. 'Swear you're not making it up?'

'Not likely,' Tess snapped at him and he laughed.

'All right then. Don't you follow us, we'll find it ourselves.'

He and his friend set off towards the stile. The woman who'd been listening came closer, looking worried, and Reenie glanced around at the other onlookers with a brief look of embarrassment before turning her attention back to Tess.

'Honestly,' she said, 'you're soaking wet. Look, get inside and change those jeans and I'll make you a cup of tea, all right?'

Tess hesitated and their neighbour said quickly 'I've got a kettle boiling right now. Let me make it.' She looked hopefully at Reenie. 'Then maybe your daughter will tell us some more about it while we wait for the men to get back?'

'Thank you,' Reenie said as Tess turned her back and headed inside. 'I've got all this washing to do for one thing . . .' Her voice trailed off for a moment and Tess's ears pricked up, waiting for what Reenie would have to say next. 'She's not mine though – my brother's child.'

'A bit of a tearaway, sounds like.' The neighbour had dropped her voice but Reenie didn't bother to.

'That's for certain. My lot are boys, and you know where you are with them, don't you? But madam in there's been a right handful ever since she was a tot. I thank my lucky stars I only have her once in a while. It sets my hair on end the things she gets up to.'

Tess struggled with the knots in her laces and kicked her boots off on to the floor. Her right foot was soaked through and she peeled off both her socks before skinning out of her jeans. As she changed clothes she could hear the voices continuing outside. The neighbour had brought out tea and Reenie was using it as an excuse to gossip. Fragments of sentences floated in through the door, which was still ajar.

'. . . her dad's up north somewhere . . . blood's thicker than water . . . had to take her in . . .'

'. . . nowhere else she could . . .?'

'. . . not the only one . . . sends her to whoever'll have her . . . no end of trouble . . . just like her dad . . .'

'I can hear you out there!' Tess shouted suddenly through the walls. 'Telling my business . . .'

She pulled her boots back on and came out of the trailer. Reenie looked annoyed, but the neighbour was embarrassed and stood up to bring Tess her cup of tea.

'Get that down you, love,' she said uncomfortably. 'You'll feel better then.'

'Fetch out those wet things so I can wash them as well,' Reenie added in a conciliatory tone of voice. 'No sense in leaving them for later.'

○

It took the men over an hour to get back and by then the news had spread across the Traveller site, from the temporary pitches on Tess's side to the permanent ones at the far end.

People gathered around Reenie's trailer, casting dark looks at the prefab huts that formed the site supervisor's office.

'It's the council,' one woman said bitterly. 'They never wanted us to get this site in the first place. Didn't matter that we'd been using it for hundreds of years . . .'

'Yeah, now they've come building their new road or whatever it is right up against the back of our site,' a man agreed. 'If they can't get us out legally, they'll force us out with traffic fumes and road noise.'

'Don't go jumping to conclusions,' someone else warned. 'We don't know that this building work has anything to do with us.' But around the circle people snorted. Tess could feel trouble brewing as thick as the cups of strong tea being passed around.

People were still discussing the situation when Reenie's husband came back from the pub and looked askance at the signs that dinner would be late. Hurriedly bundling up the bags of wet washing, Reenie shoved them at Tess and started clanking and crashing pans on the stove.

Hefting the bulky bags awkwardly, Tess made her way across the Traveller site. The short fence that ran down the middle divided the temporary side from the permanent pitches, but on both sides there were clusters of people with worried expressions.

The Travellers had long fought the council over the right to a site here. Tess had seen the saga progressing year upon year as she came back to Accleton with Reenie or other relations. A lot of people had got disillusioned and given up, but there were always some willing to fight, to struggle with the masses of paperwork needed to prove that gypsies and Travellers had been using the land to the west of town for as long as anyone could remember. Eventually they'd won half of what they'd been trying for. Half the site was now officially recognized as permanent, and the Travellers who lived there could keep their pitches year upon year. The second half, Tess's half, was different. You couldn't use a pitch here for more than six months and there were stricter rules about how and where you parked. And the Travellers were painfully aware that it might not be theirs forever – in the future, they might have to fight for it all over again. Both sides were administered by a supervisor appointed by the council: a woman whom everyone united in disliking.

It was the same in lots of places. Travellers didn't get much provision anyway and most councils seemed, to Tess, to want to make their lives harder still. Tess's dad said it was racism, pure and simple, and that people had been against gypsies and Travellers so long now that they didn't even notice it any more and there wasn't a cat's chance in hell things would ever change. But to him Travelling wasn't something you chose, it was something you were born to. Even some of the Travellers weren't really gypsy enough for him. When he'd got worked up enough, he would tell Tess about her history. She had Romany blood in her, he said, even if it came from way back. Romany and Tinker and Irish all together, her dad claimed.

'You're descended from the freest people in the world, darlin', and don't you forget that. You don't have to live by anyone's rules.'

She hadn't forgotten. Maybe Reenie didn't get it, but all those rules were made to be broken: the no-smoking signs, no-trespassing warnings, no ball games on the grass, no running in the corridors, no over-elevens on the swings. They were rules made by narrow minds to keep you down. So, like her dad, Tess did what she wanted. Tess was free.

But as she reached the main entrance, where the site joined the Accleton ring road, Tess looked back and saw the Traveller site from the outside. It was a miscellaneous assortment of caravans, trailers and cars, each with their own arrangements of washing lines, lean-tos and collections of random stuff that people used or traded or had simply picked up. Kids and dogs played between the trailers and the only way in or out for the vehicles was the entrance; chain-link fencing blocked off all the other sides.

Despite their partial victory over the council, the Traveller site still wasn't considered part of the town, Tess admitted to herself. Out on the edge, no one saw it and no one wanted to. Other people only came here on their way past to somewhere else. Whatever the council were building out by the motorway, they had put it there thinking the Travellers' land nearby wasn't important.

But, Tess remembered, there was something else her dad had always told her. They may be exiles in their own country, pushed to the edge, backs against the wall. But that was why they had to stand their ground. Or lose it. A chill went through her and Tess imagined the bulldozers moving up the hill, tearing through the scrubland, men laying concrete as they went. This was her space and she wasn't going to let anyone take it from her.

Back at the site Reenie and the others had looked scared and resentful, but they'd still tried to tell each other it was probably nothing to worry about. Tess wanted them to get angry, as angry as she was, so that they'd fight if the bulldozers came. Her dad would have done, Tess was sure; he'd have rallied the others together, got them to build barricades or something. But most likely the rest of the Travellers would just let it happen, swearing a bit the way they did when the police moved them on but giving in all the same, as if there wasn't anything they could do about it.

'We have to fight,' Tess said out loud, clenching her fists as she looked at the grey blockish buildings of Accleton and the dismal little parade of shops that was all there was on this side of town. 'We've got rights, same as anyone else. We've just got to stand up for them.'

2

B-ROAD

The heavy grey roar of the motorway dulled as the trailer pulled away into the gentler stream of traffic on the A-road. The stops and starts of waiting for lights or the right lane rocked Jo awake. Rose-yellow light filtered through the curtains and through her eyelids. Opening her eyes properly, she shifted up on the trailer couch, lifting the edge of the voile curtain to peer out. Cars rushed by in the faster lane. A small boy twisted halfway around in his seat belt to watch Jo through the back window of his parents' Citroën as it sped away. Jo met his round blue eyes, trying to make her expression blank with disinterest as the boy stuck out his tongue.

When she was younger she'd used to wave at kids through the windows. It was a game Tess had invented, getting people to wave back at them and keeping score. Kids were one point because they looked out the most. Old people were two. Three points for anyone else and five if they blew you a kiss. But you lost points if, instead of waving, the person made a rude gesture. Still muzzy from sleep, Jo tried to remember what the minuses were.

Her mouth tasted dry and musty and she got up to get some water just as the trailer changed lanes. The shift threw her off balance and she half fell back on to the couch, cracking her head sharply against the edge of the overhanging cupboards. Her eyes watered from the sudden pain. Stupid. Technically she shouldn't even be back here while the trailer was on the move and she'd lived in one long enough to know to watch out for sudden changes in the road.

She licked the fingers of her right hand and felt the back of her head, wincing as she found the tender place. Her fingers came away pinkish with blood. It was almost certainly not serious; it was simply that head injuries bled a lot. Just a couple of weeks ago Sandy Donovan had fallen out of a chestnut tree, cracking his head on one of the branches as he came down. Blood had poured from his forehead and down his neck but half an hour later he was back up the tree, wearing a huge yellow plaster and a macho grin.

All the Donovan kids were wild, shaking off cuts and scrapes as if they were nothing. Jo had hung out with them since last autumn, racing their bikes up and down the steep hills of the Devon village they'd been staying in and camping out at night in the woods. The Donovans had invited her family to join them when they went north for the summer to a place they knew, but Jo's parents had said no.

'They're fine people and the place sounds like a good

one, but Jo's getting a bit old to be hanging around with that pack of boys,' her mum had said when her parents discussed the idea late at night. 'Her marks are down again this term and that school's written twice about her attendance.'

'Those boys might be wild, but they're not bad,' her dad said soothingly. 'So what if she bunks off school a bit? High spirits is all it is.'

'I'm not denying it,' her mum said, and Jo had crossed her fingers in the dark of the caravan, holding still so they wouldn't realize she was eavesdropping, 'but there's a time and a place for fun, and Jo's too eager to forget her responsibilities and go running off at a word from one of those boys. In case you hadn't noticed, she's growing up now . . .'

At that Jo had uncrossed her fingers and clenched her hands into fists. It wasn't her fault she was getting older. Her mum wouldn't even have noticed if she hadn't got so tall. Last year she had been one of the shortest in any school class she went to. This year she towered over everyone, even the boys. Her chest had hurt when Jock Donovan kicked a football straight at her too and it had gone on hurting even after the bruise had gone.

Growing up sucked if you were a girl. When her brother Dan had turned fourteen, her parents had bought a second van for him to sleep in. But for Jo growing up meant her parents watching her sideways when Jock Donovan hugged her goodbye.

'Cheer up,' her dad had said when the Donovans left, waving and pulling faces through the back of their trailer.

'It's not as if you won't know anyone in Accleton. There'll be plenty of Traveller kids about your age.'

'Yeah, dumb girls,' Jo had muttered, earning herself a sharp look from her mum. But all she'd meant was that she wanted mates to have a laugh with, ones who wouldn't fuss about getting their clothes dirty.

Once the decision had been made on where to spend the summer, her mum had written or phoned family and friends to find out who'd be in Accleton this year. By the time she'd got the replies she was looking worried again. It had been a battle to get a pitch at all and even then it was only on the 'temporary' side of the site, a short-stay only. More and more Travellers were turning to council houses now that site provision was so hard to find, while others camped illegally in fields and lay-bys, risking the anger of farmers until the police moved them on.

The Travellers in Accleton were a mixed bunch. Some were conformists, who'd given up their trailers and joined the settled community living in houses. A few lucky ones had permanent pitches and others were stubborn enough to fight through the forms and regulations to get a place on the temporary site. Jo knew many of them from her previous stays at the town and from sites around the country, but none of them was on her list of top people to spend the summer with.

Tess Lovett was the only one of the kids with any spirit, but because of that it was impossible to be sure if she'd be there. She was a couple of years older than Jo and got passed around from relation to relation like a badly addressed parcel. Jo liked her all right when they were out in the country – Tess could climb and swim as well as any boy and she never shirked her turn. But in town she was different, flirting with boys and shouting at girls, getting up in people's faces and pissing them off. Tess came up with plans that sounded fun until you were trapped ten miles from anywhere after dark and had to beg for change for the fare home. She seemed to think the day had been a bust if it didn't end with a screaming knockdown row. People said Tess was 'trouble with a capital T'.

Tess didn't make friends easily, although stacks of people knew her by sight or reputation. But despite her bad behaviour she'd managed to make and keep one best friend, of whom she was jealously possessive. Magda Lakely was certain to be in Accleton – the Lakely family had spent the past three summers there.

Magda was fifteen and the oldest girl of the Lakely children. Between church and school and looking after all her little brothers and sisters she never seemed to have much time to herself. But what free time she did have she spent with Tess, to whom she was unfailingly loyal. Magda's soft pleading had often stopped Tess getting into serious trouble when she'd done something wrong. Everyone liked beautiful Magda; they couldn't help it. She was always so sweet and good, doing what she was told, never forgetting anything and always back home by six. Jo didn't understand how Magda and Tess could be so tight when they were so different, but whenever she was around them she felt like a third wheel.

Still, there wasn't really anyone else Jo would even consider hanging out with. The local kids at school weren't friendly with the Travellers and Jo had never had much use for school anyway. She groaned now when she remembered her mum's comments about her marks. The last time they'd been in Accleton she'd bunked off so much her parents had made her walk to and from school every day with Gwen Hughes and Carly Dixon.

Gwen wasn't a Traveller, not really, although she was related to some of the people on the site. Her mum had Travelled for a while, but she'd left Gwen's dad and settled in Accleton years ago. They lived in a flat and Gwen's mum worked two jobs. Gwen worked as well. She'd had summer and after-school jobs even when she was little, as well as getting straight As at school. Jo's mum was always holding her up as an example. Unfortunately she was also an example of a bossy swot without any real friends. And Gwen would be doing GCSEs this term. She wasn't someone to hang out with. Not unless homework was your idea of fun.

Carly wasn't any better. She was Gwen's younger cousin and her parents had settled in Accleton five years back. When Jo was young she'd liked going to Carly's house and hanging out. But Carly was a bit of a baby, whining if she didn't get her own way. Jo had accidentally on purpose ignored her the last time she visited the town, except when her mum had forced them to spend time together. Even so, Carly had written her letters all over the winter. She had written pages and pages about school and how she'd made friends with some town girls who played tennis, but Jo wasn't sure whether to believe her. Carly told a lot of lies. Even if it was true, Jo sneered at the idea of poncing around in tennis whites with a bunch of girly townies.

Flopping back on to the couch, a bit more carefully this time, Jo sighed. She missed Devon. She and Jock Donovan had built a den in the woods and not told any of the others about it. On wet days they'd sat there, listening to the rain drumming against the tin roof, not talking. Sometimes Jock had looked at her as if he might be going to say something important and then just shaken his head or offered her a stick of gum. But Jo hadn't minded. Sitting there in the rain, she'd felt relaxed and excited at once, the complete opposite of how she felt now. She was tense and bored, waiting for them to finally arrive, knowing she wouldn't care when they did get there.

○

The clock over the door read half three when the trailer finally pulled off at the turn-off for Accleton and into the Shigwell Gap rest stop. Getting up awkwardly from her seat on the couch, Jo shook the cramps out of her neck and raked her thick brown hair back before searching her pockets for a rubber band. Her hair felt greasy and she grimaced as she knotted it back into a messy ponytail and shoved her feet into her boots. She unlocked the door of the trailer and dropped out on to the ground.

Dan was leaning against the bonnet of the car, smoking a cigarette. Her parents were standing by another couple of trailers and Jo recognized them as belonging to the Lakelys.

'Have you seen Magda?' she asked, joining Dan at the front of the car.

'She's taking the kids to the bog,' he told her and added, 'Mum says you're going to ride in with them lot and stop off at the shop. Do you know what to get?'

'There's a list,' Jo said vaguely. 'I'll get it. Did Mum give you any cash?'

'I've got some,' he told her. 'Can you get baccy as well?'

'Mum won't like it.' Jo shook her head. 'And they won't sell it to me anyway.'

'Get someone else to buy it then,' Dan said, passing over three crumpled notes. 'Here's sixty to spend on what Mum wants, and I want to see the rest back.'

'Yeah, yeah, all right.' Jo rolled her eyes as she took the money and went back into the trailer to get a bag and the list. She stopped to look at herself in a little wall mirror. Licking her fingers, she rubbed the sleep grit from her brown eyes and pulled a face at her reflection. There was a knock at the door and she looked over her shoulder to see Magda shading her eyes to peer inside.

Magda's face was damp and she was wearing a daisy chain in her wet hair. Even after hours of travelling, Jo thought, she still looked like a fairy princess crowned with flowers.

'Hey, Jojo,' Magda said. 'Mam says you're coming in with us to the shop.'

'Looks like it,' Jo agreed. 'You all right?'

'So-so.' Magda rocked her hand and Jo saw she was wearing daisy-chain bracelets as well, the flowers damp with water and hardly wilted at all. 'But I've been watching the kids all day.'

The youngest Lakelys had swarmed over a picnic bench on the small patch of grass. Their T-shirts and heads were soaked with water and Jo grinned.

'What did you do, stick their heads under the pump?' she asked.

'They got themselves soaked,' Magda protested. 'They were all splashing each other in the toilets.' She nodded to the concrete conveniences over at the side of the lay-by and added, 'Do you need to go?'

'Yeah,' Jo decided and ran a few steps before turning and walking backwards to call out, 'I was playing Tess's game while we were on the road earlier. I'm minus one point.'

'That little kid.' Magda didn't look surprised. 'We saw him too . . . our lot were provoking him. But I'm plus five as well.' She hid a smile with her hands. 'A lad in a BMW – lucky for me, Da didn't see.'

Jo laughed as she turned and jogged up to the toilets. Inside, the grey-tiled floor was splashed with water and her mum was standing in one of the few dry spots, checking her reflection in the mirror.

'There you are, love,' she said. 'Did Dan tell you I want you to go along with the Lakelys to the shop?'

'He gave me cash.' Jo nodded. 'And I've got the list.'

While Jo was in a stall she heard someone else come in and recognized Magda's mother's voice.

'Magda said the kids had left the place in a state, splashing water around,' she said. 'Sorry about that, Sue.'

'If you ask me, it could use it,' Jo's mum replied. 'No one seems to bother with cleaning these lay-bys.'

'All the same, it doesn't look good to let the kids mess about,' Pam Lakely went on. 'I'm sure no one wants to stand in a puddle when they pay a visit.'

'If we leave the door open it'll dry up in no time,' Jo's mum was saying as Jo came out of the stall.

'Hello, Mrs Lakely,' Jo said, going to wash her hands at the sink.

'How are you, love?' Magda's mother smiled at her. 'All set for school?'

'It's still the Easter holidays!' Jo said, grinning back. 'Give us some freedom, will you?'

'Jo, cheek,' her mother frowned warningly, but Mrs Lakely laughed.

○

Magda's da was driving the Lakelys' big trailer, and one of her grown-up brothers was driving a car hitched to the small one. Mrs Lakely went to the battered Volvo she'd been driving and, as Magda joined them, the younger kids ran up behind her to ask if they could come too.

'I want to come along of you,' Marianna, the six-year-old, complained, trying to get in the back of the car and Magda bent down to her, her blue-grey eyes gentle.

'No, you won't, Mariannanna,' she said. 'But be sweet and I'll bring you back something sweeter.' Marianna pouted but Magda turned her gently around, saying, 'You haven't said hello to Jo yet. Show her your bracelets.'

Marianna held up plump arms wrapped round with

daisy chains and Jo smiled. All the kids were garlanded with flowers and she glanced at Magda. 'What did you do, pull up half a meadow?' she asked.

'We had to stop over at a pub,' Magda told her as they got into the car. 'Under-sixteens allowed in the garden only. I told them to pick daisies and we threaded them on the way here.'

'And I don't know what they'll look like when they get to the site,' Mrs Lakely said, getting into the driver's seat. 'You know what that site-manager woman will say.'

'I can't see how it would matter,' Magda said vaguely, winding down the window as Mrs Lakely switched on the ignition.

The car pulled out of the rest stop and back on to the B-road, heading towards Accleton. They reached the turn-off for the ring road much faster than the trailers would have and coming round the ring road Accleton itself appeared on the right, the town shaping itself into familiar space. It always happened. Sites blurred in your memory, only a few snapshot images staying clear, but when you came back to them the rest of the picture filled in. The Traveller site was on the wrong side of the ring road, just beyond the western edge of the town, near the council estate, a garage and a row of shops.

Mrs Lakely pulled off at the shops and stopped the car.

'OK, girls, you take the supermarket. You know what to get,' she said. 'Meet me here again when you're done.'

'Thanks for the lift,' Jo said as she climbed out. Mrs Lakely walked off towards the garage shop and Jo and Magda headed into the mini-supermarket together. Inside it was cool among the frozen cabinets and Magda shivered a bit in her thin cotton shirt. Jo walked up and down the shelves, consulting her list and ticking things off. Magda was much faster, seeming to know where to find everything she wanted by memory. Jo wasn't even halfway done when she heard Magda over by the checkout, chatting to the boy at the till.

Jo watched them as she searched the shelves for the last of the things she needed. Magda was smiling as she bagged groceries quickly, her eyes cast down and her long blonde hair swinging over her face. Her replies to the boy's questions were almost inaudible.

'I know you, don't I, from school?' the boy was saying. 'Is your name Marie?'

Magda shook her head, glancing up for a moment through her lashes, then smiling and turning her head away.

'Come on, tell me your name,' the boy persisted.

'Not if you don't know it already,' she said softly.

Jo moved along to the next aisle and by the time she reached the checkout Magda had made her escape. The boy at the till met her eyes over her basket of groceries and asked, 'Was that your friend?'

'No.' Jo shook her head. She recognized the boy from school, although she couldn't remember his name.

'You're gypsies, aren't you?' he went on, beginning to pass her groceries through the bar-code reader. 'Your lot go to our school.'

Jo hesitated and a voice came from over her shoulder.

'It's *Travellers* to you, and it's none of yours where she goes to school, Mr Supermarket Man.'

Jo blushed and grinned at the same time, turning to see Tess standing in the shop entrance with a hand on her hip. Coming across to the till, she hitched herself up to sit on the end of the checkout, challenging the boy with her dark blue eyes.

'What is this, the Spanish Inquisition?' she asked. 'Do you give every girl who comes in here the third degree?'

'And who are you then?' The boy finished with Jo's stuff and rang out a receipt, without taking his eyes off Tess. 'I haven't seen you around here before.'

'That's because I've got more sense than to be associating myself with the common masses,' Tess said grandly. 'Pay the man, Jo.'

Jo grinned despite herself, handing over a couple of notes, and the checkout boy raised his eyebrows at her as he made change.

'Is she your sister?' he asked and Jo shrugged.

'Like she said,' she replied, jerking a shoulder at Tess, 'none of your business if she is.'

'That's told you, Mr Supermarket Man,' Tess agreed, jumping down and linking her arm with Jo's companionably, proclaiming as they walked out through the automatic doors, 'Open sesame!'

Magda was waiting outside by the car and as Jo went to stack her bags in the boot Tess ran over and wrapped her arms around her friend affectionately.

'How's my Mags then?' she asked.

'Just grand, Tessie Tess,' Magda said, hugging her in return.

'When did you get here, Tess?' Jo asked, joining them.

'Oh, not long ago,' Tess said, releasing Magda and taking Jo's hands before stepping back to look at her. 'How's the lovely Joanne then? Starting early, are you?'

'What?' Jo looked away and Tess tilted her head deliberately to look at the supermarket. 'He wanted to know *Magda's* name,' Jo said quickly and Magda widened her eyes.

'You didn't tell him, did you, Jojo?' she said and Jo frowned.

'Of course I didn't. But he is at school here, you know. His name's Darren or Ian or something.'

'I know.' Magda looked at Tess. 'What do you think?' she asked, quirking her lips into a sudden smile.

'A three. Maybe a four,' Tess said dismissively. 'But we'll need a new scoring system for you, Magsie, the way the boys swarm in your direction.'

Magda laughed and blushed, lifting up her hands to shield her face protestingly.

Jo looked back at the supermarket window, where she could see the boy still watching them from behind the cigarette counter. That reminded her of something.

'Shit,' she said under her breath. 'Dan gave me cash to get rolling baccy. Though I told him they wouldn't sell it to me.'

'I'll get it,' Tess said instantly. 'Give us the money.'

Jo pulled out the rest of the notes from her pocket and Tess tweaked a twenty from her grasp.

'Back in five.'

'She's such a flirt,' Jo remarked as Tess walked off. Magda looked at her in surprise.

'Do you really think so?' she asked uncertainly and Jo looked away. Magda always defended Tess, even when it was completely ridiculous.

Mrs Lakely came out of the hardware shop while they were standing there, her canvas bags bulging with a new set of plastic bowls. Jo quickly opened the boot of the car for her.

'Thank you, love,' Mrs Lakely said as she loaded the bags inside.

'Tess is in the supermarket,' Jo told her and Magda came out of her daze suddenly.

'Is it all right for us to walk back with her, Mam? Instead of going in the car. I'll be back in time to help with tea.'

Mrs Lakely's expression softened into a smile. 'All right,' she said. 'But you girls stay together and don't speak to anyone you don't know.'

'Yes, Mam.' Magda rolled her eyes and Mrs Lakely petted her hair lightly.

'You can go too, love,' she said, turning to Jo. 'I'll give your shopping to Sue.'

'Thanks,' Jo said and stepped away from the car to join Magda at the kerb, watching as Mrs Lakely reversed out of the small forecourt and rejoined the stream of traffic heading into town.

Behind her she heard the sound of the supermarket

doors opening and bouncing footsteps coming out. She turned to see Tess swinging a carrier bag.

'Got your baccy, Joanne,' she said, tossing a packet at Jo before turning to Magda. 'And I've told him you'll go to a party, Mags.'

'Tess!' Magda started laughing and she shook her head, hiding behind her hair. 'You didn't . . . you know Da will never let me.'

'Never fear, Tess will find a way,' Tess told her. She looked back at Jo and said airily, 'Tell Dan I got us some stuff with the rest of his cash, right? I'll pay him back later.'

Jo stared at her and Tess grinned, swinging her bag again before linking her arm through Magda's. 'Where shall we go then, Magsie, on this fine day?' she asked.

'We could go past the sports centre,' Magda suggested, 'but I have to be back for tea.'

'No reason not to watch the boys until then,' Tess agreed, shooting a glance at Magda. Then she turned and looked over her shoulder at Jo. Hitching her bag up to her elbow, she extended a thin brown arm, her blue eyes meeting Jo's thoughtfully. 'Come along with us, Joanne. There's room for three.'

'Just barely,' Jo said, but she let Tess take her arm and fell into step on her right. The pavement wasn't really wide enough and she walked almost in the road, placing her boots one in front of the other along the kerb like a tightrope walker.

There wasn't space for three in other ways too. Tess's arm might be linked through Jo's, but her head was turned away, already teasing Magda again about the checkout boy's party.

'You're so bad, Tessie' Magda giggled.

'And you're too good,' Tess retorted.

Jo shook her head and slipped her arm out of Tess's. 'I'll walk by myself,' she said as the other two turned to look at her. Magda frowned and Tess narrowed her eyes, but Jo was already turning her back on them, swinging her arms and increasing the pace to a jog. They'd think she was sulking, but she didn't care. She didn't want to go and watch boys anyway. She'd go into the woods and look for a place to build a den: somewhere to sit and listen to the rain on her own.

3

THROUGH THE ROSE WINDOW

Sacred Heart Roman Catholic Church in Accleton was old and grand, with a floor of patterned tiles and columns of different-coloured stone stretching up to a high vaulted ceiling. But the scuffed wooden benches in the lady chapel and the rows of battered chairs in the nave were old and familiar and the hassocks that littered the floor between the seats smelt of old people, hymn books and floor polish.

Inside, the sounds and smells of the town were muted by the thick stone and muffled by incense and smoke. The little rows of votive candles, paintings of the saints and statues of the Blessed Virgin belonged to a different world from the one outside. People spoke softly, not whispering but murmuring, so that the sound dropped away into the depths of the church and settled like dust. Old people came and went from the seats and altar rail, lowering themselves painfully, one knee at a time, to pray. Black-robed priests would come in and out of the vestry or the choir stalls or sometimes from one of the curtained confession boxes. Occasionally a group of nuns would be sitting praying in silence or lighting intercession candles. Young and old, their faces were all the same under their white wings.

When she'd been younger Magda had told everyone that when she grew up she wanted to be a nun. She'd worn a white tea towel folded over her hair and carried her rosary around the trailer, passing the beads through her fingers as she repeated Hail Marys. She'd imagined herself in church, hands folded into her sleeves, face calm and eyes humbly on the ground, sitting in the side pews with the Sisters and not speaking to any of the young men from the congregation who would watch her admiringly.

'Nuns aren't allowed to have long hair,' her mam had said, whisking the tea towel off her head. 'Or to wear perfume or jewellery, and they have to wash with carbolic soap, which smells like turps.'

'And why shouldn't a God-fearing Irish girl want to be a Bride of Christ?' her da would say sometimes.

Her mam always shook her head. 'It's no life I would want for a daughter of mine.'

Her mam's words had troubled Magda. Was it really not allowed for a nun to be beautiful? It didn't seem fair to have to shave off your hair, if you covered it up anyway. Perhaps they would let you keep it if you promised not to look at it in mirrors, or to brush it only at night.

When she was eleven Magda had gone to a Catholic girls' school in the north for a while. All the teachers were nuns or priests. She'd only been going to the school for a couple of terms when her mam had convinced her da that work would be better down south and they'd moved on. Mam had given her a pair of gold earrings as a consolation, but Magda hadn't minded leaving. In her imagination a school run by nuns had been quiet and serious. Seeing the nuns gossip together had taught her that the reality was different.

But she still liked to spend time on her own in church. On Sundays she had to look after the little ones. But on weekday afternoons only the old people, the priests and the nuns were about and Magda could walk slowly up and down the side aisles of the churches, looking at the painted lives of the saints and the inscriptions on the tombs. Besides, going to church was something allowed. Her da liked the idea of her going there much more than going shopping in the town centre or to the sports complex or out with Tess. Her mam still worried that she wanted to be a nun, but she wouldn't stop Magda going.

When Magda was younger the others had teased her about being holy. Now they didn't even seem to notice it. They expected her to go to church, the same way Gwen was always studying and Jo always wanted to be outside. Only Tess ever still asked her why she went, and Magda had tried to explain.

'Because it's quiet. And beautiful.' She wondered if Tess was expecting her to say something about God. 'You just have to think and pray.'

The truth was that Magda didn't really pray any more at all. Now when she wandered around churches she day-dreamed instead: wondering about the people named in the inscriptions and counting the years they'd lived and seeing who'd survived them; looking at the icons and the stained-glass saints and deciding which had the best faces. She had a favourite part of every church she'd ever visited and could remember them all: a carved flower on the side of a wooden pew, a stone crusader on his tomb with a little stone dog at his feet, the memorial stone of a twelve-year-old boy dedicated by his sister, who'd lived to be ninety-one.

She'd only been back in Accleton for a couple of days when she'd slipped off to Sacred Heart. As always, she saved her favourite thing in the building for last. Now she came to the back of the church and, turning away from the altar, lifted her head and looked up.

Light streamed through the rose window in red, yellow, purple, blue and green. The great round window had the shape of a rose drawn out in curves of leaded glass, like a colouring book. In all the other stained-glass windows the black lines were filled with solid blocks of coloured glass, but the rose window was webbed with a crazy tangle of thinner lines in which different tiny pieces of coloured glass shimmered like dragonfly wings. From a distance the full-blown rose glowed a vivid red, but closer to it you could see that the red contained flecks of almost every other possible colour, even the ones you'd never think to use for a rose. The colours shone in patches on the patterned floor to make a mad swirl of shades like an oil slick or a peacock's tail.

Magda was wearing a summer dress of blue and white gingham. Standing under the stained glass, it was splashed with light, the different colours trembling and shifting like silk. Her arms were tattooed with bright patches and her hair dyed in a riot of streaks and shades, moving and changing no matter how still she stood.

A shuffle from the seats behind her brought her back to life and Magda walked through the pool of colours and into the shadows at the edge of the church. Dipping her fingers in the Holy Water stoup, she crossed herself as she came out of the main door and into the street outside.

It was a grey day. Pale, watery sunshine leaked through the clouds, but the air was cold enough to raise the hairs on her arms. Magda's route was along the main road and back to the Traveller site on the outskirts. Just a few streets away from the Sacred Heart lay the town centre, but her da had forbidden her to wander around the shops alone.

Turning to look at the church again, Magda was caught in a sudden shaft of sunlight that washed the church steeple with golden light. The slope of the hill rising behind it looked like a poster in a travel agent's window. The red tiled roofs of the houses were layered up the hill between the deep greens of gardens and trees. Squinting up at the sun, Magda guessed it wasn't much past five yet and her feet drew her up the hill.

The houses at this end of town were the smartest in Accleton. Big semicircles of windows curved out at the front where the gravelled yards had parking space for three or four cars. On the west side of town, near the Traveller site, the houses were all identical, like dolls' houses from Toys R Us. Here, on the hill, each house had something that made it a little different from the next one along: a proper garage, a balcony jutting out from the top floor, or a stone urn on the gatepost.

Crossing over Florence Lane and continuing up Nightingale Hill, Magda tried to pick and choose between the houses. For a while her favourites were a row of four with stained-glass sections in half-moons above the front doors, but she took that back when she saw some further up had doorways shaped like keyholes, built with a pattern of coloured bricks.

The streets were almost empty. One man, washing his car, said, 'Good afternoon,' as she walked past. But that was it. There was none of the bustling activity of the Traveller site.

A sudden breeze threw a scatter of apple blossom over her shoulders, like pink and white confetti, and Magda realized she had reached the top of the hill. The twin rows of trees at the edge of the pavements now curved round in a circle to make a cul-de-sac. The houses here were set even further back from the road, almost out of sight, so that she seemed to stand in a simple ring of trees. Their branches stretched up to the sky, dappling the ground with patterned shadows.

The air was clean and Magda took a deep breath and let it out, suddenly feeling free and light. She stretched her arms wide and spun around in a circle, and then stilled suddenly. She was not alone. Someone was sitting on a bench at the edge of the circle. A boy in a dark woollen coat.

Magda flushed and then realized that he couldn't have seen her. The bench faced the other way, where the view opened out between two houses and beyond the trees. She moved a little closer. The boy's hair was black, razored up at the back under the longer strands. He sat in the centre of the bench, feet stretched out in front of him, as he looked down at the town.

Madga followed his gaze and was surprised at how high they were. The sun was setting and the houses and streets were touched with gold. The green slopes and red roofs lay below her, descending towards the church steeple, where the light glittered and flashed on the outside of the rose window. She stared at it, imagining the sunshine streaming down the hill half an hour ago and shafting through the coloured glass to paint her own uplifted face with a mask of colour. Her eyes shifted to the boy on the bench and she felt the heat on her face as she thought of him looking down the hill while she looked up. As she thought of it, he turned and saw her. She dropped her gaze quickly to the ground. Out of the corner of her eye she saw him move. She stiffened, ready to walk away if he came over. But instead she heard him say, 'You can sit down if you want.'

When she looked back at him he had moved to the end of the bench and was looking out at the town again. She hesitated, but it seemed rude to walk away after he'd moved for her, so she sat down.

Magda wasn't comfortable with boys her own age. Tess never seemed to have a problem, but then she wasn't scared of anything. She'd speak out just the same to a boy as she would to a girl, or to a teacher or a priest. But

Magda felt nervous around them. They always *stared* so. She never knew where to look to avoid their leering eyes.

The boy on the bench didn't seem interested in her however. He kept looking into the distance as if she wasn't there and this only made her even more uncomfortable. She looked down at the town, trying to make out the Traveller site in the distance and forget the boy was there. But she could feel his presence, a dark shape in her peripheral vision. In his long black coat he was dressed for the weather and she shivered in her thin cotton summer dress.

She felt suddenly stupid. He must live around here, in one of the smart houses, and had come outside to sit in private. She was the intruder. Shifting on the bench, she decided she'd stay five minutes more so it didn't look as if she was avoiding him, and then she'd go.

It was silly to be so conscious of someone who wasn't even paying her any attention now. Magda wondered if it meant that she was vain. Some of the girls at school in Accleton last summer had called her a tease and a flirt. One of them had even gone around telling everyone she was a slut until Tess had found out about it and threatened to beat her up if she didn't stop.

'Those cows are jealous because you're gorgeous and boys like you, Magsie,' Tess had said, after the girl had mumbled an apology and run off to find her friends. 'Forget them.'

She tried, but sometimes she wondered if the girls were right. She didn't intend to flirt, and her da would never let her out again if he thought she was leading boys on. But when she felt their eyes on her it made her more conscious of what she was doing, even just smiling or walking or sitting at her desk, knowing that she had an audience. Being watched was like having a secret, she decided, a secret that everyone wanted to know. Even if you'd sworn not to tell, it only made people more desperate to know what it was. It made you drop little hints, or shake your head and purse your lips, or smile when people pressed you to tell them. Even if it wasn't that important a secret, other people wanting to know made it special.

That was why Magda thought she might be a flirt because she knew that boys liked looking at her, because she felt them watching even when she pretended not to. And even when it embarrassed her, she liked it too, because if people looked at you it showed you were worth looking at. She'd never really realized that before now, when she'd expected that attention and hadn't got it.

She smiled to herself, thinking how ridiculous it was. The sunset glowed pink and gold and red in streaks across the sky and she felt a surge of the same happiness and freedom that had spun her in a circle under the trees. She wished Tess was here so she could tell her how free it felt to be up so high, as if everything she worried about had been left behind at the bottom of the hill. Suddenly it didn't matter if boys noticed her or girls envied her or her school marks weren't good or that her parents wouldn't let her go out except to school and church. Sitting here at the edge of the hill she felt like flying and she stretched her arms out along the back of the bench, looking up at the coloured sky.

Her left hand brushed against something and she

snatched it back, but rather than blushing she laughed as she realized what she'd done. 'Sorry,' she said to the boy, whose face she'd touched with her hand, and he smiled, showing straight white teeth.

'No worries,' he said. Then added a moment later, flicking his eyes back to the horizon, 'Cool sunset.'

'It's glorious,' Magda replied and then dropped her eyes, aware that her voice showed too much of what she was feeling. From under her lashes she saw the boy push back his coat sleeve from his right hand and reach out to her.

'I'm Seb,' he said expectantly.

'My name's Magda,' she told him, taking his hand awkwardly. She'd never met a boy who'd tried to shake hands before and it was strange to feel his warm brown hand close around her own pale fingers. It took a moment for her to realize she'd told him her name, something she never did with strangers.

'You live around here?' he asked as he released her and she shook her head, wondering how he could have mistaken her for a rich townie like himself.

'Over that way,' she explained, pointing across town and then worrying that he'd think less of her for coming from the Traveller site. But if he realized where she was pointing, he didn't seem to care.

'I saw you coming out of the church,' he said and Magda felt a shiver across her skin as she followed where he was looking to the rose window and the wooden arched doors of Sacred Heart. 'You're a Catholic?'

'Yes.'

'Me too,' he replied, surprising her into looking at him and he twisted his mouth into a half-smile. 'I mean, my mother is. My dad isn't much for church so I don't go, except for at school.'

So, Magda guessed, he went to a church school for posh kids. At the same time she noticed with curiousity that when he mentioned his father a flash of something passed across his eyes.

'You live here, don't you?' she said slowly, turning to look at the circle of houses.

'Yeah,' he shrugged. 'That one.' He pointed to one with a keyhole door.

'It looks nice,' she said and he shrugged again.

'I guess,' he replied. 'My mother's had it done up though and she's a bit obsessive. You can't sit anywhere without thinking you're going to break something and she screams if you get the tiniest speck of dirt on the floor.'

'That's not so good.' Magda thought of her own family's trailers and the little kids and their friends running in and out while she made them messy jam sandwiches at the kitchen counter. 'But it must look lovely.'

'Well, we have a pool,' Seb said, 'so it's not as if there's nothing to do, but most of my friends live out in the country and I haven't been driving long.'

'You can drive then?' Magda said, wondering how old he was.

'I'm seventeen,' Seb stated, as reading her mind.

'Fifteen,' Magda said quietly. It was another bit of information she normally didn't provide.

'So,' Seb smiled again, the same half-smile as before, 'do you swim?'

'Sometimes, at the pool at the sports centre.'

'You mean Bluewater?' Seb's face closed up suddenly. 'I don't go there.'

'I suppose not, if you have your own pool at home,' Magda said, laughing nervously.

'Something like that.' He hesitated and Magda blushed before he spoke, guessing what was coming next. 'Would you like to come in for a drink?'

'Oh no. I can't.' She stood up quickly, the sky was getting darker and she thought about all the chores she still had to do back home. 'I should go.'

'I guess I didn't exactly make it sound appealing,' he said, not trying to persuade her, 'but you don't have to go.'

'I do. I've got things to do.' She lifted her hands helplessly and then stepped back when he stood up. 'Really. I'm late already.'

'Will I see you again?' Seb asked and Magda realized with surprise that he had been flirting with her, or maybe she had been flirting with him. She blushed again at the thought.

'No, no, I don't know . . . probably not.' She looked away and said, 'I have to go.'

'If you must.' He sat back down, this time on the arm of the bench, though he smiled at her as she backed away. 'But I think I will see you again. Maybe I'll come to your church . . .'

She laughed and covered her mouth with a hand, shaking her head again. She just managed to stammer a goodbye before turning. She walked quickly, but she could feel his eyes on her as she went and she turned at the corner of the circle of houses to see him still watching. She waved and then turned and ran, her sandals clacking against the pavement as she hurried back into town.

4

UNDER THE GLASS STAIRS

The reception area in the leisure centre always smelt of chlorine when Gwen arrived, although by the time she went off shift she'd usually stopped noticing it. Pushing through the glass side door from the car park, she always paused to inhale deeply.

Main reception was where everyone signed in and first thing in the morning staff were already clustered near the desk, chatting. Stepping around the edge of the group, Gwen bumped into one of the lads and he turned to grin at her over an oiled and gleaming shoulder.

'Sorry, Craig.' Gwen smiled back widely. It paid to be friendly to the lads. Not too friendly or they chatted you up all the time, but if you seemed stuck up you got it even worse. They were all practical jokers and the leisure centre was full of handy material for embarrassing set-ups. But Gwen knew these guys and Craig just flexed an eyebrow at her and jerked his chin at the multicoloured timetable pinned by the desk.

'We pulled lifeguard duty together this week,' he said,

'and Charmaine wants you to do a late night on Thursday.'

'Sure.' Gwen glanced across the scrum to catch the receptionist's eye and Charmaine leaned over the desk to speak to her.

'It's a private booking for a hen night,' she explained. 'They want all female lifeguards, so if you can, Gwen . . .'

'No problem.'

Gwen's duties floated around main reception, lifeguard duty and rolling reception for the outside and inside pools. It was all downstairs work. The best wages were paid upstairs in the gym and health club, but it was hard to get in without an instructor's certificate. She was working on that. Craig was gym staff and he and some of the others had taken her through the preliminary material. But there were only so many hours in the day and she was a way away from getting there any time soon.

The crowd around the desk gradually pulled away. Joining Charmaine at the desk, Gwen started working through the pile of morning post. By nine the smell of chlorine had faded and she was washed back into the regular routine: the shuffling of paper and the occasional *bring-bring* of the phone while voices hummed in the distance and staff ran up and down the stairs. This early in the morning there weren't many customers, but every now and again the automatic doors swung open, hurling a gust of air into the lobby as one of the senior staff arrived.

Mr Swayland came through the car-park side door with a jangle of keys as he tucked his car beeper back into his pocket. Although he wore a suit he carried his papers in a sports rucksack and he dropped it casually at his feet as he stopped by the desk. He was usually early in the mornings – he only had to come round by the ring road from the smart end of town.

'Hello, girls, how's it going?' he asked as he always did. Gwen jumped when the phone chose that moment to ring. It was a routine enquiry, but as she answered it she ignored her own voice smoothly shifting through the gears, answering questions and explaining times. Her eyes flicked up and down from her notepad to the computer, catching glimpses of Mr Swayland talking to Charmaine. She thought she'd blown it when the phone call was still dragging on as he picked up his rucksack, but when she finally replaced the receiver he was still standing there.

'I hear you're going back to school again next week, Gwen,' he said, leaning across the desk to look at her sitting on the tall stool. 'Does that mean we'll be losing you then?'

'Well, I have exams this term,' Gwen explained, fiddling with one of the cheap leisure-centre biros that littered the front desk, 'although I'd still like to come in for lifeguard duty and maybe I could take a few shifts . . .' She paused, but he was still watching her expectantly so she went on. 'But after that I'm finished at school and I'd like to come back full time.'

'But aren't these only your GCSEs?' he asked, smiling at her. 'I'm surprised a girl of your abilities doesn't want to go on to university . . .'

He was leaning even further over the desk now. Gwen looked at the heavy Rolex watch on one of his tanned wrists and then at her own hands, fingers dyed blue from the leaky biro.

'I'd rather have a job, be out in the world,' she said and he smiled again.

'Of course you would,' he agreed, white teeth gleaming. 'Come and see me sometime. We'll talk about what you can do for us after school . . . Well, see you later, girls.'

Slinging his rucksack over his shoulder, he headed up the glass atrium stairs to the executive offices. It wasn't until they heard the muffled thud of the doors up there shutting that Charmaine murmured softly, 'Yeah, see you later, you old letch.' She cut her eyes at Gwen and giggled.

'He's not that bad,' Gwen said and Charmaine stared.

'He's lethal! He makes passes at all the girls upstairs. Lucky for us he only floats through here a couple of times a week. But ask Jaycee about the time he gave her a lift home; she'll tell you.'

Gwen shrugged and after a moment the phone rang. As Charmaine answered it she looked back down at her ink-stained fingers and then headed for the women's toilets.

It was soft lavender inside and every surface that wasn't padded was mirrored. Scrubbing her hands at the sink, Gwen looked up at her reflection and smiled at it. On pool duty she had to tie up her hair and her face looked pale and freckly without make-up. But on reception you were supposed to look smart, so she wore her hair loose, the red-gold waves falling thickly to her waist. She was small and her cloak of hair made her look even more delicate.

She sometimes caught the other girls eyeing her resentfully. They all had crops and streaks and styles and somehow seemed to think it unfair that hers was so extravagantly natural.

Gwen took a dark brown eyeliner pencil out of her make-up bag and retouched her green eyes carefully. She put on lip gloss as well. Looking in the mirror one last time, she admitted she didn't have Magda's beauty or Tess's dramatic flair, but when she made the effort she did all right for herself.

○

It was a slow morning and Gwen was able to read through her biology notes. But business would pick up over the summer once the weather improved and Gwen chatted to Charmaine about taking shifts during her exams.

'You won't be able to get any revision in,' the other girl warned her. 'Not when it's busy in here.'

'I know,' Gwen said, feeling annoyed. 'I only do it when it's slow anyway.'

'I'm not criticizing,' Charmaine said quickly. 'I think it's great that you do all that work. I'm surprised you're not going to stay on at school – since you're that into it.'

'You have to be kidding!' Gwen made an effort to give the other girl a friendly smile. 'I want to get out on my own. I'm not living at home any longer than I have to.'

'Oh?' Charmaine leaned forward, looking to gossip. 'Do you not get on with your folks then?'

'It's only my mum and me,' Gwen said slowly, 'and we

get on fine. I just want to be away from the rest of it . . . you know.'

'Yeah, too right.' Charmaine was already nodding. 'Like, I'm living with my boyfriend now and, although he's a complete slob, at least I don't get hassled by my mum any more about eating right and wearing a coat and cleaning up my room.'

'My mum and I don't talk about that kind of thing.' Gwen wondered if there was any point trying to explain. 'It's just our place is small and . . . bringing back boyfriends . . .'

'Ah.' Charmaine grinned at her. 'Say no more.' She paused for a second and then said, 'You know, if you're looking for a flat or something, there's a couple of the girls in the gym who're sharing together but they argue all the time, so I reckon Kelly's going to move out before long.'

'Is that so?' Gwen said.

Charmaine went on, 'If you want to come out to the pub with us later, I'll introduce you to the other girl – that's Jaycee.'

'Isn't she the one you said . . . ?' Gwen dropped her voice suddenly and glanced up at the glass stairs to the offices.

'Yeah, that Mr Swankipants made a pass at.' Charmaine giggled. 'You should get her to tell you that story. It's a riot.'

'All right.' Gwen smiled. 'I'll come. Thanks.'

'No worries.' Charmaine grinned.

A lot more people came in at midday, using their lunch breaks to exercise. It meant that Gwen didn't get much of a break herself, but she covered the desk while Charmaine went to the cafe and got sandwiches for them both.

Mr Swayland had a business lunch booked into the diary and Gwen was just finishing the last of her sandwich when a middle-aged man in a suit came in and up to the desk.

'Councillor Kevin Chalmers,' he said crisply, barely looking at her. 'Here to see Mark Swayland.'

Gwen dialled the extension from memory. He answered after only two rings. 'Your lunch appointment is here,' she said.

'Thanks, Gwen. I'll be right there.'

She watched out of the corner of her eye as he came down the stairs to shake hands with the man waiting. Then they headed out through the main doors together, towards Mr Swayland's red Lexus.

'What do you reckon that's about?' Charmaine asked and Gwen looked at her blankly. 'He's met with about half the town council in the last couple of months. Darren reckons he's going to try to run for the council himself. You know he owns a lot of property about town, right? Not just the sports centre but a block of flats and stuff like that. He's a right wheeler-dealer, that one.'

Gwen would have liked to ask more, but sometimes Charmaine got a weird look on her face if Gwen asked too much about the boss, and she didn't want to sound

54

naive. Instead she settled back to her biology. Through the glass of the atrium she could see the clouds gradually receding to leave the sky a pale blue-white. Mothers and little children began to troop past towards the main pool, several stopping to ask if the outside pool was open.

'Not yet, I'm sorry,' Gwen said as she always did. People seemed to think one clear day meant summer had arrived. Of course none of them realized how expensive it was to keep the outside pool going.

The noise of a group of teenagers coming in made her look across at the doors and she felt her face tighten as she recognized them. It was embarrassing how tatty they looked as a group. Tess was in jeans and T-shirt. Magda was wearing a peasant blouse over indecently short cut-offs and lugging an ancient beach bag, filled almost to bursting point. Jo was in running clothes and Carly in a bright orange sundress that clashed with her slightly frizzy ginger hair.

'Hey, Gwen,' Carly shouted from across the lobby. 'Look who's back.'

'Hi,' Gwen tried to keep her voice low, hoping that they'd follow suit. 'How are you all?'

'I'm good,' Magda said, smiling as she reached for her purse. 'Is the outside pool open?'

'No, not yet,' Gwen told her briskly. 'So, four under-sixteens for swimming?'

'I don't have any cash on me,' Tess said predictably and leaned on the edge of the reception desk to add wheedlingly, 'Can't you just wave me in, Gwen. You could do it easily.'

'No.' Gwen frowned at her and flicked her eyes sideways, to where Charmaine was on the phone, hoping she hadn't heard. 'And don't ask again. I don't want to lose this job.'

'I'll spot you, Tessie,' Magda said, counting the coins out carefully. Carly paid for herself and then turned to stare at Jo, who had produced a wad of notes.

'I want a swim pass for the summer,' she said and added, 'Dan gave me the money for it, and you still owe him at least fifteen quid, Tess.'

'Yeah, whatever, all right?' Tess said, looking away.

As Gwen printed out a season pass for Jo, she saw the double doors open behind them and Mr Swayland come back from his lunch. Her heart sank as he approached the desk. Just her luck to be surrounded by a group of ragged gypsies right now.

'Any messages?' he asked Charmaine, and as she was printing them out he looked from Tess's trainers to Magda's long bare legs and then glanced over at Gwen. His mouth curved in a smile as she gave Jo her pass and the group jostled and barged past each other to get to the changing rooms. Gwen smiled back and shrugged her shoulders a little as he slung his bag over a shoulder and headed up to his office.

'What a letch,' Charmaine said again. 'Did you see him looking at that girl's legs? You know he's married with a little kid back home.' She shook her head dubiously before turning back to her work.

Gwen felt a stab of irritation. Charmaine was making it all up about Mr Swayland, she told herself. After all,

Gwen had been working there for a year and she'd never heard him mention a wife or a child. Charmaine liked to gossip, that was all. And, Gwen decided, she just wouldn't listen.

5

WALKING THE BUS ROUTE

Carly felt sick on the first day back at school after the Easter holidays. The white blouse she'd picked out for the bits of lace on the collar suddenly looked stupid and drippy and her school skirt hung in stiff pleats to her knees. Even when she rolled the waistband up a couple of inches it didn't look much better. She felt hot and cross and her reflection in the mirror looked tragic. At least her hair looked good, she hoped as she crammed her books into her school bag. She'd dried it with her mum's hairdryer so it wouldn't frizz up. But then she glanced at the window in time to see the rain start.

'Mum!' she called, grabbing her bag and hurrying down the stairs.

'Must you come down like a herd of elephants all the time?' her mum asked, gulping the last of her cup of coffee as she put on her shoes for work.

'It's raining,' Carly told her. 'Can't I have a lift to school?'

'Your father's taken the car already,' her mum said unsympathetically. 'It's only ten minutes. You won't melt.'

'More like twenty,' Carly grumbled.

'Oh, just keep the hood up on your new coat and you won't get wet.' She hustled Carly out of the house and in five minutes was walking quickly down the road in the other direction.

Carly made a face at her mum's departing figure and swung around crossly, heaving her rucksack up on one shoulder and then wincing as her hair got caught under the strap. There was a bus stop just outside the housing estate, but this far out of town any journey cost more and her mum always said, 'It won't hurt you to walk,' whatever the weather was like. Carly set off. She could feel her hair slipping out of her too-small hood and already frizzing up from the rain. With a growl she yanked it back and stuffed it down inside her clearly useless new anorak, where it bunched up uncomfortably in an itchy mass. Suddenly she heard shouts from over the road. She looked around to see three figures waving at her.

Carly watched them as they waited for a gap in the traffic. School uniform was supposed to make everyone look the same, but the three girls on the other side of the road were unmistakably different. Jo was wearing a battered school blazer and a man's white shirt and instead of the regulation blue pleated skirt she had a pair of black tracksuit trousers, probably planning to claim her school skirt was torn or lost. Magda's uniform was hidden under a short pink duffle coat that would have fitted one of her little sisters better and her bare legs looked cold and exposed beneath it. Tess was in black jeans and a red jumper, her blue eyes challenging under dark lashes heavy with mascara. Carly wondered how Tess always seemed to get away with it; no one else would dare break the uniform code as blatantly. At the same time she suddenly felt very young, prim and silly-looking compared to the three of them. How come none of *them* had frizzy hair?

They ran across the road the second there was a break in the traffic. A couple of cars hooted their horns and Tess swung round and glared at the drivers, making Carly cringe.

'Hey, Carly,' Jo said casually. She glanced at Carly's rucksack and laughed. 'What've you got in there? Rocks?'

'Just books,' Carly said awkwardly.

'Same old Carly,' Magda said. 'You're getting to be as brainy as Gwen.'

'Where *is* Gwen?' Tess asked and Carly shrugged.

'I bet she got a lift in with her mum,' she said. 'She's probably been at school for an hour already.' Jo started walking and Carly followed when Magda did, turning to add over her shoulder to Tess. 'How come you're here anyway? It's not as if you care about school.'

'Got to be there on the first day,' Tess said with a knowing look as she came up beside Magda, her hands rummaging through her jacket pockets for something. 'Get registered properly.'

'Besides, it's wet,' Magda added softly, looking up at the grey sky from which the rain was still drizzling down. 'What's the point of bunking off?'

'Truant officers spot you if you hang around the

shops,' Jo chimed in, turning around and walking backwards.

Tess stopped and hitched herself up on a low wall. 'Hang about, you lot. I'm not facing the first day of school without a cigarette.'

Magda stopped obediently and Jo came to a reluctant halt, fidgeting with her feet against the paving slabs and improvising a kind of hopscotch.

'We'll be late,' Carly pointed out, shifting her bag about awkwardly on her shoulder. 'On the first day. You always get us in trouble, Tess.'

'I don't see anyone keeping you here.' Tess shot her a look. 'Go on ahead if you like.'

○

Carly wasn't late, even with the others delaying her. But once they reached school they all peeled away from her. None of them had been there for the spring term, so they had to go to the office for registration cards, Jo for year 9 and the other two for year 10. They didn't even notice Carly walking the other way.

'Them lot are the gypsies,' a voice muttered and Carly turned quickly and defensively. A couple of the girls were walking past, but they weren't even looking at her; they were watching Tess instead. Her boots were muddy and had tracked noticeable footprints in through the front doors. Carly glanced down at her own shoes but thankfully they were still clean. She grimaced. Why did she have to have embarrassing gypsy relations and connections who made everyone stare?

Carly didn't need to register specially. She'd been living in Accleton for almost as long as she could remember, ever since her parents moved into the housing estate. Dad hadn't wanted to but her mum had said Carly wouldn't get a good education moving around, putting it all on her as usual.

Lugging her rucksack into class, she looked around, trying to work out what desks everyone had picked already. Last term she'd sat next to Amy and Deborah and thought they might be becoming friends. But now they were sitting near Genevieve and she could hear they were all talking about tennis. She knew they'd been spending time together over the spring holiday but she hadn't let them see her when she'd spotted them in town. It would be too embarrassing if they knew she'd been watching them.

Instead Carly slid into a seat on the edge of the second row, next to the lockers. The boy in the seat next to her looked over as she sat down and then looked away again and Carly pretended not to notice.

Her class teacher, Mrs Verny, walked with them as they went down the stairs to assembly and Carly asked, 'Did you have a nice holiday, miss?'

'Holiday? With all the marking I had to do it wasn't much of a holiday,' her teacher said. Carly blushed and looked away, hoping the girls behind her hadn't heard.

They had to cross the playground to get to the hall and it was then Carly saw the other three again, running from the door of the school office towards the hall as well. Magda's pink coat and Tess's red jumper seemed all the more noticeable against the streams of uniforms heading the same way and Carly cringed.

'Aren't they your cousins?' a boy said.

'Not exactly,' Carly muttered, glancing at him to see if he was getting at her.

'My brother fancies one of them,' he remarked conversationally as they went into the hall. 'The blonde one.'

'Her dad doesn't let her date,' Carly snapped.

'Well, get you,' he said, laughing. 'Think your cousin's too good for my brother?' He whispered something to one of his friends and they looked back at Carly and laughed. She cringed down into her seat, feeling large, frizzy and obvious.

Assembly seemed to last forever – there were a hundred announcements about sports and outings and auditions for *Romeo and Juliet*. Carly pulled a strand of hair into her mouth and started chewing it. Like biting her nails, it was a habit she kept promising herself she would break. But today she didn't have the will power. In the playground afterwards the classes were streaming back to their form rooms. It was a shock when a voice said suddenly:

'Carly Dixon.'

It was Mrs Sutcliffe, the deputy head, who was staring at her with the bad-smell expression that meant she wasn't happy about something. 'Your *hair*, Miss Dixon,' the deputy head emphasized, grabbing a strand of her own short brown hair and shaking it. 'You know the rules about hair, or you should by now. What are they?'

'Long hair has to be tied back,' Carly said miserably.

She hadn't exactly forgotten, it was just that almost no one kept to the rule. Genevieve wore her long fair hair loose but kept a scrunchy around her wrist so she could tie it back if a teacher looked at her.

The deputy head produced an elderly-looking rubber band. 'Now tie it back and keep it back, is that clear?' she commanded, her voice carrying across the playground.

Everyone else was already at their desks when Carly got back to her form room and she slid into her place as quickly as she could.

Miss Verny raised her eyebrows and asked, 'What happened to you, Carly? Did you get lost?'

'Mrs Sutcliffe was telling her off,' one of the girls sitting next to the window contributed, before Carly had a chance to say anything. 'About her hair.'

Everyone turned to look at Carly and she hunched her shoulders. The stupid rubber band was too tight and she was sure it was tearing her hair. Not to mention making her look like a dumb little kid. She burned with anger. It wasn't fair the way she kept being singled out. She just knew that Genevieve was whispering about her now with Amy and Deborah.

Before they started lessons Miss Verny read out some more school notices.

'Students below year ten may not leave the school grounds at lunch or break time,' she announced. 'Last term there were a lot of people going out regardless and lying to the prefects on duty. This term anyone found sneaking out will be given a week's detention.' There were groans from the class.

'Smoking is absolutely forbidden,' Miss Verny went on. 'Any student found with cigarettes, matches or lighters will have them confiscated and the headmaster will be sending a letter to your parents.'

Someone called out, 'It's not fair, miss. People might have matches for all sorts of reasons.'

'Name three,' Miss Verny replied and people laughed.

'It's those gypsies who're always going out and smoking,' someone said and Carly stiffened in her seat as the girl continued. 'I don't see why we've got to be punished for what they do.'

'That's a very ignorant remark,' Miss Verny said sharply, 'and I'd better not hear it repeated.'

Carly ducked her head as Miss Verny looked around the class, a couple of spots of colour on her cheeks showing that she was really cross.

'The rules are for the benefit of *everyone*,' she said. 'And the Travellers at this school will be treated the same way as the rest of you. If I hear any more comments about another person's culture or ethnic origin there'll be serious trouble, is that understood?'

'Yes, miss,' the class mumbled, and Miss Verny started to give out some books.

Carly kept her head down, trying to pull some of her hair out of the rough ponytail to conceal her face. For one moment she'd been certain she was about to be singled out again, that Miss Verny would say something like, 'Carly's from a Traveller family.' Instead it seemed like her teacher didn't even know she was one of them. Her eyes stung.

She was always attracting attention for the wrong reasons, but being invisible hurt even more.

○

Carly had to collect her free pass at lunch time and used it to get sandwiches and crisps, which she ate in a corner of the dining hall near the year 7s. She didn't want to be seen by anyone in her class or by Magda, Jo and Tess. After lunch, when Carly hauled her heavy bag to the library, she found lots of people loitering there, hiding inside from the dreary weather. She'd *expected* to find Gwen there, since she was library assistant. But it was a surprise to see Tess lolling against the front desk chatting to her. Watching Gwen from across the room, Carly wondered if any people at school knew that Gwen's mum had been a Traveller before she'd settled in Accleton. The teachers knew, and Gwen had told Carly that they were even keener for her to stay on because of it. Lots of Traveller kids left at the first opportunity, but Gwen got such good grades they said it would be a waste.

There was a long line of people queued up to return books and Carly wandered up and down the shelves, waiting for them to finish. Tess stayed at the desk the whole time and it wasn't until the sixth-form lunch patrol had come along to chase all the people who shouldn't be there out to the playground that she sloped off somewhere and Carly finally came out from the shelves.

'Hey, Gwen,' she began and her cousin looked up in surprise from stacking books on the library cart.

'I thought I heard those sixth-formers tell everyone to

leave.'

'I was choosing books,' Carly pointed out, dumping them on the desk. 'And I have all these to return as well.'

'Why didn't you bring them earlier then?' Gwen went round to the other side of the desk again and started running the books through the scanner. 'And I'll get in trouble if I stand around chatting with all this work to do.'

'There was a queue earlier!' Carly reminded her. 'Anyway, I saw you talking to Tess.'

Gwen glanced at her but didn't say anything and Carly felt annoyed. She wanted to talk to Gwen about what had happened in class, but her cousin was making it difficult.

'Gwen,' she began slowly, 'do you think people can tell you're a Traveller by looking at you?'

'What?' Gwen's face set into sharp annoyance. 'Of course they can't. Why should they?'

'I don't think my teacher knows I am,' Carly tried to explain and Gwen flicked another quick look at her and frowned.

'Well, isn't that what you want?' she asked. 'You were complaining over the holidays that you didn't want the town girls to know you had relations at the Traveller site, weren't you?'

'That's different.'

'I don't see how,' Gwen told her. 'Honestly, Carly, why don't you make your mind up about what it is you want?'

'That's not fair!' Carly was about to launch into her explanation when Mrs Mills, the librarian, came in. She smiled at Gwen in a distant way and then her eyes travelled to Carly.

67

'Hello, Carly, did you enjoy your holiday?'

'It was OK,' Carly said, remembering how her class teacher had reacted when she'd asked the same question. If she were to say, 'Not much of a holiday when you have lots of homework,' Mrs Mills would think she was being rude and probably send her to the head. But there weren't any rules about teachers being polite to kids.

'If you've finished here you should really run along to the playground,' the librarian said as Gwen handed Carly her new books.

'But it's raining,' Carly pointed out and Mrs Mills gave her a cool look.

Carly didn't try to protest again. But as she was getting ready to go she saw Tess hadn't left the library. Instead she was skulking between the non-fiction shelves.

'Coming, Tess?' she asked loudly, feeling cross at being shooed out, and both Gwen and Mrs Mills glanced up at her.

'No,' Tess said, narrowing her eyes at Carly nastily. Then she looked at Mrs Mills and pasted on the smile she used when she was trying something on. ''Scuse me, miss . . . have you got any books about the city council? You know, about what they're allowed to do and stuff like that.'

Carly couldn't help rolling her eyes. What a stupid question. It ought to be obvious to anyone that Tess was just making something up to be allowed to stay in and chat to Gwen. But Mrs Mills was completely taken in.

'It sounds as if what you want is the operational procedures for local government,' she said. 'That's a bit

68

sophisticated for a school library, Tess. Is it for a class project?'

'No.' Tess shook her head, shaking out her long dark hair, which she hadn't even pretended to tie back. 'I'm just interested in finding out my rights.'

Mrs Mills beamed at her, swallowing Tess's story hook, line and sinker. 'You'll need to go to the library in the town centre for that,' she explained, 'but I might have some pamphlets in my office that can help you. Why don't you come with me and we'll talk about it there.' She beckoned Tess to follow her and paused at the doorway to look at Carly. 'Run along now, Carly, or do I have to tell you again?'

Carly flushed hotly and picked up her bag. Tess smirked as she passed and Carly pulled a furious face. It wasn't fair. Mrs Mills thought it was so great that Tess actually wanted to learn something because she was usually a troublemaker. No one cared about Carly – because she did what she was told.

○

At the end of the day it was still raining and Carly's bag was just as heavy as it had been at the beginning. Rather than wear it she bundled her horrible anorak – that she'd thought so trendy and wanted so much only weeks before – under her arm and walked out of the school doors. Outside she dragged the horrid rubber band out of her hair and chucked it away, shaking her hair into a wild tangle of ginger curls.

A stream of parents' cars was pulling up, fouling the

bus lane as they idled their motors outside the main gates. Genevieve from her class was sitting in the front passenger seat of a black Saab. For an instant her eyes met Carly's through the window as the car pulled out into the road. Carly narrowed her eyes at it and then looked away.

'Hey, Magda,' she called, recognizing the blonde figure in the pink coat waiting at the gates. 'Want to swap coats? Yours'll fit me easy and I'm sick of this stupid anorak. It doesn't suit me anyway.'

6

REFUSE AND RECLAIM

Tess was watching from the top of a pile of broken old cars when the others came up the dirt track to the dump on Sunday morning. Officially it was the Accleton Council Collection, Refuse and Reclaim Centre. But naturally no one actually called it that. It was the dump, or the wrecking shop, or the tip. On Saturdays the place was humming and you couldn't hear yourself think for the crashing of bottles, broken furniture and scrap metal into the massive waste bins. But on Sundays the dump was almost deserted, closed to everyone except employees. Tess had hitched a lift up last week with some of the Travellers who worked as sorters and had instantly recognized it as one of her places. The pile of wrecked cars was like a fortress from which she could survey the rest of the tiny junk kingdom. The dirt track led past it and around in a circle so that people could take turns to unload the contents of their cars into the big yellow skips, bottle banks and Portakabins. She even liked it on Saturdays, the crashing din and exhaust fumes and the knots of people that formed around an especially large or interesting piece of rubbish.

The first time she'd come up here some of the town men who worked at the dump had given her dubious looks.

'Oh, she's all right,' one of the Traveller men had said, unexpectedly coming to her defence. 'That's Tess Lovett. She's into everything – you'll only waste your time trying to keep her out.' There was a pause as the man lowered his voice so only the other Travellers would hear him and he added, 'She's the one that spotted the roundabout.'

'Is that what it's supposed to be?' another of them asked and Tess answered quickly.

'A roundabout to connect the motorway directly to the ring road, that's what I heard. A big one with slip roads and a link round to the overpass, so big it's bound to affect us. Imagine the noise while they're building up near our site. Not to mention once it's in use – a busy junction like that.'

The Traveller site had been full of rumours ever since Tess had discovered the work signs and the area of churned-up earth. She'd listened to all of them, joining in whenever people let her. But to her disappointment hardly anyone seemed to be up for a real fight. They just talked endlessly or sent the council letters which were never properly answered.

'We need to protest,' Tess continued, her eyes flashing dangerously. 'Some people are signing a petition to take to the council. We should have a huge march with it, and a rally and sit-in – show them what we're made of!'

'The council approved the roundabout over the winter,' the man who'd supported her said, giving Tess a look that meant 'quiet down'. 'There's plans drawn up that you can see in the town-planning department, but the first we heard of it was when work started.'

'That's not the worst of it,' another man put in darkly. 'You know there's Travellers on the road-gang? It's a betrayal, that's what I call it.'

'I hadn't heard that.' Tess was livid. 'That's well out of order!'

'If it's already approved I don't see why it shouldn't be us that get the work,' one of the group argued and the others closed in around him, gesturing furiously as they explained how wrong he was.

Tess wanted to stay and hear more, but after a moment they noticed her again and a man said, 'All right then, we've work to be doing. Tess, you can stay if you want, but don't mess about and don't get in the way.'

She'd done as she'd been told. She'd smoked a couple of cigarettes out of sight in one of the abandoned cars and in the middle of the morning, when the sun burned away the clouds, she'd gone down to the shops and come back with two litre bottles of cold water that she'd carried around to the men from the site. At lunch they'd called her down from her post and shared their sandwiches with her and by the end of the day she'd been working as well, lending a hand here and there to the people unloading their cars. Traveller kids were supposed to help with the family's work and, although Tess usually ducked out of helping Reenie with the wash, it had made her feel good to be accepted by the men. But today she had more on her mind than helping out and she waved impatiently when the other girls finally appeared at the entrance, beckoning them over.

Magda spotted her before the others did and waved back, but Jo was the first to jump up athletically on to a car bonnet and climb the scrap mountain. She was the only one who'd dressed sensibly, in a faded T-shirt and old ripped jeans, but she looked different somehow. It took Tess a minute to spot that she was wearing black eyeliner and it looked as if she'd put lipstick on and rubbed it off again.

Tess grinned, staring challengingly down at the others. 'So, are you coming up or what?' she asked.

'Is it safe?' Magda asked, looking doubtfully at the heap of cars.

'It's rusted solid, trust me,' Tess said. 'But you're not exactly dressed for climbing.'

Magda shrugged her shoulders, and pulled a face at her white blouse and long green skirt.

'Da said my shorts were indecent,' she said. 'Mam gave me this to wear instead.' Taking hold of the hem, she bunched up a length of fabric before tying it in a knot that pulled the rest of the skirt up to well above her knees, showing more leg than her old shorts had. Tess came down halfway to meet her as she scrambled from car to car and Jo reached down from above to help her up the last bit.

At the bottom Carly and Gwen were eyeing the car mountain dubiously. Gwen was dressed in her work clothes and she hitched herself up to sit on one of the lower cars before saying, 'That's as far as I go. I've better things to do with my day than play king of the castle on a rubbish dump.'

Carly hesitated, torn between joining Gwen's protest or the others at the top of the pile. Her purple mini was short but so tight she had difficulty just climbing up on to the first car. She was complaining by the time she reached the second.

'For Christ's sake,' Tess said, rolling her eyes. She gave Carly a pull up that made her moan 'ow' before scrambling up the last bit on her own.

Balancing on the roof of the topmost car, Tess looked out across the dump and then further. The sun was clearing the last wisps of cloud away, leaving a beautiful, sunny day. Over to the west she could see the drab bridge of the overpass between the high verges of the motorway and in the other direction, towards the town centre, she turned to see the gleaming white blocks of the sports centre, with the outside swimming pool a square of brilliant blue beside it.

'So . . . what do you think?' she asked, turning to the others.

'I like it,' Magda said, looking up with sparkling eyes from where she'd sat down. She had spread her long skirt out again, underneath her legs to stop them being burned by the hot metal, and she looked as if she was at a church picnic.

'It's cool,' Jo agreed, shading her eyes as she looked around as Tess had been doing. 'Like a metal tree house.'

'Yeah.' Carly nodded her head enthusiastically. 'You know, we could get blankets and food and like a radio and stuff and keep them up here in one of the cars and—'

'And what, play make-believe?' Tess looked scornfully at her. 'It's not a Wendy house, Carly.'

'I'm not sure any of you should be up there,' Gwen put in. 'It's probably trespassing.'

'Oh, come *on*,' Tess said, disgusted. 'How old are you anyway, grandma? Live a little.'

Gwen flushed crossly and looked as if she was about to snap back when Magda intervened.

'It might not be a Wendy house, but it is kind of like a castle, isn't it? Look, down there's the treasure chamber.'

They looked, following her pointing arm, to the largest bottle banks, big skips full of smashed bottles. From up here they did glitter and sparkle like emeralds and diamonds, in all shades of green and clear glass.

'Then the scrap-metal bin's the torture chamber,' Tess agreed, losing her irritation and sitting down next to Magda. 'All those rusty hooks and spikes, right?'

'I don't like the state of the library,' Gwen said with a smile, gesturing at one of the paper bins, where different colours and types of paper were heaped up into a rats'-nest tangle.

Then Jo looked beyond the dump and asked, 'Is that that construction site, Tess?'

At the casual way Jo mentioned it, Tess had a fleeting urge to push her off the car pile and see her bruise and scrape herself all the way down.

'Yeah, that's it,' she said, scowling and tossing her

head. 'It's s'posed to be a massive motorway roundabout. Can you imagine what'll be like to have that round the back of the site? It'll be like living in a multi-storey car park.'

'Maybe it won't be that bad,' Magda suggested, reaching out to touch her arm but Tess wasn't ready to be consoled and she twitched away.

'Maybe it'll be worse,' she said. Standing up again, she stabbed a finger in the direction of the construction site. 'Look,' she said, 'there's where the works road comes off the motorway –' she swung her arm round to the left – 'there's the Traveller site –' and brought her arm round again to point at the ring road – 'and there's where it'll link up with the town traffic system.' She turned angry eyes back at the others as she continued. 'No one's saying it out loud, but there's no way the council can build it without cutting into the Traveller site. They'll have to cut a huge chunk out just to fit everything in.'

'They can't do that, though, surely?' Jo said, frowning. 'The site's ours; they can't just build over it.'

'It's not ours,' Tess told her. 'The south side's an official Traveller site. But we live on the other side in temporary pitches, right? All that isn't officially ours. It didn't get included in the rules, so the council can do what they want with it. And if the roundabout goes through it, all the people that live there will have to move, now do you see? And even those left on the permanent site will be boxed in by roads and flyovers.'

'If we have to move, maybe we can apply for a

permanent pitch on the other side,' Magda said slowly, thinking about it. 'But not if everyone else wants one as well.' She looked up. 'There'll never be enough space for all of us here.'

'Maybe you can get a house?' Carly suggested. 'Like me and Gwen.'

'There wouldn't be room for all of us in a council house,' Magda said vaguely, her eyes staring into the distance, across the town. 'I reckon Da might want to go across to Ireland. Work's hard to find, but at least there's still places you can stay. More than here anyway.'

'I wouldn't want to live in a house,' Jo said, 'but I wouldn't mind leaving this stupid town. I wanted to go to Scotland, but Mum and Dad thought we'd be better off coming here.'

Tess clenched her fists with frustration. How could they miss the point like this? 'Look,' she said, trying to take control of the conversation, 'I've been talking to people all over the site and some of them are willing to go to the town hall and complain that we weren't consulted about the roundabout. We should have a rally or a proper march and you could all come.'

'Why?' said Jo, she was picking at a hole in her jeans and looked uninterested. 'Since when are you all about joining in?'

'Travellers should stand up for their rights,' Tess insisted, through gritted teeth. 'If we don't, who will?' The others still seemed unconvinced and suddenly Tess snapped. 'You're all pathetic,' she snarled. 'My dad . . .'

Magda's arm around her shoulders stopped Tess and

Magda said softly, 'I'll come with you, Tessie. If there's a protest. Just as long as I don't have to make a speech or anything.'

Tess let her tensed shoulders drop. 'Just be your beautiful self,' she said, eventually smiling. 'Maybe we'll make the front page.'

Magda laughed, but when Tess looked towards Jo challengingly the younger girl just shrugged.

'Maybe,' she said. 'If it happens.'

'It's going to happen!' Tess poked Jo hard in the arm, and Jo pushed her hand away roughly.

'You don't know that,' Jo said. 'And even if it does, it probably won't make any difference.'

'You should go, Jo,' Carly piped up. 'Us Travellers should stand up for our rights, like Tess says.' She had a serious look on her face but Tess felt annoyed at the way Carly had parroted her words and made them sound stupid.

'Oh, what do you know about it anyway?' she said. 'You with your house and your townie friends.' Suddenly she was annoyed with all of them again. 'You don't understand anything.' Jumping down from the top car with a clang, she turned her back on Carly's protests. 'I'm going to the shop.'

'I have to go too,' Gwen said, standing up. 'My shift starts in an hour.' She was brushing the dust off her clothes and Tess frowned at her, trying to remember when Gwen had become so uptight. 'I'll see you later.' Walking past Tess, she waved a hand dismissively. Her first few steps were slow, but she soon sped up and as she came out of the dump gates and turned in the direction of the sports centre she was walking fast, her heels clicking on the pavement in quick staccato beats. Tess wondered why she was in such a hurry. Perhaps she fancied one of those muscled lifeguards. That would explain why she didn't want Carly hanging about all the time.

'I'm going to the shop,' Tess repeated now. 'I'll be back in ten minutes, all right?'

'Sure,' Magda still hadn't moved, her skirt hiked up to display long freckled legs just beginning to get a touch of the sun.

'Wait!' There was a pounding of feet on the dirt track a few seconds later and Carly called after her. 'Wait up, Tess. I'll come with you.'

Tess glanced at her, fighting the impulse to say something savage. It wasn't Carly's fault she was young and annoying. Or rather it was, but it wasn't like a criminal offence. Tess just got bored of the way the younger girl whinged all the time. She was always down on someone for something, or telling stories about people so that she'd look better by comparison. The trouble was, she was so obvious about it that it only won her enemies.

○

At the mini-supermarket Tess took a wire basket from the stack and pushed it at Carly. 'You can make yourself useful.' Pausing, she looked at her. 'You said you could pay for your own swimming, so you've got cash, right?'

'Five pounds,' Carly said. 'I saved it out of my pocket money . . .'

'Then we can get Coke and crisps and that,' Tess said. Grabbing a six-pack of crisps, four cans of Coke and a box of jaffa cakes, she dropped them in the basket.

'What about you? How much have you got?' Carly asked, and Tess shrugged.

'Not much,' she said. 'Travellers don't get *pocket money*.'

'That's . . .' Carly blushed. 'That's OK, I'll get it.' Taking the basket up to the checkout, she put it down on the counter.

'Here,' said Tess, dropping a packet of Maltesers into it from the rack of sweets at the counter. 'Let's get these as well.'

She wasn't looking at Carly and neither was the boy serving. He grinned at Tess as he began to ring up the purchases.

'Having a picnic?' he asked and Tess rolled her eyes.

'No, we're starting a girl group and these are our accessories,' she said. 'She's Jaffa Cake and I'm the Malteser.'

Carly giggled nervously and the boy grinned widely.

'That I'd pay to see,' he said. 'What about your friend, the blonde one? What's she going to be?'

'She's Coca-Cola,' Tess said, picking up a plastic bag and putting the Coke cans in as he passed them to her. 'Sugary, sweet and bad for you.'

Carly looked completely confused. 'Do you mean Magda?' she asked, flicking her eyes from the boy to Tess.

'Aha, I knew I'd find out her name sooner or later,' the boy said and Tess nudged Carly with her elbow.

'Now look what you've done,' she said. 'Now he'll probably ask her out and you know what'll happen.'

'Sorry.' Carly fumbled to get her money and dropped some on the counter. As she was picking it up again the boy frowned at Tess.

'Three pounds eighty-five and why shouldn't I ask her out?'

'Coca-Cola doesn't date,' Tess smirked. 'It would hold back her musical career.'

'You're a riot,' the boy laughed again, accepting Carly's money and ringing it up on the till. 'Maybe I should ask you out instead.'

'Oh yeah?' Tess grinned back flirtatiously. 'I'll tell Magda that . . .' Picking up the bag, she swung it to and fro, stepping back from the counter. 'Come on, Carly. Let's leave Mr Supermarket Man to his work.'

'So that's your name,' the boy said quickly, looking at Carly for the first time. 'What's hers?'

'It's Tess,' Tess answered herself as she headed towards the door.

'Wait up,' he said hastily. 'What about my party? Remember you promised you and your friend would come,' he dropped his voice as he added less certainly, 'if I sold you that tobacco.'

'Yeah, like that'd hold up in court,' Tess said, but when he continued to stare at her she added, 'I've told her about it. I can't force her to come, can I?'

'Saturday the twelfth of July,' the boy said emphatically. 'Don't forget.'

'It's going to be hard to, with you reminding me every time I step in here.'

Carly was looking at Tess strangely as they left the shop. 'Does he really fancy Magda?' she asked.

'All the boys fancy Magda,' Tess said grandly. 'The ones that aren't after me, anyway. But neither of us are going to waste ourselves on some spotty schoolboy.'

'He wasn't spotty,' Carly objected and Tess snickered.

'Ohh, so you fancy him then, do you?'

'I do not!'

As they approached the dirt track to the dump again Tess suddenly said, 'Listen, don't go telling other people's names in public again, all right? If Magda wants him to know what her name is, she'll tell him herself. And she doesn't, so she won't.'

'OK, OK.' Carly pulled her arm away. 'I didn't know it was a big secret. And you told him my name anyway.'

'Like that matters,' Tess said scornfully. 'It's not you he fancies.'

'Well, it's not you either, Tess Lovett,' Carly retorted. She narrowed her eyes as she added, 'What are you, Magda's keeper? Here, give me the stuff. I paid for it, didn't I?'

Reaching out, Carly grabbed the bag of food and began to run up the track, leaving Tess behind. Tess glared at her pale pudgy legs pounding up the path. Then, breaking into a run, Tess loped up the track, passing Carly easily, even with the younger girl's head start.

Tess grinned to herself, the sting of Carly's words fading already. She wasn't Magda's keeper; but they looked out for each other. Tess made the decisions, and when they got into trouble Magda did the apologies. No one seemed to notice that Magda always went along with what Tess suggested. So she hadn't been flirting with that boy for herself, she'd been doing it for Magda. Magda would never agree straight out to come to the party, but that boy would keep asking and Tess would keep bringing it up, and they'd go in the end. Magda might look like a good girl, but she wasn't quite as innocent as everyone else thought.

Magda and Jo were still sitting on top of the car mountain sunning themselves, and Magda looked down and smiled as Tess arrived. 'We could see you coming from miles away,' she said. 'This is a great place, Tessie.'

'It's a dark tower and you're the enchanted princess,' Tess said, grinning back at her. 'Magsie, Magsie, let down your hair . . .'

Magda laughed and leaned forward over the edge, shaking out her long blonde-streaked hair as Tess began to climb up the cars. Behind her, Tess could hear Carly trying clumsily to get on to the bonnet of the first car.

'Wait for me . . .' she whined. But Tess ignored her, ruffling Magda's hair as she reached the top of the pile once more.

'Now I'm the king of the castle,' she said.

'Then who's the dirty rascal,' Jo asked, and Tess glanced back behind her. The youngest girl's lip quivered and for once Tess couldn't be bothered to hold the grudge.

'Whoever the filthy swine is that came up with this whole roundabout plan,' she said. 'That's who.' And reaching down a hand, she helped Carly up to join them.

7

BEHIND THE CHOIR STALLS

After a week of golden sunshine the rain had come in again as if it regretted giving them a break. At night it hammered on the roof of the trailer and by day it spat at the school classroom windows. Magda sat trapped behind a desk at school, or trapped with the kids in the trailer at night, longing for it to stop so she could escape. She spent breaks and lunch behind the school bike sheds, huddled under the tin roofing while Tess chain-smoked.

They'd discussed bunking off but there was nowhere to go, at least nowhere dry. Jo had built a den somewhere across the overpass, but she was being sulky again and refused to tell either of them where it was. Carly spent her breaks hanging around in the library, annoying Gwen so much that she'd begged Tess and Magda to include the younger girl.

'It's hanging around with you that's started her making a big deal about being a Traveller all of a sudden. She's trying to fit in.'

But Tess had refused. 'She'll spend the whole time talking about the dangers of smoking,' she said. 'You know she will. Or talking about her gypsy ancestry, like a tourist.'

'At least she's for Traveller rights and against the roundabout,' Magda had pointed out, but Tess had just rolled her eyes and Magda hadn't pushed it. Tess was sensitive on the subject and at the slightest opportunity she'd flare up at them for not caring enough or caring the wrong way.

Poor Carly. Magda couldn't help feeling sorry for her – she didn't seem to have any friends in her class. But even Magda had to admit it was embarrassing the way Carly was acting. She'd got her first-ever detention that week for mouthing off to the deputy head when she was spotted wearing massive gold hoop earrings in assembly.

'It's cultural jewellery, miss,' she'd insisted. 'Cos of my Romany heritage. I'm allowed, aren't I?'

School policy only allowed plain studs, although Tess had two tiny gold rings. But what had made it so silly was that Carly's were clip-ons. The deputy head confiscated the earrings. Tess had been annoyed.

'You might as well come to school with a crystal ball and start telling fortunes,' she'd said cruelly later that day, when Carly's face was already blotched from crying.

With all the roundabout mess people's feelings were churned up anyway, like the earth and sand barricades out at the construction site. Travellers were suddenly an issue at school in a way they hadn't been for a while. Magda had thought they were accepted here, but some people were making it plain they thought it wouldn't be a bad idea if the Travellers were forced to move on.

'That's what you lot do anyway,' one of the other smokers had said to Tess when they'd argued over who should have the shelter of the bike shed. 'Move on, right? So why don't you get on out of it.'

Tess had flung herself at the smoker girl then – her dark hair streaming out behind her – ready to fight. It was only Magda's intervention that stopped her and saved her from a detention, if not a suspension. 'You'll only make things worse,' she'd said.

'They don't know anything about us,' Tess said bitterly afterwards. 'Nothing at all. It's all crystal balls and painted wagons to them. Just like it is for Carly.' She stormed off, and Magda didn't try to go after her. You couldn't talk to Tess when she was in a mood like this. The only hope was to wait for her to calm down and switch back to sunny again.

Magda tried to persuade herself to do something nice for Carly, take her to the rec or to the swimming pool maybe. But she had to look after little kids so much at home that she didn't have the energy to take on another, and her younger sisters and brothers were a nightmare at the moment. They grizzled to be allowed to go out and then came back filthy with mud ten minutes later. She seemed to spend half her life wiping muddy footprints off the floor. Thinking about this, she remembered again the boy she'd met on the hill. Seb. He'd told her his house was supposed to be spotless, like it was a bad thing, but right

88

now Magda could see the appeal. Anything had to be better than sticky fingers clutching at her skirt.

Today after school she should have gone home to help with tea. But she'd turned right instead of left out of the main gates and asked Tess to tell her parents she'd gone to church. She was wearing the anorak she'd swapped with Carly, but she shivered as she walked quickly through the town centre, trying to avoid the umbrellas of passers-by.

It was chilly inside the church, even though someone had put electric heaters up and down the aisles. It was also busier than usual, probably people taking the opportunity to get out of the rain. Standing by one of the heaters, Magda took off her anorak and folded it inside out, so it wouldn't drip, before looking for a place to sit. She crossed herself automatically as she passed the high altar and walked up the steps to the row of high-backed choir stalls.

It was warmer in the stalls and she put her anorak under the seat before leaning back against the carved wood. There was a hymn book on the bench in front of her and she picked it up. It always interested her how many different kinds of hymns there were: for saints' days and seasons, for absent friends and use at sea. Pausing at Hymns for Rough Weather, she read the words of one of them, trying to remember the tune. Each verse ended with the line 'peace, be still' and her hands stilled on the book as she felt herself relaxing. Peaceful and still, that was how she wanted to be.

As she warmed up Magda felt drowsy and her eyelids drooped. Dreamily she looked around the church.

She started as a shadow blocked out the light at the end of the stalls and looked to see someone sitting down. As he slid along the bench to join her, her eyes widened and she whispered, 'What are you doing here?'

'Visiting church,' Seb said, stretching his legs out in front of him as he turned to look at her. 'I told you I was a Catholic.'

'Oh yes?' Magda raised her eyebrows and he shrugged and showed his white teeth in a grin.

'Besides, it's filthy weather out there – you really think all these people came in to pray?'

'Maybe,' Magda said even as she looked at the girl in smart clothes who'd taken off one of her high-heeled shoes and was looking at it ruefully, and the woman with a double buggy who was leafing through the postcards at the door '*I* did,' she said, feeling as if someone should have at least. She felt Seb frown even before he spoke.

'I'm sorry, am I disturbing you?' he said, catching her off-balance again.

'No, no, that's fine.' Why was she always so worried about seeming rude to him?

'You haven't been up the hill for a while,' he said softly.

'I had chores,' she said. 'I've little brothers and sisters I have to watch after school.'

He leaned closer every time he spoke, whispering conspiratorially so that the stalls felt like a small cave of warmth they shared together. 'At least I don't have that at home,' Seb said. 'I'm an only child.'

'And you a Catholic.' Magda smiled at him, but when his face set uncomfortably she realized she'd said something wrong.

'I think my mother would have liked to have had more but my dad said no.' He shrugged. 'He doesn't like kids. Me being so old, it makes him feel older. You know, he tells people he has a little boy, like I'm five or something. It's embarrassing when they phone up; I can tell they're confused and think they've got it wrong, but it's all him.' His voice had got hard and fierce, rising out of a whisper.

'My parents don't like thinking about me growing up either,' Magda offered. 'They worry, you know, about me going out, who my friends are . . .'

'Meeting boys?' Seb asked.

'That too,' she admitted and she put up a hand to hide her smile.

'Bet they didn't think you'd meet anyone in church,' he said.

'My da would go spare.' She felt guilty even as she said it and glanced around to check they weren't being watched. If someone did see them and told her parents, the joke wouldn't seem so funny.

Seb moved even closer and Magda felt his shoulder pressing up against hers as he leaned to look past her hair and smile at her again. 'Not even a nice Catholic boy?' he asked and Magda laughed softly.

'It's not just that,' she said. 'It's more that you're . . .'

'What?' His blue eyes were staring into hers and she felt flustered and confused by them.

'You're not like us,' she said uncomfortably. She raised her head to meet that stare and said clearly, 'Not a Traveller.'

'Oh.' Seb blinked and then she saw comprehension dawning. 'You're from the gypsy camp? The Traveller camp,' he corrected a moment later.

Magda sensed him draw back, moving away from her. His expression was shuttered and she felt a dropping sensation inside herself at the thought that he might not like her because of her background. People talked a lot about prejudice but she'd never met it in someone she . . . liked.

'That's near where the building work is happening, isn't it? For the roundabout?' he said and she blinked, surprised that it was *that* he found interesting. 'You know about that, right?' he said slowly, not quite meeting her eyes.

'My friend Tess is furious about it. She says we should all protest. She thinks if it's built we'll lose half the site.'

'And what about you?' He lifted his head to look at her. 'What do you think?'

'Everyone at the site's against it,' she said, emphasizing her words. 'If the roundabout gets built, half of us might lose our spaces here, and the others will be living right next to the roundabout and road. We'd have to find somewhere else to stay and that's never easy.'

He shook his head and she felt that slow dropping again, sure that he was disagreeing, but then he said, 'That's so wrong.' His mouth twisted unpleasantly. 'I'm really sorry.'

'It's not your fault.' Magda smiled at him, relieved to find he was on her side after all.

'I'm still sorry,' he said quietly, and his hand covered the small distance that had momentarily opened up between them to take her hand and hold it.

○

Magda knew the rain had gone when people began to leave the church and dyed sunlight floated down through the great rose window at the back. Looking at her pale fingers, twined through Seb's brown ones, she didn't want to move.

'I should go,' she said.

'You always have to go,' Seb said. 'When can I see you next?'

'You can't.' Untangling her fingers, she let go of his hand and clasped her own together. 'My parents wouldn't like it.'

'You know I'll find you again – here or on the hill.' His blue eyes challenged her. 'So you may as well say that I can.'

'What if I asked you not to?' she asked and he replied at once.

'Then I wouldn't. But you won't, right?'

Magda sighed. This was what the Our Father meant about temptation. Once you're led into it, it's hard to turn back. It was better not to be tempted at all. Once the devil spoke to Adam and Eve, they couldn't help themselves from listening. But Seb wasn't the devil. And she liked him.

'I won't say you can see me,' she said. 'Not when my parents wouldn't like it.'

'But you're not saying I can't,' Seb said, putting his hand over hers once more.

Magda looked up at him sideways, through her lashes. 'I'm not saying you can't,' she agreed.

She moved a little and Seb took his hand away again, leaving her feeling cold. To cover her brief shiver of doubt she reached for her coat. It was damp and clammy and she said 'ugh', laughing a little.

'Take mine,' Seb said instantly, shrugging his shoulders out of his black jacket.

'I can't.' Magda coloured and he smiled at her mischievously.

'Of course you can,' he said. 'You know I only live up the road. You can give it back to me next time.' He put an arm across her shoulders, draping his jacket over them.

Her breath caught and she felt light-headed. She had to resist the urge to lean back into his arm. Instead she stood up, sliding her arms into the sleeves of his coat. Searching for something to say, she teased, 'Perhaps I'm a thieving gypsy and you'll never see me again.'

'I'll see you again,' he said and she remembered him saying that before.

'Goodbye,' she said softly. He didn't try to touch he, but he watched her as she edged out from the choir stalls and she could feel him still watching as she walked down the nave towards the doors.

She thought about him as she walked out of town

and back past the school – Seb sitting in the church, waiting for her. Or up at the top of the hill, watching the sunset and thinking about her. Now, reaching a hand to stroke the dark material of his coat, he seemed more real to her than she did to herself. The girl who laughed and flirted with Seb wasn't the same Magda as the girl who had walked alone into church and tried to feel at peace. She didn't know which of them she was any more.

Back at the site she checked the mailbox at the staff prefab and Peggy, the site supervisor, watched her from her desk.

'How are you then, Magda?' she said. 'Bit late, aren't you?'

'I've been to church,' Magda said, feeling like a liar. Her mother was always on edge around Peggy, claiming she looked down on them when the kids ran wild and would have them off the site if she could. But this was the first time Magda'd noticed the woman's accusatory tone herself. Probably because it's the first time I've felt really guilty about what I've been doing, she realized. But Peggy was looking embarrassed now, the way people often did when Magda mentioned going to church. It made them feel judged for not going themselves.

'Say hello to your mum from me,' Peggy said. Magda nodded and walked away.

At the trailer door she stopped, took off Seb's coat and rolled it into a ball, stuffing it in her school bag. Putting on Carly's old anorak, she shivered as the chilled fabric touched her bare arms, then she opened the door.

'Hello, Mam,' she said. 'Sorry I'm late.'

'It's all right, love,' her mother smiled, getting up to pour another mug of tea. 'Tess told us you'd gone to church.' She nodded to the other end of the table.

Tess was sitting next to Marianna, drinking a cup of tea, and her dark eyes lifted to meet Magda's lighter ones. 'You were ages,' she said. 'Reenie's having a strop and your mam said I could stay over with you tonight.'

'Oh.' Magda sat down and summoned a smile. 'That's fine.'

'You don't mind, do you, love?' Her mother gave her the tea mug and Tess laughed.

'Course she doesn't mind.'

'You're not to talk all night though,' her mam added, passing her a plate of food. 'Seconds, Tess?'

'That'd be great.' Tess held out her plate for more.

Magda looked down at her own food and suddenly felt not hungry.

'Keep mine warm for me,' she said. 'I'm all wet from the rain.' She stood quickly and picked up her school bag, holding her mug in her other hand. 'I'll drink this while I change.'

'Don't be too long or I'll eat yours as well.' Tess grinned at her. 'I'm starving.'

'I'll make sure to hurry then,' Magda replied, opening the door with her shoulder and going across to the other trailer.

But as she reached her room and put down the mug of tea on the dresser unit she knew she'd be doing the opposite. Tess would be sleeping in here tonight, she thought, putting her bag away in the back of her closet. She would probably want to talk and Magda would listen. She wondered how she knew already that she wasn't going to mention Seb.

8

COLD RECEPTION

The Travellers had agreed to hold the protest in the middle of the week of half-term. A weekend would have been better, so that most people wouldn't have to take time off work, but the police had said that would disrupt traffic too much.

'We're supposed to be walking up the high street to the town hall, right through the middle of town,' one of the men working at the dump had told Tess. 'You'll make sure to get your friends to come along, won't you, Tess girl?'

'No problem,' Tess agreed. 'I've already told them they've got to.'

But on Wednesday morning it didn't seem as if a lot of the Travellers were that bothered. The sun was shining for the first time that week, and around the site grown-ups were getting out washing tubs while the younger kids were kicking a football about. A group of women had cut up a sheet and were painting 'Travellers against the roundabout' across it, but it wasn't exactly the frenzy of activity Tess had hoped for.

Reenie was sat outside with a neighbour, drinking tea, and Tess headed over to look down at them.

'You're going on the march, aren't you?' she said and Reenie looked at her coldly.

'Waste of time,' she snapped. 'The building work's started already.'

'We might go later, love,' the neighbour said placatingly, 'but I've got to take my kids to the sports centre first. They'll riot if we don't take advantage of the special offer.'

'What offer?' Tess frowned.

'Half-price entry to the outside pool,' the woman explained. 'They've opened it at last. A man was down here this morning putting flyers up all over the fence.'

'What?' Tess turned to stare at the fence and then set off at a run towards it. Pieces of paper had been sticky-taped across the chain link, facing in. They all said the same thing.

Bluewater Sports Centre
Outdoor pool opens Wednesday 28 May.
Half-price admission for under-16s.

Looking away from the signs, Tess saw that a couple of kids mucking about with a hose were wearing swim things and some of the washing lines already up were strung with bikinis and trunks like brightly coloured flags. Heading through the gate to the payphone, she passed Mrs Lakely with a bunch of the younger kids, all carrying towels and inflatable rings and toys.

'You're going to the pool?' she said and Mrs Lakely stopped to look at her apologetically.

'Sorry, Tess. I can't exactly take this lot to the protest, can I? Not when it's the first decent splash of sunshine we've seen. But Magda's going with you lot, I think. She went off to the shop to get something, but she'll be back any minute.'

'Thanks,' Tess said grudgingly. She did sort of see that the little ones wouldn't want to go on the protest, but maybe if Mrs Lakely had explained to them how important it was . . . She shook her head and jogged up to the phonebox.

The phone rang about nine times before it was picked up and a familiar voice said, 'Bluewater Sports and Fitness Centre. How may I help you?'

'Gwen, what the hell's going on?' Tess demanded. 'How come you've opened the pool today? You never do until June.'

'Is that you, Tess?' Gwen's voice dropped to a whisper and Tess had to cram the phone up against her ear to make out what the other girl was saying. 'Look, what's your problem? Mark thought it would be a good promotion, take advantage of the sunshine. What's wrong with a special offer?'

'What's wrong with it is that the protest's today!' Tess shouted down the line, hoping everyone on the other end would hear her. 'We're supposed to be marching to the town hall, not going swimming!'

'Keep your voice down,' Gwen hissed. 'Just get over it. I'm sure lots of people will go on your march.'

'Yeah, right. You're a traitor, Gwen Hughes.' Tess slammed the receiver back on the cradle and turned round, fuming.

A pile of placards saying 'Save Our Site' in photocopied pages stapled on to plywood lay abandoned by one of the trailers, but there was no other sign of people preparing to protest. Stopping at the Rowlands' trailer, Tess banged on the door but no one answered until Jo's brother got out of the van parked next to it.

'What's up, Tess, you looking for Jo? She's gone out already.'

'I was looking for all of you,' Tess told him angrily. 'You know it's the protest today. We're all off to the town hall.'

'I know,' Dan said, surprising her. 'I'm coming. But that's not till one, is it?'

'Yeah, but no one seems to be taking it seriously,' Tess ranted. 'And the sports centre's having a half-price day, so everyone's going there instead.'

'Maybe that's where Jo's gone,' Dan suggested, before shaking his head. 'No, she's got a season pass, hasn't she? Talking of which –' he fixed Tess with a hard look – 'don't you owe me fifteen quid? Jo says you borrowed it out of cash I gave her.'

'Yeah, keep your hair on,' Tess said, tossing her head. 'You'll get it back, all right? Look, I've got to find Magda – she said she'd come on the march. I need her help to persuade other people to come.'

'Well, she's got a better chance than you,' Dan said, looking darkly at her. 'Maybe you could try actually asking people when you want something from them.'

When Tess got back to the Lakelys' trailers they were still empty. A group of adults had assembled near where the women's banner was and were drinking tea and talking about presenting the petition. But they seemed more interested in moaning than actually doing anything. Tess had signed her name to the petition days ago. Reenie hadn't signed and Tess had waited until no one was looking before signing for her too, forging her handwriting as she'd done on notes for school a hundred times.

There was still no sign of Magda. Then at eleven thirty Tess saw a figure in a pink duffle coat hurrying along the path and went to meet her, relieved.

It wasn't Magda, it was Carly. She was carrying a weighty shopping bag and a banner taped to bamboo poles.

'What are you doing here?' Tess snapped. 'And why are you wearing Magda's coat?'

'We swapped, ages ago,' Carly said. 'And I'm here for the protest, of course. I made a banner. Look . . .' Dropping her bag, she opened up the banner, sticking one of the poles in the earth and unrolling the sheet carefully. The letters were black felt and had been neatly ironed on.

Accleton Travellers and Residents
say NO to the roundabout!

Around the edges of the banner were coloured-in drawings of cars and trucks on a long looping snake of grey with white lines down the middle.

'What do you think?' Carly asked, grinning nervously.

'Why did you put that bit about residents?' Tess asked. 'People round here don't care about Travellers.'

'No one in the development wants the roundabout either,' Carly said, looking surprised. 'They don't want a roundabout across the road any more than you want to be next to one. I told a couple of people about the protest, but there weren't any signs up about it so I don't know if they'll come. Just those Bluewater fitness posters. Have you seen them?'

'Yes, I've bloody seen them,' Tess snapped before storming off to the Lakelys' trailers again.

They were still closed and empty. It wasn't like Magda to just vanish like this and Tess wondered if she'd forgotten what day it was and gone off to church. Tess looked around; someone had made a round of sandwiches and a bunch of men were drinking beer while they ate. It was more like a picnic than a protest. What would they look like when they finally got going?

By one o'clock about fifty people were gathered around Alan Hughes's trailer. Alan was organizing people into groups and as Tess came up he waved her over. 'There you are,' he said. 'I was wondering where you'd got to. You're coming on the march, right?'

'Of course I am.' Tess scowled at him. 'I've been here all morning, trying to get people to go.'

'Good, good.' Alan hardly seemed to hear her. 'We're

off in a moment. Why don't you get alongside of Carly and hold up that banner? We can stick the two of you in the front, so the news'll get a good shot of you kids if they take photos.'

'I was waiting for Magda . . .' Tess began to explain, but he'd already moved on to telling the group of men they had to get rid of their beer cans before the march.

Tess turned and looked around the gathering. Carly was standing a little to the edge of the group, still holding her banner although she'd managed to ditch her huge bag. 'You've been ages,' she said as Tess came over. 'Hasn't Magda shown up yet? Do you want to hold the banner or not? It's not going to work right if it's just me.'

'Yeah, yeah, I'll help with the bloody banner,' Tess said. She kicked angrily at the ground. 'I'm just going to have a fag first.' She started to rummage in her pockets and Carly opened her hazel eyes wide.

'You can't,' she said. 'It'll look bad. Uncle Alan said so.'

'He's not your uncle,' Tess snapped, before remembering that actually he was, sort of. At least, he was Gwen's uncle and Gwen was Carly's cousin. 'Anyway, he's not looking.'

Just then Alan's voice boomed out over the chatter and people started to move forward. Alan had got hold of a loudhailer and was repeating stuff they already knew about walking into town and then up the high street.

'Come on,' Carly said, holding out the banner and Tess took the other side of it with a sinking feeling.

Peggy from the site office came out of the door to

watch as the Travellers formed up at the entrance. Peggy wasn't one of them and she seemed to be making a point of it as she watched them go.

Tess and Carly were at the front of the protest near the mothers with pushchairs and had to keep dodging the pushchair wheels as the marchers clustered on one side of the pavement. It would have looked better to be able to walk up the centre of the road, but there weren't enough of them, and at least bunched together on the pavement they seemed like more of a group. People coming out of shops had to move back into the entrances and watch as they went by and the drivers of cars slowed down to look at them.

Alan was using his loudhailer to encourage people to make noise and a group of the men responded resoundingly with shouts of 'NO' when he asked, 'What do we say to the roundabout?' and, 'What do we say to the council?'

'This is great.' Carly was grinning all over her face as she looked across at Tess. 'You know what? We should have had a "Hoot if you support us" sign. That'd be really good.'

'Those people don't support us,' Tess sneered at her. 'They think we look like idiots. That's why they're watching.'

Her mood soured further when they got to the high street. One side of it had been blocked off with police barriers and there were about six policemen at the beginning of the route. 'I thought there'd be more of your lot coming,' one of them said as the protest straggled into the road.

105

Tess glowered, looking back over her shoulder. There weren't very many of them. It didn't look anything like the marches she'd seen on TV that went on for blocks and blocks of people.

As the protesters got nearer to the town hall there were more police, lining the barriers with their arms folded behind their backs and bored expressions on their faces.

'Travellers say no to the roundabout!' Carly shouted as they went past and other people started yelling things as well. But Tess felt sick. She wanted to yell stuff out but the angry words in her head, about standing united and people's rights, didn't seem to apply to this straggly group of day trippers. This wasn't a march of rebellion, it was an orderly stroll. Instead of making them look powerful, Tess thought, it made the Travellers seem pathetic.

When they got to the town hall there were more barriers and police, and people sort of milled about in the space between the car park and the front steps while Alan collected up pages of the petition.

'You can't all go in,' a policeman said, coming up to the barriers. 'You can send four people inside. The rest of you have to stay here.'

There was a confused huddle. Suddenly Tess had had enough. She turned to Carly. 'Tell your uncle he should pick us,' she hissed. But Carly shook her head.

'You tell him if you want to go,' she said unhelpfully.

Tess dropped her end of the banner and pushed her way through to Alan. He'd already selected two other men and a woman and they were walking up the town-hall steps.

'Alan!' she said, running up alongside him, her hair wild about her head. She grabbed his arm. 'I've got some things I'd like to say to the council – you need someone in there with you who's not afraid to speak up for our rights!'

Alan frowned. 'Calm down, Tess. I'm not sure that's such a good idea—'

'This is pathetic,' Tess heard her own voice rise angrily. She pushed past Alan up another step. 'This ridiculous little stroll, this polite petition, isn't going to get us heard. If my dad was here he'd have come up with something better; he'd have said—'

'Shut up!' Alan grabbed her by the shoulders and spun her round so she was looking back down the steps. 'See that?' he said. He pointed at a policeman making his way through the small crowd below them, his eyes fixed firmly on Tess. 'And that?' he pointed at a newspaper photographer lining up for a shot. '*That's* not going to achieve anything either – a picture of a Traveller teenager being arrested on the steps of the town hall! What do you think that will do for our popularity with the town? Do you have to make trouble everywhere you go?'

Tess clenched her fists but Alan's face was implacable, staring her down. Eventually she dropped her eyes, her dark hair falling forward to hide her face. She heard him walk up the stairs without her. She glared at the steps, trying to compose herself, wishing she had one ally in the crowd. Her thoughts went bitterly to Magda, who had promised to stand beside her and failed to turn up.

When she finally started back down, she saw the man with the camera was taking photos elsewhere now.

'I'm from the *Accleton Gazette*,' he was saying to one of the mothers with pushchairs. 'So what's this protest about anyway?' But he didn't seem that interested when they told him.

'Are we going to be in the paper?' Carly asked him when he'd finished.

He shrugged. 'As long as nothing more exciting comes along.'

Shortly afterwards, Alan and the others came back down the town-hall steps.

'That didn't take long,' someone said and Alan looked annoyed.

'They didn't let us in to see the council,' he said. 'Two councillors came down and took the petition but they didn't hang about. They said the development's perfectly legal, all sewn up. We haven't got a leg to stand on.'

Tess bit her tongue. Why hadn't they let her go in? She'd have *forced* the council to listen.

'Well, we've made our opinions felt – that's something,' Alan said.

'It's not anything,' Tess muttered bitterly under her breath.

People were already beginning to leave, the mothers with pushchairs off to go shopping and the men heading in the direction of a pub. The policemen were leaving too, taking their barriers with them. The whole protest had lasted about an hour and a half and that was a generous estimate. Carly rolled up her banner neatly and came over to Tess.

'So, what do you want to do next?' she said. 'You could come back to my house if you want.'

'I don't want,' Tess snarled. 'I'm out of here.' Turning, she began to walk away.

'See if I care then, Tess Lovett,' Carly shouted after her. 'Who needs you anyway?'

Tess stamped her feet as she walked round the corner. It was true, no one seemed to need her around. She'd thought she'd be doing something useful in the protest. After all, it was her who'd found out about the round-about in the first place – but no one seemed to remember that. It just didn't matter to them. Tess scowled blackly as she walked down the road, barging past people when they got in her way. At the pelican crossing on the other side of the road from the Catholic church she waited for the cars to stop. Then a head of blonde hair opposite caught her eye.

It wouldn't be Magda, she thought, looking over. She'd hoped she'd seen her a couple of times already today and each time it hadn't been her. This girl was coming out of the graveyard, wearing an expensive black jacket and walking beside a tall boy with dark hair. Obviously not Magda, Tess told herself as her gaze skipped over the girl. Then she looked again, ignoring the cars that had stopped for her to cross the road. It was Magda.

Magda had turned and was looking up at the boy through her long lashes, in the way that made her appear so demure. She was smiling and laughing. Tess turned away savagely, dodging out of sight in case Magda looked her way.

She should have stopped, she thought, even as she was running, taking the short cut in back of the library towards the cycle path that went south. She had a right to be angry. She should have stopped and told Magda what she thought of her. But, as she wiped her sleeve across her stinging eyes, all she could think of right now was getting away.

9

BESIDE THE STONE ANGEL

Jo made it to second break before she couldn't take any more. One of the things about moving schools was that you ended up repeating stuff. Her class at Accleton seniors was doing *Catcher in the Rye* in English. The teacher kept singling her out because her last school had passed on her notes and she was supposed to know the book already. But she hadn't read the stupid book last time she'd done it, back in Devon.

As soon as the bell rang Jo was out of there and she got to the playground ahead of anyone else. The sun was shining, but a wind was blowing in blustery gusts so that she was warmed and chilled alternately. Looking across the empty playground to the main gates, Jo found herself walking towards them. She didn't even make a real decision to bunk off until she was through them and walking down the main road towards town. If she'd bunked off first thing in the morning she'd have headed out across the motorway to her den in the woods. But now if she went that way she would most likely run into someone she knew as she went past the Traveller site. So she continued in the other direction.

The wind whipped past, casting her mane of tangled hair into her face as she walked. Looking at her reflection in the shop windows she passed, she grimaced at her own body. She was wearing blue jeans with her white shirt so it wasn't obvious she was in uniform, although if a truant officer saw her that wouldn't fool them. But it was embarrassing the way her shirt didn't hang straight, the wind pulling it tight around her front so that her breasts pushed out from under the fabric. Jo never used to care about how she looked, though when she gave it a thought she was pleased that she was skinny, not lumpy like Carly. But now her own body looked rude to her, and the bra her mother had bought her just made it worse. Bras were supposed to hold stuff in, weren't they? But hers just seemed to make her stick out more.

As she stared at herself in a shop window, an assistant fixing the display turned to look at her and Jo stepped back quickly. It was too exposed, being on the street. To the right was the Catholic church the Lakelys went to. Jo wasn't interested in churches, but around the side an iron gate led into a graveyard. She crossed over the road and went through.

The graveyard was empty, the flowers people had planted or left tossing in the winds and the long grass rustling like ghosts. At the far end of the graveyard there were tombs, like little houses for dead people, with pillars and metal doors. Ivy grew over the older graves. Jo supposed the statues were supposed to be angels, but most of them looked like soppy young men: holding books or harps or flowers. She sneered at them and was turning to go on when a movement caught her eye. Behind the soppy statues was one that did look like an angel: a woman with a smooth oval face and hair carved in gentle waves that the wind couldn't touch. Her hands were folded in front of her like someone's at church and the wings that grew from her back were folded forward as if they were protecting the gravestone at her feet.

It was a tiny gravestone, child-sized, and sitting in front of it, sheltered by the angel's wings, was Magda.

She was looking straight at Jo, with the same calm expression as the angel, so it took Jo a moment to realize that Magda wasn't actually seeing her. In the end she had to wave an arm to attract her attention. Only then did Magda's light grey eyes glitter into life as she recognized her.

'You bunking off as well?' Jo asked, coming to stand in front of the angel, and Magda looked sheepish. 'How come Tess isn't with you?' Jo went on as she sat down next to Magda. The other girl shrugged and looked away.

'She's still mad at me about the protest. Because I didn't go with her,' she said.

'Why didn't you go?' Jo asked, surprised. Magda and Tess were always so tight, she hadn't doubted they'd both go. 'You decided it was lame, or what?'

'I had something else I had to do,' Magda said softly. 'And it wasn't lame. It's brave of Tess to fight for our rights.'

'Yeah, well, she likes a fight,' Jo shrugged, then added, 'and you'll make it up, bound to.'

'We've never fought before,' Magda said. 'I feel bad. I should have gone with her. And now she's not even speaking to me. I didn't expect her to be so angry. I should have realized how much it mattered to her.'

But Jo didn't feel like talking about Tess. It wasn't often that she saw Magda alone and she felt a rush of liking for her that made her ask a different question straight out.

'Mags, do you wear a bra?'

'Yes, of course!' Magda's face went slightly pink at the question and she giggled, lifting a hand to cover her mouth. 'Why?'

'Oh, it's just I hate my stupid body,' Jo said, picking a stem of grass and twiddling it between her fingers. 'Mum bought me this bra and she said I have to wear it and it makes me look . . .' she stripped the piece of grass of seeds and scattered them. 'I don't see why girls have to change shape.'

'It's natural,' Magda said, smiling. 'And you shouldn't hate your body. You're pretty, Jo.'

'I'm too tall.' Jo tore the piece of grass into short sections and dropped them on the ground. 'Even the boys in my class are shorter.'

'Girls mature faster,' Magda said. 'That's why they date older boys.' The look on her face was knowing and Jo felt surprised. Magda was the good girl; it never seemed as if she was interested in boys, for all that they were fascinated by her.

'I'm not into dating,' Jo said. 'I just want things to be comfortable again. You know Mum made us come here because I was hanging out with the Donovan boys? She told Dad I was growing up.'

'Well, you are,' Magda smiled. 'Everyone is, all the time.'

'You know what I mean,' Jo objected and Magda lifted her shoulders in something between a shrug and a sigh.

'At least your parents will let you date when you want to,' she said. 'Even if they don't like it, they admit you're growing up. Ma wouldn't let me wear a bra until one came in the jumble and I took it.'

'Do you *want* to grow up?' Jo asked curiously and Magda shook her head, letting her long blonde hair swing loose about her face.

'Not the way Gwen does – leaving school and having a job. I'm not ready for that. But . . .' she hesitated.

'What?' Jo leaned forward, sensing confidences, and Magda laughed nervously.

'I'd like to be allowed to be me,' Magda said. 'My real self, not someone else's idea of how I should be.'

Jo was surprised; she'd never heard Magda talking like this before. 'You seem real to me,' she said slowly. 'Like you know who you are and what you're doing.'

'No, I don't,' Magda's voice was sad. 'I don't at all.'

○

The wind died down as the afternoon sun crept across the graveyard, and Jo lay on her back looking up at the sky above. The remaining cotton-wool clouds were streaked

115

into streamers by the contrails of aeroplanes and, although she could hear traffic on the road beyond the church, it was dim and distant.

'This is a good place,' she said. 'Do you come here a lot?'

'Sometimes,' Magda said. 'My parents don't ask me questions if I say I was at church.'

Jo wondered how many times they'd all thought Magda was praying when she was actually just sitting in the graveyard on her own.

'It's peaceful,' Magda went on. She was leaning back against the angel now, looking completely relaxed. Her skin wasn't sunburned like Jo's but a kind of honey-brown and it made her look prettier than ever.

'Do you really think *I'm* pretty?' Jo asked suddenly.

'You are when you're happy,' Magda said softly, 'but you don't smile enough.'

'What's there to smile about?' Jo retorted.

'Oh, I don't know. Sunshine, sunsets . . .' She laughed suddenly. 'Getting out of school?'

'Yeah, that's pretty good,' Jo admitted.

'You could probably leave if you wanted,' Magda said slowly. 'A lot of Travellers do. The schools make allowances. My parents would let me . . . they know I'd be useful at home.'

'I don't feel like being useful at home,' Jo said crossly again and Magda's voice came like a whisper on the rustling breeze.

'Me neither.'

A fat grey cloud crossed the sun and the air cooled. Jo

sat up as the iron gate clanged on the other side of the graveyard. Magda looked up too, and they watched together as a boy in grey and black school uniform, complete with a tie, came up the graveyard path. He was turning his head as if looking for someone and his eyes met Jo's for an instant before moving on past her. Then he changed course to come towards them.

'Jo,' Magda said, in a low voice. But before she could add anything the boy had reached them.

'Hey,' he said, smiling at Magda. 'How's it going?' And he sat down next to her.

Jo was thinking it was a bit out of order to come up to complete strangers like that when Magda spoke, looking up at the boy with a smile that was just for him.

'Fine,' she said and added, 'This is Jo.' She nodded in Jo's direction and, meeting Jo's eyes, she went on, 'This is Seb.'

'Hi.' Jo was amazed and then suddenly not any more. She met Magda's look and grinned at her, thinking again about all the times Magda had come here alone.

'Hey, Jo.' Seb smiled at her.

He was very good-looking, Jo thought now, watching with fascination as he leaned closer to Magda and touched her arm lightly. Jo saw the brown hand slide familiarly across the golden skin and realized she was in their way.

'I should get back,' she said quickly, not minding the interruption as she might have done if it had been Tess.

'You don't have to go, do you?' Seb asked quickly, looking at Magda, and she shook her head.

'Not yet,' she said. 'Jo . . .'

'I'll tell your parents you went to church after school,' Jo assured her. 'See you later, OK?'

'OK.' Magda smiled and Seb glanced up to nod a goodbye.

'Nice to meet you,' he said politely.

Jo suppressed a laugh, thinking what he really meant was, it was nice she was going – leaving them alone.

At the gate Jo turned and looked back. It was hard to see between the stones and statues, but beneath the angel Seb had moved closer to Magda, black hair shining against blonde. Jo grinned as she crossed the road. Her shirt was still flapping about her hips with the wind and she reached down to undo the bottom buttons and knotted the front tails together around her waist. Catching a glimpse of her reflection in the window of Boots she saw her own smile, conspiratorial, like a secret she shared with herself.

10

INSIDE AND OUTSIDE

Even though her parents both worked late, Carly didn't have a key to her own house. She had to go to the Homework at School Club – in the library – or to a friend's house to wait till her mum got home. But this term Carly hadn't had friends who'd asked her round. So the first Friday back after half-term, when everyone else was rushing away, Carly picked up her bag and trailed dismally across to the school library.

Earlier that day she'd asked Gwen if she could come round to her's instead, but Gwen had rolled her eyes and said curtly, 'I'm working later.' She'd tried to find Magda to ask if she could go home with her, but she wasn't anywhere to be found. In fact, Carly thought, Magda seemed to have turned into a complete nun recently – she went to church practically every day and was more dreamy and vague than ever.

As for Tess, Carly wasn't even speaking to her any more. At the protest the older girl had made it clear that she was embarrassed to be seen with Carly. She'd spent the whole time complaining that Magda hadn't come and at the end she'd just stormed off. It wasn't as if any of the others had turned up, but she'd acted as if Carly was worse than no one because she wasn't a 'proper' Traveller. Besides, Tess had barely shown up at school since.

Carly didn't want to see Jo either. When they'd been in junior school, Jo and Carly had been friends, even though they weren't in the same year. But nowadays Jo was blanking her and everyone else. Most of the time she didn't seem to want friends full stop, though she wasn't a complete outsider. The sporty girls all liked her and sometimes she could be seen tearing around the playground playing football with the boys.

Carly didn't understand it. Gwen hardly spoke to people in her year, she was always so busy working, but she had made friends at the sports centre. Magda was shy and Tess bunked off, but they had each other. Jo played sports instead of talking to people. But Carly, who wanted to have friends, didn't. She'd tried and tried. She always volunteered to show new girls around, but after a couple of weeks when she'd have lunch with them and they'd sit together in lessons, they always went off with someone else and later she'd see them whispering together and giggling. She didn't know what she was doing wrong.

In the library Carly slunk into a seat by a window and mechanically unpacked her books from her bag. A hand on her shoulder made her jump and she turned to see the librarian standing with a stack of books for shelving.

'Hello, Carly,' Mrs Mills smiled. 'Good to see you here.

And just as I was wondering whether Tess has had any more luck with the council. Do you know?'

'After the protest they made a statement saying the roundabout wouldn't be a problem – that it would only come up to the edge of the permanent site – but,' Carly admitted, 'the Travellers are still worried about space, and noise, and pollution and stuff. And Tess is getting aggro about it because she reckons there's stuff the council aren't telling, especially since they rushed it through so we didn't have time to stop it before it was too late.'

'She's probably right.' Mrs Mills shook her head. Moving further down the shelves, she continued to put books away.

A month ago Carly would have offered to help, but things had changed and now she couldn't be bothered.

○

Carly did a page and a bit of her geography homework but then she got bored. Getting up from her desk, she wandered along the shelves, pretending to look for a book and checking out what everyone else was doing. But as she rounded a corner she came face to face with Jo, sitting with a stack of science books around her and a scruffy-looking school notebook. Jo had been staring into space and her eyes met Carly's blankly at first before properly noticing her.

'Oh, hi,' she said dully.

'I didn't know you were going to be here.' Carly came closer to Jo's table.

'The school sent my parents a letter about me bunking

121

off.' Jo made a face. 'Now they're making me stay longer to make up the work. What are you in for?'

'Mum doesn't want me coming back to an empty house,' Carly told her and then blushed. It sounded so babyish. To change the subject she asked quickly, 'So how come you weren't on the protest?'

Jo shrugged. 'I said I wasn't going to be.'

'Were you with Magda? You know she wasn't there either, even though she said she'd come?'

'Maybe I was, maybe I wasn't,' Jo said, her eyes narrowing. 'What business is it of yours anyway?'

'Tess was really annoyed she didn't show,' Carly protested. 'Why won't you say where you went?'

'Since when do you care about Tess?' Jo asked. 'You never used to. Now you're hanging around her all the time. Letting her boss you about.'

'I'm not!' Carly glared back at Jo. 'I just happen to care about the council building on gypsy land. That's all.'

Jo looked sarcastic, but before she could say anything the teacher on duty appeared round the corner of the bookshelves.

'What do you two think you're doing?' she demanded. 'You should be working, not chatting. Socialize on your own time, girls!'

Back at her own table Carly rested her head on her arms, feeling hard done by. A group of boys got up and went noisily out into the corridor. She could hear doors banging in sequence and from her window seat she saw them spill out into the playground. As they walked together towards the rows of bike racks Carly recognized one of them as the boy who worked in the mini-market near the Traveller site, the one who had asked Magda's name.

Remembering the scene in the mini-market made her feel embarrassed all over again. Tess had criticized her for that too. It was as if they were all growing up and trying to leave her behind and Carly couldn't understand why. She was growing up too, wasn't she? Yet the others seemed to think of her as a baby.

As she watched the playground, the side door opened and Jo came out. She looks like Tess, Carly thought suddenly, for all her criticisms of her. It wasn't just the way she was dressed but the way she walked, as she headed across the asphalt and stopped where the boys were standing about by the bike racks. She looked older, more confident, and the boys had stopped kicking a ball around to talk to her.

Carly stood and picked up her bag, sweeping her stuff into it. Why should she bother to sit around here? As long as she was outside the school gates at six fifteen when her dad came to collect her, how was anyone to know what she'd been doing in the meantime? It wasn't as if she ever got any credit for being the good girl. She put on her pink duffle coat and shook out her frizzy hair as she headed outside.

The boys and Jo were still talking on the other side of the playground, kicking the ball back and forth between them lazily. They were all laughing about something and, slowly, Carly walked towards them. Jo's back was to her and none of the boys was paying her any attention.

Instead the boy from the mini-market was saying, 'You should come, it'll be great. My parents are going away, so it'll only be my sister in charge and she's hopeless.'

○

'Maybe.' Jo stuck her hands in her pockets casually. 'It's not for ages though, is it? Tell me again when it's closer.'

'And get your friend to come too,' one of the other boys said. 'You know, the pretty one.'

'Magda.' The boy from the mini-market looked past Jo suddenly and saw Carly. 'Hey, you,' he said. 'Your friend's name is Magda, isn't it?'

Jo turned round and gave Carly a cold hard look and Carly blushed. Jo was wearing eyeliner and for a moment she had the same expression of contempt in her eyes as Tess always did.

'I can't tell you,' Carly said and the boy laughed.

'It is Magda all the same.'

'You seem to know everyone,' Jo said to him. 'Even *Carly*. But Magda won't come to your party. She's got a boyfriend, you know.'

Carly frowned. Why had Jo said that? Everyone knew Magda's parents didn't let her go out with boys. There was no way she could have a boyfriend. But before she could say anything, Jo caught her eye.

'Just don't,' she snapped. And to the boys she added, 'I'm off. I've done my time.'

'Well, think about the party yourself,' the first boy said, completely losing interest in Carly. 'I'll remind you.'

'Sure.' Jo was smiling now as she met his eyes. 'See you later, Ian.'

She gave Carly another hard look as she picked up her school bag. She swung it in her hand as she set off across the playground and tossed it in the air and caught it again. The boys watched her go and Carly crossed her fingers, hoping Jo would drop the thing and spill her stuff all over the ground. But of course she didn't.

11

ACROSS THE OVERPASS

Tess hadn't been to school in over a week. Early that morning she'd collected the post from the boxes at the site office and found a letter for Reenie with the school's postmark on it. She'd ignored Peggy watching her through the window as she'd shoved it into her pocket.

Leaving the site, she walked in the opposite direction from school, along the ring road. It was half past eight in the morning and the sky was a clear pale blue, but the air was thick with car fumes as people made their way to work or dropped off their kids. Tess walked quickly, as if she knew where she was going. But she didn't actually have a plan. She couldn't go to the dump – it'd be obvious she was bunking off again – and she didn't feel like going near the roundabout. There was an access road to the construction site on the town side now, coming off the ring road near the overpass. As she passed it, Tess turned her head away. All she wanted was to get out of Accleton, to leave the whole mess behind her and start somewhere new. But she had nowhere to go.

Ever since Tess's mum had left without a trace when she was too young to remember her, Tess had been passed around the family from relation to relation. Her dad was known for his charm and his way with words; he could always talk someone into taking Tess on, just for a few weeks that inevitably became months. But it never took Tess long to outstay her welcome, so there wasn't exactly a wealth of homes for her to head off to now. No one wanted or needed her – not here, not anywhere.

Whenever Kieran appeared out of the blue, either to visit for a couple of days or to collect Tess and take her to the next place, she always asked why she couldn't stay with him. At first the reason had been that she was too young. But as she got older Kieran had other excuses. The place he was staying didn't allow children, or he had a major job on that took all his time. That was the way it was with true Travellers, he said.

'But some day,' he'd told her many times, 'we'll find a way for you to come with me. We'll go a-roving together through the country, pitch up wherever we like.'

When she was little Tess had drawn pictures of her and her father travelling the country together. But when Reenie had found them she'd thrown them away.

'You think that good-for-nothing father of yours will ever have time for you?' she'd snorted. 'You're fooling yourself. I can see through his blarney if no one else can.'

'I don't believe you,' Tess would scream, refusing to hear her.

○

127

Almost without thinking about it, Tess found herself walking across the overpass. At the far end the paving ran out and she found herself walking through the grass of a rough verge as cars zipped past. If the roundabout was built then this whole area would have to be reconstructed in concrete, so that cars could loop off and on from either side of the motorway. She could imagine it all too well and she didn't look back as she strode onwards, her dark eyes stormy.

Ahead the road curved out of sight. But here the grass verge ran up to a plain wooden fence and Tess swung herself over it. Under the shadow of the trees the noise from the A-road and the motorway behind seemed to drop away. Her footsteps crunched on bracken and the desiccated remains of last autumn's leaves. In the trees birds were twittering to each other.

Tess picked up the pace as she walked through the woods, all the reasons why she wanted to get away piling up in her head. But the worst reason of all she couldn't even bear to think about: Magda's betrayal. All these years she'd been the one person Tess *could* count on and instead she'd gone off with some boy, someone she hadn't even mentioned meeting.

'She's not the person I thought she was,' Tess said aloud bitterly.

She pushed on through the woods as the day got warmer and brighter. She didn't know where she was going, except *away*. She'd run away before. The first time she'd been ten and she'd packed a bag with chocolate bars and crisps and set off, planning to walk from Lincoln to

Scotland to find her father. She'd got about a mile and half before a policewoman had stopped and questioned her for long enough to see through her obvious lies. When she'd been driven back home, Reenie had rolled her eyes and told the policewoman Kieran probably wasn't in Scotland anyway.

It hadn't stopped Tess running away again and again. But sooner or later she'd always run out of money or places to bunk, and then she'd be back at Reenie's, or another family member's door. Reenie said it was something else she had in common with Kieran, wanting to run away from her problems. But Tess didn't see it like that. She thought she could understand why her dad didn't want to stick around people who criticized him all the time. Reenie threw cold water over his plans, whatever they were, calling him every bad word under the sun. They didn't understand him any more than they understood Tess.

By mid-morning Tess had made it to a rise of ground where she could see across the trees and scrubland to the surrounding countryside. Accleton was a grey mass beyond the ribbon of the motorway, but in the opposite direction villages clustered here and there on country roads, nestled into the side of hills or among squares of farmland. Coming out of the woods, she dropped down on to a winding road and began walking along it. She wasn't sure where she was, but it wasn't as if she was lost. She knew where Accleton was, after all. As the road curved around she had a view of fields on her right and looked out across them to see a cluster of what looked like trailers parked haphazardly in a rough circle.

Tess climbed the fence into the first field and began walking towards them. If they were Travellers, chances were there would be someone she knew.

By the time she'd reached the second field she was already planning what she'd say in order to win a ride, but when she reached the trailers she was disappointed to see that they looked empty. There were no cars or trucks about, which suggested that people had gone off to work, but during the day you could generally expect to find a couple of women and children around. The camp must belong to a group of Traveller men, she realized. It sometimes happened that men on a short-term job would make a temporary camp like this, often without the permission of whoever owned the field.

Tess was pretty confident of her ability to handle herself, but she didn't much like the idea of trying to join up with a group of strange men. She was about to leave when she heard the sound of someone inside one of the trailers. She turned in time to see the door open and a man start carefully down the steps, one arm held against his chest by an improvised sling. As he moved to face in her direction Tess caught her breath.

He saw her at once and stared for a moment, then came quickly towards her.

'Well, here's a turn-up for the books. What are you doing here, Tess?' He sounded almost nervous.

'Dad?' Tess stared back at him as he gave her a

one-armed hug. 'I was just out walking. What are *you* doing here?'

'Well, I'm on my way to see my darling daughter,' he laughed suddenly, relaxed now, the same dark blue eyes as hers twinkling at her surprise. 'Got a job in the area, haven't I? Only just as I was planning to take a trip to see you and Reenie, I got me arm mangled.'

'Is it broken?' Tess looked at the sling and Kieran shook his head.

'Just banged up. I'll be fit as a fiddle next week.'

'Why didn't you call?' Tess felt a smile breaking over her face as she realized it really was her dad standing in front of her, just when she'd been wishing for him. 'I'd have come to see you.'

'And so you have,' Kieran pointed out quickly.

'I bunked off school,' Tess told him. 'There's all this stuff going on right now . . .'

'And you found your way to me.' Kieran grinned at her. 'Well, put up a chair and tell me all about you.'

In fact he got two deckchairs himself, awkwardly with his left arm, and unfolded them. There was a case of beer under one of the nearby trailers and he took two cans, offering one to Tess.

'Pete's a mate, he won't mind,' he told her.

'Mind if I smoke?' Tess said and Kieran laughed.

'Filthy habit,' he said. 'Make your old dad one, eh?' Sitting back comfortably with her beer and cigarette, Tess wondered if this time Kieran would finally let her join him. There couldn't have been a better moment for him to turn up, just when things in Accleton seemed unbearable.

But coming out with it straight off wouldn't be a good idea. So she started her tale with her discovery of the construction site.

Kieran was unusually silent as she told the story. She didn't leave anything out and it made for dismal retelling, especially the pathetic anticlimax of the protest. When she reached seeing Magda and her secret boyfriend Kieran finally spoke.

'Got to expect that, Tess darlin'. Little girls have best friends, big girls have boyfriends. That's the way life is.'

'But . . .' Tess tried to wrap her head around this. 'Magda's not like that.'

'All girls are like that sooner or later,' Kieran said and Tess frowned.

'Anyway,' she went on, 'don't you think it stinks about the roundabout? It's just like you said, about the way people push us out to the edge and then take even that away from us. *You* wouldn't have let it happen, would you, Dad?'

'It's the way of the world all right,' he said. 'Happens again and again. I'm not surprised you couldn't get that lot at the site to fight it properly. There's not a true Romany among them. I've come up against their type myself, time and again.' He sighed heavily.

Tess frowned even more deeply. She'd wanted her dad to agree with her, but she'd also wanted him to suggest something else she could try. Instead he sounded almost as defeatist as some of the people at the site – the only difference was that he blamed the Travellers instead of the council.

'If they won't fight, they deserve what they get,' Kieran said, finishing his beer and crunching the can in his fist. 'Some people will just lay down so others can walk all over them.'

'Not me,' Tess insisted.

'That's because you take after your old dad,' Kieran told her, getting up to fetch another beer. 'You've got the fire for a fight. But you're wasting your time with that lot. Back in the old country you might be able to stir 'em up. But here . . .' He shook his head.

'So what should I do?' Tess asked. 'If the roundabout gets built it'll be like living in the middle of a motorway. And I don't see any way it can be built without taking space from the Traveller site too.'

'That's right.' Kieran nodded. 'There isn't the space. From what I remember anyway,' he added quickly.

'Dad . . .' Tess looked at him, meeting the blue eyes that were a match for hers. 'If Reenie loses her pitch, what do you say I come along with you for a while? I'm nearly done with school and I'd be useful. The men at the dump say I'm strong for my age and I can work hard.'

Kieran looked at her thoughtfully. He took a gulp from his beer and stayed silent for so long Tess wondered if he was going to answer her at all.

'I'll be honest with you, darlin',' he said eventually. 'Your old man's got himself in a spot of trouble. The kind that means I've got to be keeping a low profile.'

'What sort of trouble?' Tess dropped her voice even though there was no one around for miles. 'With the police?'

'Something like that.' Kieran gave her a twisted grin. 'That's why I couldn't come round and see you earlier. I can't risk being seen in town.'

'But I don't have to go back to town,' Tess pointed out. 'I could just stay here.'

'And what about when Reenie lists you as a runaway and the filth come calling?' Kieran said, shaking his head. 'I can't risk it, Tess girl.'

Tess's shoulders slumped. She thought of the walk back to Accleton and the letter in her bag. The last thing she wanted to do was go home to a bunch of Travellers so pathetic even her dad had given up on them. He was right – they weren't worth the effort. But if Kieran wouldn't let her stay, what choice did she have?

'Tell you what, darlin',' her dad said. 'Once I've got myself sorted out, we'll take a trip together. Maybe go to the seaside. I've got a couple of mates down in Brighton I haven't seen for a while. What do you say?'

'Sounds great,' Tess said. 'But when?'

'Hard to say.' Kieran scrubbed his free hand through his curly hair. 'Got a job on at the moment, so I've got to stay put. But I won't go without you. I wouldn't leave me only daughter living on a roundabout, would I now?' He grinned at her and Tess managed to smile back.

'So I suppose I'd better be heading back,' she said. Then something occurred to her: 'If you can't come into town, how will you let me know when your job's over?'

'I'll work something out.' Kieran winked. 'You mustn't underestimate your old man's resourcefulness. I've still got some tricks up my sleeve.'

'OK.' Tess stood up.

Kieran tipped his head back to look up at her. 'I won't see you out,' he said, waving a hand. 'Take care, Tessie. Give 'em hell.'

'Yeah.' Tess nodded. But she didn't feel much like a hellraiser right now. 'Hope the arm gets better.'

'A couple of days rest should see me all right,' Kieran said, lifting the beer can and winking.

Tess threaded her way back between the trailers and across the field. When she reached the road she turned, but she couldn't see her dad. For a fleeting moment she had an urge to run back, to plead with him to let her stay. But Kieran hated scenes. She started walking down the road.

Seeing her dad hadn't lifted her spirits as much as it once had. Probably because he had made her see just how bad things had got in her community. Did she really have to go back to that . . . ? Though there was Magda. Tess wondered if her dad was right about her best friend too, and realized that on this, just this once, she wasn't pre-pared to accept his point of view. Magda had been her friend for too long. She'd have to talk to her, she realized. Even if her dad was right about boyfriends changing things, she couldn't afford to lose Magda's friendship for-ever. Especially not now.

She hadn't intended to run away anywhere specific, she'd simply started walking. Now she wasn't exactly planning to go back. But she knew that her feet would take her along the country roads and across the overpass. There was nowhere else to go.

12

BUTTERFLY HOUSE

The mobile turned in the slow air currents, coloured butterflies on threads moving around and about each other,
wings held rigid. Lying on her bed looking up at them, her
blonde hair spilled over the pillow, Magda watched the
sunlight through the half-open curtains glitter and corus-
cate from the glass wings. Seb had given it to her the last
time they'd met, and she smiled at the memory. She'd told
him casually one day that she liked watching butterflies.
He had remembered and given her this. It had been hard
pretending to her parents that she'd bought it from a
charity shop.

One of the butterflies rotated around another, the
threads supporting them tangling together, and Magda
sighed. All her feelings for Seb were tangled right now.
Her parents would be furious if they knew she'd been seeing someone without their permission and she hated lying
to them. But she couldn't stop herself. And Tess seemed to
have vanished off the face of the planet, still angry about
Magda's desertion of her on the day of the protest. But

she hadn't been able to stop herself then either. She'd never felt so far in the wrong before.

Outside the trailer, she could hear her brothers and sisters shrieking and yelling as they played chase around and about the site. Her mother was watching them. Magda had said she had a headache, another lie, and had been sent inside to rest, away from the hot sun. She was supposed to be meeting Seb in less than an hour's time but now, as if determined to make the lie the truth, she was beginning to feel ill. She shouldn't go. She should never have spoken to him in the first place, never let him meet her at church, never let him hold her hand or put his arm around her. He was all she could think of and she'd turned her back on everything else for him. She'd been skipping school at least twice a week since half-term and now her class teacher had written to her parents. Magda had intercepted the letter, collecting it from the post area at the site entrance and hiding it, promising herself that she would stop bunking off. But the very next day she'd done it again.

It was impossible to concentrate on school projects anyway when the June sunshine turned the fields to a dazzle of glory and her classroom into a grey prefab prison. She hated the work they were doing, especially in English – it was easier not to go, to hide out where no one would call on her and ask questions she didn't know the answers to. And all the time her feelings for Seb either made her feel light as air or lay on her like a weight, so often she felt the ache not in her heart but in her bones. Lying on her bed, watching the butterflies dance, she tried to find the energy to move and couldn't. Perhaps she wouldn't go this time, would leave Seb to wait.

Putting an arm over her face, Magda bit her lips hard, trying to drive out the guilt and pain. A sudden bang of the outer trailer door startled her and she twitched as it was followed by a softer knocking on the door to her room.

'Hello?' She pulled her arm down and looked at the door as it opened. For a second she thought it was Tess and sat up suddenly before realizing that the figure wearing a red top and black shorts was Jo.

'Hey,' Jo murmured. 'Your mum said you weren't feeling well.'

'I'm OK,' Magda said, lying back down. 'I'm just . . .' She tried to smile. 'I've a lot on my mind.'

'Seb?' Jo asked, coming to sit next to her on the bed and Magda looked away.

'Yeah,' she whispered. 'Him and other things. Tess as well. And my parents and . . . just everything.'

'You shouldn't feel bad for liking him,' Jo said and Magda looked back at her, surprised. 'Well, you shouldn't,' Jo insisted, blushing slightly. 'Not that I know anything about it but . . . he seems nice.'

'Yeah,' Magda said. 'He is.' No longer feeling so crushed, she sat up and shifted back on the bed to sit cross-legged and give Jo more room. 'I'm supposed to be meeting him in a bit.'

'How are you going to get away?' Jo asked, lowering her voice and glancing at the window, and Magda sighed.

'I don't know . . .' She lifted her hands and then

dropped them back in her lap. She didn't want to use church as an excuse any more – it felt wrong. Usually she could have used Tess as an alibi, but right now she couldn't ask that, even if she knew where Tess was.

'Why not say you're coming with me?' Jo said, and Magda met her eyes with a start. Jo shrugged and added, 'I've got a den in the fields. Kind of like Tess's car mountain, only not exactly. But you could say you were coming with me. I don't mind.'

'You'd have to wait for me to come back,' Magda protested and Jo shrugged again.

'I don't mind,' she said. 'Really.'

○

The way her mam smiled at them when they came out of the caravan made Magda feel guilty all over again.

'You're looking a bit better, love,' she said, looking up from a pile of mending. 'How's your headache?'

'OK.'

'I thought it might help if we went for a walk,' Jo said, lying as brazenly as Tess ever had. 'I know a place in the fields that's cool and shady. I thought it might help if she wasn't so near the kids yelling and everything.'

'Well, that's true enough,' Magda's mother agreed. 'That's sweet of you, Joanne.' She turned to Magda and said, 'You go along with Jo if you like and I'll hold the fort here.'

'Thanks, Mam.' Magda's voice came out in a whisper and Jo linked an arm in hers possessively, pulling her away. Instantly, Magda felt like turning and running back to the trailer, sitting down next to her mam's chair and staying where it was safe. But already they were nearing the stile that led to the footpath out and Jo was turning to ask, 'Where are you meeting him?'

'The ring-road turn near the overpass.'

'Let's go this way then.' Jo grinned as she climbed over the stile and added, 'I think your mum bought it.'

'She trusts me,' Magda said sadly. But as she followed Jo over the stile something of her dark mood dropped away.

Running her fingers through her hair she pulled a handful of it around to look at it. She hadn't brushed it before leaving the house, or changed out of her crumpled white sundress.

'How do I look?' she asked.

Jo rolled her eyes. 'You always look good,' she said. 'I don't know why you're worrying.'

They reached the road and sat together on a low wall, watching the passing cars.

'I'll try to be back by five,' Magda said. 'Shall I meet you here then?'

'Sure.' Jo nodded. 'Have fun.'

Just then a red Lexus pulled up at the side of the road, the sound of music with a heavy bass rolling out of it from the open top.

'Cool car,' Jo said, with a lift of her eyebrows.

'It's his dad's,' Magda whispered back. At the same time she realized she didn't know what his father did to be able to afford such an expensive car.

Seb leaned across to open the passenger door for her

and, as Magda got in, he waved to Jo, before starting the engine and pulling away.

'He's a businessman,' Seb said, turning his head towards her when she asked about his father a moment later. His eyes were hidden behind expensive sunglasses and his face was expressionless, as it always was when he mentioned his father. 'He runs the sports centre.' He pulled out on to the ring road.

'I didn't know that,' Magda said, surprised. 'A friend of mine works there.'

'Oh yeah? Is her name Jaycee?' he asked.

'No, it's Gwen.' Magda's hair was whipping about in the wind and she smoothed it back down behind her ears. 'Maybe you've seen her?'

'I never go there.' Seb shook his head. 'I wish I had though, if you've been there all this time. Why don't you come back to mine later today and we can swim in our pool?'

'I can't.' Magda blushed a little at the thought of swimming with Seb. 'I promised Jo I'd be back by five. She's covering for me at home.'

'That's cool,' Seb said easily. 'I still think you should let me meet your parents though. Let me convince them my intentions are honourable . . .' He turned to grin at her and Magda smiled back.

'Watch the road,' she said. 'And no, it's not going to happen.'

'You're probably right.' Seb's mouth thinned down into a grim line and his voice was tense as he added, 'They wouldn't like it much that I'm a Swayland.'

'What?' Magda was puzzled and Seb shook his head.

'Forget it,' he said. 'I mean . . .' He shook his head again. 'Never mind. Let's not talk about my dad. Sorry.' They turned off the ring road heading west and it was a minute or two before Seb looked away from the road again. 'Guess where we're going?'

'You said a park,' Magda reminded him.

'I know. It is a park. There's a big country house called Westercott and it has gardens and a lake where we can take a boat out if you like. But there's something else as well, and that's a surprise.'

'OK.' In the ensuing silence Magda felt her gloominess threatening to come back. She shook it off with a toss of her head. She was here now. There wasn't much point in feeling guilty about it. 'Should I have changed? I feel underdressed for this car,' she asked instead.

'You look fantastic,' Seb said, turning away from the road to look at her again. 'But there's a spare pair of sunglasses in the glove compartment if you want them.' Reaching out across her knees, he pressed the button so the compartment flipped open, his hand brushing her thigh on the way back.

'Thanks.' Magda didn't bother much with sunglasses, but she had started a bit when he touched her and needed to disguise the movement.

The spare sunglasses were designer as well and she checked out her reflection in the wing mirror and felt surprised at the girl who looked back. Her sun-streaked blonde hair framed hidden eyes and a secretive smile.

By the time they reached the place Magda was feeling like someone completely different, and more than a little wild. If she was going to break the rules, she might as well have fun. Westercott made it even easier to pretend she was someone else. It was a huge mansion in grey stone with a great big drive leading up from the car park across a lawn that was as green and lush as a water meadow. Seb held her hand as they walked up the drive and looking around Magda could see that there were lots of other couples about, although most of them were older. She relaxed a bit, thinking that no one she knew would be likely to see her here.

She hadn't thought to bring money, not that she had much anyway, but Seb seemed to assume that he'd pay for her. He bought two tickets at the main gate and brushed off her thanks.

'It's nothing,' he said. 'Guilt money from my dad.' He winced and added quickly, 'I didn't mean . . . wow, that sounded spoilt . . .'

'Well, if you are, you can spoil me too,' Magda said, trying to laugh it off. 'Look, there's an ice-cream place. Shall we get some?'

Eating their ice creams and still holding hands, they walked in the park. It was peaceful, Magda thought, and beautiful too.

'My mum likes this place. It was her who told me about it,' Seb said. 'She says she likes how "English" it is – it intrigues her, even after all her years here.'

'She's not English then?' Magda said and he shook his head.

'I'm half Spanish. That's the Catholic part. My full name is Sebastián.'

'Sebastián.' Magda repeated it slowly. 'I like the way you say it.'

'I like the way *you* say it,' he countered. 'Come on, I promised you a surprise, remember?'

He led the way through the gardens towards a white wood and glass pavilion at the back of the house. As they passed a wooden signpost he threw an arm around her shoulders and put himself between her and it.

'Don't look,' he said. 'It'll spoil the surprise. Close your eyes.'

Magda closed her eyes nervously. She felt a sudden cool shadow pass overhead as they went through a door. Then they crossed a room and went through what sounded like another door and she felt something brush around her shoulders, plasticky and unpleasant.

'What was that?' She opened her eyes in time to see a curtain of plastic strips falling away to the side, and ahead a jungle of plants and flowers inside the pavilion. Sunlight shone through glass panes and it was warm. From some-where ahead there was the sound of water rushing, and around the pavilion boardwalks led over small bridges and artificial ponds.

'Look.' Seb caught her hand again and turned her a little to the left, where a huge black and red butterfly was sitting on the broad green leaves of a plant. There was another one on the next leaf, a brown tabby sort of colour, and as Magda watched a third fluttered past.

Looking after it, she saw that they were everywhere. Not glass and wire like the ones on her mobile but alive in glimmering glimpses of vibrant colour, alighting here and there on the trees and flowers.

'It's the butterfly house,' Seb said.

'It's beautiful,' she told him, looking in all directions at once as she caught sight of more and more butterflies.

He led her along the boardwalk as some people came in behind them. It curved and wound through the plants so that they seemed almost alone, except for other half-heard voices through the trees. There were turtles and fish in some of the ponds and insects buzzed past, but everywhere there were butterflies and moths.

'Look,' Seb said as they passed a waterfall, a cascade of water rippling down rocks. As Magda stopped a blue and purple butterfly came to rest on her arm. She stilled instantly, watching it open and shut its wings, feeling the smile spread across her face like sunshine. After a moment the insect's feet tickled the hairs on her arm. She moved only a fraction, but it took off and flew away past Seb's shoulder. As she watched it go her eyes met Seb's.

He was staring at her intently, and now he bent towards her. He kissed her with his eyes open but Magda shut hers, not daring to be the focus of that intense blue stare. It was a long romantic kiss and her chest felt light and fluttery, like the wings of the butterfly that had landed on her moments before.

Her hand felt moist and sweaty in his as they went

onwards and she could hardly see the butterflies he pointed out. It was ridiculous to feel sad when he'd planned this as a surprise for her, but it was as if Seb lived in another world. Stepping into it made her feel enchanted, but at the same time she knew that the spell couldn't last.

'You make me feel like Cinderella,' she said softly, trying to express something of what she was thinking as Seb smiled at her.

'Except for the wicked stepmother and sisters, I hope.'

Her fingers tightened on his. 'But I have to be home by five or I'll turn into a pumpkin.'

'I'm sure that's not the way it goes,' he said. 'But I hear you. This was what I wanted you to see anyway.'

'Yes, thank you.' Magda looked back at the butterfly house and for a moment the colour blurred in her vision. But she couldn't let Seb see her cry and she opened her eyes wider instead, letting the tears dry before they could fall.

He kept his arm around her on the way back to the car and with every step she could feel how little she wanted to leave. All through the drive back and Seb's kiss goodbye and the walk down the footpath to where she had said she would meet Jo she felt as if she was still standing by the waterfall inside the butterfly house.

13

IN THE KING'S ARMS

The King's Arms was a large rambling pub that catered to various groups from the town. It had a big main bar room, made out of a number of different rooms knocked through to each other. Tables and chairs were placed in alcoves or on either side of supporting walls, giving an illusion of privacy. There was a large garden at the back too, with benches separated by trellises and the climbing plants growing up them.

When Gwen arrived it was crowded. People had claimed most of the indoor tables and she had to wait for a while to be served. She wasn't carded, perhaps because it was so busy. But looking at her reflection in the mirror behind the bar she hoped it was because she looked older than her sixteen years. After all, now she was officially done with school. She'd had her last exams that afternoon and was confident she'd done well. Afterwards she'd gone back to the flat and thrown away her revision notes. Her mother was out at work and Gwen had wandered the rooms, listening to the sounds of the town that seeped in through the windows and pretending that this was her *own* flat. She'd lost herself in a daydream of coming back after work and cooking a meal as someone opened a bottle of wine and brought her a glass. By the time she'd come back to herself she only had time to grab a quick shower and change before heading out.

But, looking at herself in the mirror again, she was pleased with what she saw. Her hair shone coppery gold and her eyes were secretive behind the dark mascara tinting her lashes. The barman winked at her when he brought her drink over and she smiled back before heading for the beer garden. The sunshine was still bright outside and there were groups of people gathered around the benches. Towards the back of the garden she saw a familiar head of dark hair and, swallowing, made her way over.

Mark Swayland was sitting on his own, already halfway through a pint of beer. He was wearing a dark blue shirt with the sleeves pushed back, showing tanned forearms and the gleam of his Rolex watch. As she approached the table he looked up and smiled widely, before standing to greet her. Gwen blushed as he bent over her, holding her shoulders while he kissed her cheek. They didn't kiss hello at the sports centre, but maybe this was different.

'So here's to you!' he said, taking his seat again as Gwen sat down opposite. 'All finished with school then?'

'Thanks,' Gwen raised her glass and he chinked his against it.

'I'm sorry we couldn't make time to talk about your

career before,' he continued, 'but this was the first gap I had in my schedule. And it makes a change from the office.'

'Yes.' Gwen smiled again. When she'd called the sports centre to discuss working there full time she'd been surprised when Mr Swayland had suggested meeting here. Surprised but pleased.

'So, tell me what your plans are,' he said. 'What're your hopes and dreams, Gwen?'

'Um, well I'd like to be able to afford my own flat,' she began.

He nodded. 'Always a good idea,' he said. 'Property's a safe investment. If you need any advice about buying, I'd be happy to help.'

'I'm a little way from that at the moment, Mr Swayland!' Gwen exclaimed in confusion.

He laughed. 'Call me Mark.'

She blushed, feeling young and silly, wishing she could be as confident and relaxed as him. She sipped her drink and listened as he talked about property. But she wasn't listening so much as watching him.

'. . . everyone starts out small, but there's no reason to think small. When I first got into fitness clubs I just had a small gym and attached pool, then I bought Bluewater. And I've never looked back.'

How old was he? she wondered. He was so young-looking, but he had to be in his thirties, didn't he, to be the owner of a sports centre and more?

'I've got various new projects under development at

the moment too,' Mark went on. He drained his pint and nodded to her drink. 'How about another?'

'Thanks.' Gwen watched him walk back to the pub with long, easy strides.

While he was gone she opened her bag and checked her face and make-up. Her reflection smiled nervously back from her hand mirror. Returning it to her bag, she realized she'd still not finished her first drink and gulped the rest of it down.

'Thinking about your boyfriend?' Mark's voice startled her and she looked up as he slid another glass of wine in front of her before taking his own seat. 'You were miles away.'

'I'm not seeing anyone right now,' Gwen said quickly and then wondered if she'd been too quick.

'We workaholics . . .' Mark smiled. 'Don't know how to have fun, do we?'

'Well, if I'm going to get the house of my dreams, I've got a lot of work to do,' joked Gwen, and Mark laughed.

'The trouble is, once you've got one dream house you start saving up for a second,' he said. 'I've got this fantasy of a house in France, a little cottage by the sea. Buying freshly baked bread, local wine, meeting a stunning French mademoiselle . . .' He laughed again, at himself.

'I wouldn't mind that myself,' Gwen said. 'Not the mademoiselle. But I wouldn't say no to a *jeune homme*.' She used her best French accent and Mark looked delighted.

'You even speak the lingo,' he exclaimed. 'You'd fit

150

right in. But I see you in a Parisian apartment. One of those chic young women, with your hair in a chignon.'

Gwen smiled and lifted her hair up, piling it on the back of her head. Mark's eyes watched her admiringly and she let her hair cascade down again, hiding her flushed face for a moment.

'Mmm, *très chic*.' He smiled and Gwen felt fluttery. Was he flirting with her? 'So, tell me more about yourself, Gwen,' he continued. 'I see you at reception with that *Mona Lisa* smile and I wonder what you're thinking about. What about your family? What are they like?'

'It's just me and my mother,' Gwen said. 'And we live, well, very separately. She has a flat in the city centre and we come and go at different times.'

'So your dad's out of the picture?'

'He's a Traveller,' she said. 'Mum went on the road with him for a while, but in the end she wanted to settle down and he didn't. He went back to Wales six years ago and we haven't seen him since. He sends a postcard now and then, when he remembers to.'

'A Traveller, as in gypsy?' Mark asked and when Gwen nodded he said, 'I've always thought there was a wonderful richness to gypsy culture, but I expect that doesn't look as alluring when it's part of the reason for your parents splitting up.'

'Yes.' Gwen was surprised he was so understanding. 'That's right.'

'So you don't have any friends in the local Traveller community then?' Mark asked, looking interested.

'A couple,' Gwen said. 'But we're not really close any more. They're still in school.'

'And you're a woman of the world.'

○

When Gwen finished her second glass of wine, Mark insisted on buying her a third. He reminded her that they still hadn't talked about what she would be doing when she came to work for for him full-time. But when he returned he started talking about holidays and Gwen was swept away by his stories of sailing across the Mediterranean and hiking through the Andes.

Around them other people came and went. It was still sunny in the beer garden and green light dappled through the trees that shaded the tables. Excusing herself to use the bathroom, Gwen walked back inside the pub and then suddenly found herself ducking behind a pillar. A group of darts players was loudly cheering one of their number and she'd recognized muscled forearms as a dart clunked into the board. It was Craig, one of the lifeguards from the pool. Sidling around the pillar, Gwen went to the ladies', feeling nervous at the idea that Craig might see her with the boss. Washing her hands, she looked at her face in the mirror, flushed and excited and a little tipsy. After splashing water on it and reapplying her make-up she left the bathroom and worked her way carefully back through the bar. Mark looked up with a smile as she arrived and she smiled uneasily back.

'Guess who's playing darts inside,' she said, wondering how he'd respond. 'Craig from the sports centre.'

Mark threw a quick glance towards the pub. 'He is?' he said. 'Well, I'd invite him to join us but I'm afraid I should be getting back.' He finished his pint and stood up.

'Yes . . . um . . . me too,' Gwen agreed. They walked together through the side gate of the garden and out on to the street.

'This was fun,' Mark dropped a hand on her shoulder and Gwen felt its warmth through the sleeve of her blouse. 'We should do it again some time.'

Gwen's eyes flew up to his. His words could be taken at face value, but they could also be the sort of thing people said at the end of a date. Gwen walked alongside him in the direction of the city centre, telling herself not to imagine things. Mark would never be interested in her.

But the things he had said implied that he thought of her as an adult. In fact, he was almost the only person who did. As they walked along the road together she wondered if passers-by looked at them and saw a couple. She was smiling to herself when Mark stopped and waved a hand towards the north of town.

'Well, this is me,' he said.

'I turn left here,' Gwen admitted, wishing she didn't have to go.

'So, when shall we two meet again?' Mark asked. 'I've just realized we still haven't settled anything.'

'I can start full-time as of Monday?' Gwen suggested and Mark smiled.

'Sounds perfect,' he said. 'But we should really hammer down the details. Get the admin sorted out. What do you say to meeting up on Sunday? There's a cafe I know not far from here, tucked away down one of the side streets. Why don't I buy you lunch?'

'I'd like that,' she said, blushing at her own eagerness.

Mark told her the name of the cafe, but she wasn't sure she took it in properly, because as he did so he bent to kiss her cheek again, quite casually. She jumped a bit and his mouth brushed against the corner of her lips.

'Au revoir, then,' he said smoothly. 'Until Sunday.'

She raised a hand awkwardly in farewell and he crossed the street, not looking back when he reached the other side. It was a moment before Gwen continued on her way home. She hoped her mother wouldn't be there when she got in. She wanted another chance to imagine her own dream house and to think about the ideal man she'd like to share it with.

14

FOOTPATH THROUGH THE FIELDS

In the last weeks of June the weather changed again. The sky shifted from a pale powder blue scattered with white woolly clouds like sheep to a deeper, richer colour like something out of a paintbox. Azure, cerulean, turquoise, a cloudless blue without so much as a wisp of white. Magda's eyes were drawn to it, drawn to keep looking up up up until a bright dot suddenly dazzled her, scattering light through her lashes. People said, 'Don't look at the sun,' though in the winter you could. A pale disc of light lost in grey clouds couldn't blind you. But the summer sun was like a pinprick stabbed through the blue and it was easy to believe that it could hurt.

The fresh green growth of spring was parched now, with brown and yellow patches in flower beds and on the verges of the roads. People were parched too. Magda collected empty lemonade bottles, going calling around the council estate to get them. She filled them with water and put them under the trailer in the shade. Every day after school she had to watch her sisters and brothers, forcing them to drink something before smearing them with sun-cream and cramming hats back on to their heads. The little kids ran riot, tiring themselves out so that they collapsed in the sun like panting dogs or splashed each other at the pump while Peggy yelled at them for making a mess.

Magda felt scorched by the sunshine, her temper unravelling like the edges of her straw sunhat. She'd shouted back at Peggy, yelled at the kids and made meals grumpily, shredding salad with sharp twists of her fingers and slamming sandwiches together into messy heaps of crumbled cheese and uneven slices of bread. She didn't have time to go to church now, except on Sunday, and then the long walk into town made her hot and headachy. Last Sunday she'd sat in the graveyard afterwards, hiding from the sun in the shadows of the graves. But it found her in the end, although nobody else did, and she'd got home late. Even then the sun had followed, burning down from the sky and up from the hot pavements.

She'd changed, just like the weather. The sun had bleached her already blonde hair and browned her skin and there was a mark on her throat where her cross had heated up enough to burn the skin there, giving her an x-shaped burn that hadn't faded yet. But those were just the outward changes, and she wondered that no one else saw the inner ones. No one commented when they heard her voice raised to a yell or saw that her eyes were red on Monday morning, or that she'd been late from school on Wednesday and, smiling again, had bought the little ones ice cream on the way home. Mam lay on the sofa inside with a flannel over her face, hiding from the sun, and praised her as much as ever. And Da said he was sorry the only time she had for herself was church, and told her to take a holiday next Saturday while he took the little ones swimming.

But maybe her Mam had noticed something after all, because she told Magda on Friday she'd arranged for Carly and Gwen to come round that weekend with Jo and take her out, and had looked so sorrowful when she'd had to tell her that Tess had cried off.

Magda had called Seb from the payphone near the office that evening, while Peggy watched from behind the curtains, and told him she couldn't meet him that Saturday after all. She felt guilty for letting him down, but not as guilty as she did about letting Tess down over the roundabout or all her other lies, or the fact that a day with the girls wasn't what she really wanted.

○

On Saturday morning she made a picnic. Then, sitting on the steps of the trailer, she smeared barrier cream over her arms and hitched up her skirt to do her legs. Pushing her sunhat back, she blobbed some on her nose and neck and closed her eyes for a moment. To her surprise she was feeling happy, the sun was warm and the cream was a cool balm, soothing away hurt. I'm happy today because I'm being good, she thought. Because I'm doing and being what other people expect me to be. But does that mean I was never really good before – when it didn't cost me any-thing? When I didn't have anywhere else I'd rather be?

A shadow fell across her and she opened her eyes. Tess

stood there, her hands on her hips. In the darkness of her shadow Magda couldn't see the expression on Tess's face, just the sun streaming round her like an aura.

'You have a halo,' she said. 'Is that because I'm the bad one now?'

'Can anything you do be bad?' Tess asked with a twist in her voice and Magda sat up properly, blinking.

'Yes,' she said sadly. 'Tessie, I'm sorry I didn't come to the march with you. And I'm sorry I lied. I didn't forget, I . . . I was doing something else.' Her voice unravelled for a moment. She could see Tess's expression now and it wasn't surprised. She was just waiting, her dark blue eyes watching and thoughtful, like a priest at a confessional.

'I was seeing someone,' Magda said. 'A boy. His name is Seb.'

'Do you love him, Magsie?' Tess asked softly. And Magda bowed her head.

'Yes,' she said. 'I've never felt this way before.'

The words ran out of her and she tightened her lips before she could say more. She didn't know how, or even if, she could admit all the feelings she had.

Tess continued to look at her. It was impossible to tell what she was thinking. Magda knew her friend could be judgemental, but she'd never been on the receiving end before. She felt as if Tess was weighing up their friendship and her heart felt heavy with all the guilt and shame.

'I'm sorry,' she said again.

'All right then.' Tess's hand touched her shoulder briefly. 'It's OK, Magsie. Love makes the world go round, right? Guess I shouldn't be surprised you'd rather be with your true love than at some cockamamie protest that isn't going to make a difference anyway.'

Something about that wasn't right. Even as she felt relief at being forgiven, Magda thought Tess didn't sound like herself. Her voice was bitter and resigned at once, all her fire gone.

'Look,' Tess said then, nodding towards where the other girls were walking down the rough track towards the trailer, 'there's your little team of chaperones. Bet your mam hasn't a clue she ruined your plans with her picnic party. She's probably not noticed that Lexus waiting for you up at the overpass every week.'

'You knew all along?' Magda gasped.

'I know everything, me,' Tess replied. 'So shall I come along on your picnic then?'

'You'd better.' Magda smiled back hopefully before raising an arm to wave.

○

As they set off along the footpath Magda realized she and Tess weren't the only ones who'd been changing.

'We'll go out northways,' Tess decreed, 'to the fields.'

'That's awfully far,' Gwen said. 'Why not just across the overpass to the woods?' She was wearing her hair loose and had on a pale lemon sundress that swirled around her slim hips as she walked. Magda looked at her with new eyes and wondered which of the lifeguards at the pool had brought such a skip to her step and smile to her lips.

'No. That's further.' Tess answered Gwen abruptly.

'How about south, to the wasteland?' Carly suggested

before adding, 'We wouldn't have to go past the round-about diggings.'

'Shut up about the roundabout,' Tess snapped, her eyes looking Carly up and down contemptuously.

Carly had on a wrap-around patterned skirt, a white peasant blouse and her frizzy hair was contained for once, wrapped up in a red bandana, showing off even bigger gold hoops than the ones she'd had at school. Yet, Magda thought, looking from Carly to Tess, despite Carly's latest over-the-top gypsy-inspired clothing, it was Tess in her ripped cut-offs and plain halter-neck top whose Romany blood showed out suddenly in the proud set of her face. Proud but bleak. Magda wished she knew what it was that had changed Tess like this.

'There's nothing south anyway,' Jo said so firmly that Magda guessed her hidden den was that way.

Jo was wearing eyeliner again and her faded cotton shirt was knotted at her waist, above her blue jeans. She didn't seem to be scowling as much as usual and after a moment Magda realized it was because she'd plucked her eyebrows. 'We could go east, if we got a bus; there's parks up near the posh houses.'

'Not east,' said Magda quickly.

'Yeah, we'd have to go through town and everything,' Jo agreed hastily after a moment, her eyes holding Magda's knowingly. Magda flushed and looked away.

'So the fields it is then,' Tess confirmed. They were already walking in that direction anyway – the others had fallen in with her as they always did.

They had to walk single file once they reached the

footpath, and the overhanging branches of leaves sheltered them from the worst of the day's heat, but as they came out at the overpass the sun hit them again like a wave. They crossed the road together and cut past the entrance to the dump, arriving on the northbound road that led out of town. Gwen glanced right as they approached the sports centre.

'How come your lot didn't put up any flyers about the outside pool by the site today?' Tess asked, narrowing her eyes.

'How should I know?' Gwen said defensively. 'I told you last time, Mark doesn't consult me about every decision he makes.'

Magda realized that Mark was Mr Swayland, Gwen's boss and Seb's father. It was strange to think that Gwen knew Seb's dad, but she kept quiet about it. Seb didn't like to talk about his father and finding anything out from Gwen would seem like spying.

Carly kept up a stream of commentary as they walked along; Magda just let it wash over her. Ahead, past the low roofs of the bungalows, she could see blue sky stretched out over the gentle swell of green hills. It had been a good decision to come this way.

'Where next, Tessie?' she asked.

'There's a footpath that goes off to the right, through a meadow,' Tess said, jerking her chin in the direction she meant. 'We'll come to it soon.'

'Good,' said Carly. 'I'm starving already. And thirsty too.'

They turned off towards the footpath soon after. It

161

began as an earth track along the side of a cul de sac of buildings. Gravel was spread across it in places, spilling out from the driveway of the nearest house. At the end of the cul de sac there was a wire fence overgrown with trees and Tess nodded at it. 'There's a golf course beyond that,' she said. 'And then the back of your sports centre.' She glanced at Gwen.

The path continued along the wire fence.

'We've come miles and miles,' Carly complained. 'Where are we going? Australia?'

'Hold your horses,' Tess said. 'We're nearly there.'

At the front of the group Jo jogged ahead and disappeared round a bend of the path before calling back, 'Hey! Not bad, Tess!'

The others picked up the pace, came round the bend at the same time and saw a wooden stile, on which Jo was half sitting, half standing. Beyond was a meadow, and beyond that the hills, divided by the different colours of grasses and crops into patches like a quilt, hedges and fences running this way and that between them.

The meadow was wild grass grown almost as high as Magda was tall. A breeze shook the grass, sending rippling waves of movement up and down the meadow and, although here and there the curves of the path could be seen, it was often lost behind dips in the land, so that it was impossible to tell which way it went.

They all clambered over the stile.

'Where shall we stop?' Carly asked, red-faced and sweating, and Gwen was looking doubtfully from the track to her own white sandals.

'Not yet,' Tess ordered, shouldering the rucksack and taking Madga's arm. 'Come on, don't want Jo to get to Australia before us.'

Magda laughed and let Tess pull her along. For a moment it was as if nothing had ever changed between them. Ahead she could see the top of Jo's head as she forged through the long grass, sending it shaking and dancing around her. She could hear the others coming behind her, but within a moment they were far enough away that it was as if Tess and she were alone together. She had a sudden urge to ditch the others. If she and Tess were to veer off the path, plunge into the grass and drop down to the ground, no one would see them.

Tess grinned at her and Magda wondered if she'd had the same thought. But then she called out, 'Hey, Jo, come back here,' and headed to the side of the path, where a flowering bush and the bare ground around it made an alternative route through the grass. Gwen and Carly arrived behind them as Tess was pushing back the undergrowth to reveal a circle of flattened grass shaded by small trees and bushes.

'I reckon it's someone's shagging spot,' Tess said, 'but it makes a good picnic spot too, doesn't it?'

'I'd never have seen it if you hadn't pointed it out,' Gwen agreed doubtfully.

'I did,' Jo said from the back of the group. 'I didn't know you wanted to stop here though; the path goes on much further. But here's good.'

'I'm not carrying this any further,' Carly announced, thumping down her picnic basket.

Magda flopped on to the grass and stared up at the blue sky. It was completely cloudless and seemed to extend forever, framed by the long grasses all around her.

'You can't even hear the town from here, let alone see it,' she murmured with relief. 'We *could* be on the other side of the world.'

○

They finished the water in the first hour and Jo's cool lemonade, and had to move on to Carly's warm Coke cans. Tess and Carly ate their way though sandwiches, crisps, biscuits and buns sticky with melted white icing. The rest of them only picked at the food. Gwen and Magda had brought suncream, but although Magda offered to share, the others refused. Jo was brown as a nut anyway, and Tess's arms and legs were already tanned, but Carly's face and shoulders went from pink to red until Gwen said if she didn't put on some cream, she'd get Jo and Tess to hold her down and squirt her with it.

'OK, OK, you're not my mum,' Carly said, but she was grinning and she took the cream.

'So you're free now, Gwen,' Jo said. 'You don't have to come back to school ever again.'

'Just to get my certificates,' Gwen said, stretching out her legs. 'The rest of you are so tanned.' She smiled at Magda. 'I don't know how you do it – you're as fair skinned as me and Carly.'

'I'm always running about after the kids,' Magda said, 'but I did get burned.' She tilted her chin to show the cross-shaped mark.

'It looks as if you've been branded a sinner, Magsie,' Tess said slyly and Jo laughed abruptly.

'I can't believe you're really leaving school,' Carly said, picking up the conversation suddenly. 'Mrs Mills keeps saying how much she's going to miss you in the library.'

Gwen shrugged. 'They all want me to stay on,' she said. 'Even my mum. She knows once I'm working full-time I'll move out instead of paying her rent.'

'But your room's not bad at home. Where would you move to anyway?' Carly said.

'I could share with someone from work,' Gwen answered, 'although I'd rather have my own place. I'd like more privacy.'

'Which means sex, right?' Tess said, which was so exactly what Magda had been thinking she couldn't help but laugh.

'N-no,' Gwen stumbled over her denial. 'It's not anything to do with that.'

'She doesn't have a boyfriend anyway, do you?' Carly chimed in.

For the second time that day Jo caught Magda's eye and smirked. This time Tess saw the glance and she frowned, looking from one of them to the other. Gwen wasn't watching, but Carly turned just in time to catch Magda's sudden shrug of discomfort.

'Jo said *you* did, Magda,' Carly said. 'She was telling some boys at school that you did anyway.'

'I only said that so they'd stop asking if she was going to their stupid party,' Jo said quickly as Tess glared at her and Magda dropped her eyes to the ground.

Magda expected an explosion but instead Tess's voice took on the same edge it had had when she'd accepted Magda's apology earlier that morning. 'Better find a boyfriend fast, Mags, so Jo won't look stupid.'

Confused, Magda didn't know what to say, but she was let off the hook as Tess sat up abruptly, blocking her from the others' view as she continued. 'I forgot about that party; it was ages ago that Ian first said anything about it, back when we met up at the shops.'

'If that was ages ago, that's ages you've had that money of my brother's, isn't it?' Jo said and Tess rolled her eyes at her.

'What party?' Gwen asked.

'Just this one some guy called Ian is having,' Jo said with studied casualness. 'You know, he works at the mini-market.'

'You mean the one that fancies Magda,' Carly said. 'His brother's in my class. So when's this party anyway?'

'You're not going,' Jo said.

'I was just asking when it was, all right?'

'Next Saturday,' Tess said. 'He's a proper flirt, he is, coming on to Magda and me and Jo. It'll be Carly next.'

'Leave me out of it,' Jo said. 'I just know who he is, that's all.'

'Oh, so you're not going either then?' Tess said.

'Leave me out of it too,' Magda interrupted suddenly, but Tess shook her head.

'No way, Magsie,' she said. 'I promised him ages ago when I was getting Dan's fags that I'd make you come.'

'I don't want to go,' Magda protested. She thought she

could guess what the look on Jo's face meant and she didn't want to get in her way. If she actually did like Ian, that was probably why she'd blabbed to him about Seb too, to make sure Magda was out of the picture.

But Tess seemed determined. 'Come on, it'll be a laugh,' she urged. 'And you owe me one anyway.'

'It's not fair to force her,' Gwen said before adding, 'It's a pity you *don't* have a boyfriend, Magda. That'd be a way to stop the other boys going on at you.'

Magda felt Jo looking at her and Tess glanced across as well. It was easy to see what they were thinking, although the idea made her feel suddenly short of breath.

'I'll think about it,' she said eventually.

'*I* haven't decided yet,' Jo said supportively and Tess laughed.

'Give it up, Jo, we all know you're going.'

'I'm not,' Gwen yawned. 'It doesn't sound like my sort of thing.'

'Too grown up for schoolboys?' Tess asked and Gwen shrugged.

'I don't see why I can't come,' Carly complained. 'I'm only nine months younger than Jo.'

'Oh, let her come,' Magda said. 'Let's all go.'

Carly beamed, while Jo glared, and Tess's expression went flat again, making it impossible to tell what she was thinking.

Magda wondered if she dared do as they wanted, bring Seb to the party. Even in her own head she didn't like to think of him as her boyfriend. It meant admitting something she just wasn't ready for.

'Don't you want to be seen with me?' Seb had asked the last time they'd met.

'It's not that,' she'd told him. 'I just need more time.'

But now she wondered if there was enough time in all the world for her to feel right about going against her parents' rules. Then again, was there was any point in continuing to be secretive when she felt now that she would keep seeing him, regardless of what anyone said?

By the time they got back to the site, Magda still hadn't made up her mind. But it didn't matter. When Tess and Jo said goodbye, she knew they'd made it up for her.

Washing off the greasy suncream and wringing out her hair in the shower, she spotted the cross mark on her skin again and remembered what Tess had said about being branded a sinner. She'd meant to be good today, yet she'd let Tess lie to protect her when Jo had nearly spilled her secret. And Tess must have wondered why Magda had confided first in someone else, rather than her. She must have hurt Tess's feelings again, even if Tess had hidden it well at the time.

It was true what people said – that once you started spinning lies, you soon got tripped up by them. She'd tripped up again today and she still didn't know how far she would fall.

15

SHADOWS BETWEEN STREET LIGHTS

Jo had bought a dress but she wasn't going to wear it. It was the first dress she'd had since she was a kid. It was black and short and had three thin straps on one shoulder and one wide one on the other. She'd tried it on that morning in her room when her parents were outside.

In the mirror at the shop she'd thought it looked good. Enough to pay over all the money she'd saved that summer. But now she thought it made her tummy bulge out too much. And what were you supposed to do about bra straps, she worried. The one on the right side was hidden by the strap of the dress, but on the other side it showed through. Jo had never thought she'd get so used to wearing a bra that she'd be worried about leaving it off. She'd hidden the dress back in the bag, underneath the jumpers in her chest of drawers.

Outside, Dan had the bonnet of the car up and was tinkering with the engine. His back was sunburned and he was sweating and Jo wrinkled her nose as she went past. The worst thing about the summer was the way everything and everyone smelt. At school, the bins by the bike sheds were overflowing with pungent rubbish. Wasps swarmed around them, droning like helicopters. Jo had seen Ian there on Friday, hanging around with his friends, too hot to even have a kickabout.

'Don't forget my party tomorrow!' he'd called out and Jo had shaken out her hair the way Tess did when boys spoke to her.

'Yeah, all right,' she'd said. 'Where is it again?'

He'd come over then and repeated the address twice, even offered to draw her a map.

'No worries,' Jo had said. 'I'll find it.' She'd waved casually before heading off and it wasn't until she was out of the main gates that she'd let herself smile. But later, on the way home, she'd wondered if all that had been for her or for Magda.

Magda was sitting outside the Lakelys' trailers sewing up a tear in a child-size skirt. Jo rolled her eyes. Magda was so domestic. She was always cooking and cleaning or shopping or sewing. At first, knowing that she wasn't as good as she seemed after all had made Jo feel closer to Magda, but now it felt like just one more thing that Magda did better. Who cared that she wasn't too bright at school when everyone at the site thought she was the perfect daughter. Meanwhile all the boys thought she was the perfect girl.

Feeling annoyed, Jo dropped down beside her and grabbed the nearby bottle of water.

'So, is he coming tonight?' she asked.

'Shh!' Magda looked up in alarm, checking right and

left to see no one was listening. 'I told him about it,' she went on softly, barely moving her lips. 'But I'm still not sure . . .'

'Oh, loosen up,' Jo criticized her. 'It's only a party.' But she dropped her voice as well before asking, 'So what are you going to tell your parents?'

'I said I was going round to Gwen's,' Magda said, looking uncomfortable, 'that she was going to give me her textbooks now she's leaving school. That's true,' she hastened to add. 'I called her earlier and asked if I could say she wanted me to stay the night too.'

Jo nodded, but she was thinking that Magda wasn't much good at lying. Even if Gwen backed her up, it would be easy for her parents to check with Jenny and then Magda would be in the soup.

'What about you?' Magda asked and Jo shrugged, gulping down water before she replied.

'Haven't decided yet.'

When her mum got back from the shops, Jo helped her carry stuff in and got a look of surprise in return.

'You're helpful today, love,' she said.

'Aren't I always?' Jo frowned. 'Or is it just compared to Magda you think I'm not.'

'Oh, don't bicker, love.' Her mum packed the last of the veg away and sat down in a chair to take off her shoes. 'I'm that hot. I don't compare you to anyone, you know that.'

It wasn't true, but Jo let it go.

'Mum, can I camp out in the woods tonight?' she asked. 'It's so much cooler there.'

'I don't know, Joanne.' Her mother rubbed her swollen feet.

'What if I got someone to go with me?' Jo pressed. 'Like Tess maybe?' She hadn't asked Tess about it, but she was pretty sure Tess would agree.

'I don't know, love. I'll think about it,' her mum said and Jo knew that was the best she'd get for now. By the time her dad got back from work she was helping Dan change the oil in the car and later she got the lunch all by herself without being asked. By six o' clock her mum had smiled when she came by and asked, 'You spoken to Tess yet about camping?'

Jo got out her tent and packed her bag, including three changes of clothes and the black dress, just in case. She found Tess near Reenie's trailer and filled her in on the plan.

'Nice work,' Tess nodded. 'All right then. We'd best make ourselves scarce until it's time to meet the others.'

○

Jo hadn't meant to show Tess the way to her den, but it was nearby, private enough to change in and they'd easily an hour to kill before it was time to even look for the others.

'Promise you won't tell anyone where to find it?' she'd insisted and Tess had looked scornful.

'Like I've got nothing better to do than shoot my mouth off,' she'd said.

That was a jab at what had happened at the picnic. Tess hadn't been pleased to discover Jo knew about Seb already, and it was even worse that Magda had trusted her with the secret and she'd then blabbed it about. But Tess was erratic these days. One moment she'd been fired up about the roundabout; now she said it wasn't worth trying to stop it. One minute she'd looked ready to kill when Jo had intruded on her friendship with Magda; the next she was agreeing to be Jo's alibi. With all the mixed signals Jo found it hard to know where she stood. No wonder she felt on edge having Tess in her personal space. Once they reached the little shack in the wasteland, she wondered what they'd have to talk about. But Tess had a six-pack of lager in her bag and passed one across to Jo before rolling herself a cigarette.

'That what you're wearing?' she asked, raising her eyebrows at Jo's old shorts and T-shirt. 'You are such a tomboy.'

Tess was wearing black jeans and a blue silky top, almost as silky as her brushed-out hair, and Jo hesitated before answering.

'I've got other clothes in my bag,' she said, 'but it's so hot. I haven't really decided what to wear.'

'Come on,' Tess chugged down about half her beer and made a grab for Jo's bag. 'Let's see what you've got.' Jo glared as Tess rummaged through her stuff: a pair of jeans, a denim skirt, a red Arsenal shirt and a plain black vest top. '*Oh là là!*' Tess said when Jo pulled the black dress out of its carrier bag. 'Sexy! I wouldn't have thought it of you, Joanne.'

'Shut up.' Jo grabbed the bag back. 'So what if I have a dress?'

173

'Chill out,' Tess said, letting the bag go and picking up her beer can. 'You don't have to be such a grouch all the time. So, are you going to wear it?'

'I don't know.' Jo shifted uncomfortably. The next question slipped out before she could help herself. 'What do you think?'

Tess looked back at the pile of clothes. 'You know,' she said slowly, 'boys are a bit weird about girls being dressed up. I mean, the dress is sexy, but if you look too sexy no one'll come near you. They get scared off.'

'Is that really true?' Jo asked.

Tess shrugged. 'If it were me, I'd wear the skirt and the black top,' she said. 'Keep it casual, let them know you've got legs and go all out on the make-up.' She paused. 'Want me to give you a hand?'

○

By eight o'clock it was cooler. 'We'd better get going,' Tess said, flicking the end of her cigarette out through the open door. 'Let's leave our stuff here,' she added. 'No sense lugging it about.'

As they forged back through the wasteland Tess looked across at the digging works of the roundabout and made a face.

'I still can't believe Travellers are working on that,' she said bitterly. 'It's treachery, that's what it is.'

'Yeah.' Jo could see what she meant for once and when Tess linked her arm in hers she squeezed it back. 'It sucks.'

They made their way through the undergrowth and

174

Jo felt odd having bare legs. Tess glanced over at her and smiled.

'Don't worry,' she said, reading her mind. 'You look good.'

They waited for the others round the side of the council estate. It was actually fun hanging out with Tess like this, Jo realized. Somehow Magda's boyfriend seemed to have opened up a gap between the two best friends, enough for Jo to get to know each of them a bit better. In fact, she and Tess had quite a lot in common.

'So, do you think Magda's boyfriend will come then?' Jo asked.

'Reckon so.' Tess nodded. 'He won't want anyone else poaching on his turf.' Jo laughed and Tess shushed her. 'Someone's coming.'

It was Carly. She was carrying a heavy bag and in the dim light they could see she hadn't dressed up.

'You guys changed already?' she called out even before she'd reached them, looking from Tess's top to Jo's make-up. 'I couldn't. I told my parents I was going round to Gwen's.'

'So did Magda,' Jo said and Tess rolled her eyes.

'Really original, Carly,' she sneered. 'I suppose you can change in the public toilets, if you must.'

Just then, Jo spotted a figure slipping out of the entrance of the Traveller site.

'There she is,' she said. They all watched as the figure crossed the road, looking right and left nervously. Magda was wearing a black leather jacket a size too large for her and a white sundress with a pattern of pale pink flowers.

On anyone else it would have been ridiculous. But Magda could never look anything but gorgeous and Jo couldn't help glancing across at Tess.

'She doesn't need to worry about scaring the boys off,' Tess leaned over and whispered in her ear. 'She's got Seb to do that for her anyway.'

Jo laughed, feeling included by the whisper. But when Magda reached them Tess linked arms with her too and said, 'Looking good, Magsie. Where did you get the jacket though?'

'Where do you think?' Magda replied a bit breathlessly. 'Come on, don't stand about here. Someone'll see us for sure.'

When they reached the city centre Carly went into the toilets to change. Magda kept her company and Jo and Tess sat outside on a park bench, watching people walk by.

'Oh God,' Tess said when Carly and Magda emerged. 'Tell me I'm not seeing this.'

'You're *not* wearing that.' Jo glared at Carly. She had on an orange and red dress with puffed sleeves and a flounced skirt.

'What's wrong with it?' Carly demanded.

'You look like a flamenco dancer,' Tess said, getting up and flicking her cigarette into the gutter. 'But if you want to make a fool of yourself, go right ahead.'

'Don't listen to her.' Magda frowned at Tess and put an arm around Carly. 'You look nice. Your hair is lovely down.'

Tess shook her head, then put her arm through Jo's.

'Come on,' she said. 'It's party time.'

176

Finding the house would have been easy even without Ian's directions. The thumping beat of the music could be heard halfway down the street and light blazed out of the upstairs windows even though the curtains downstairs were drawn.

A group of kids was hanging out in the front garden and Jo heard one of them say, 'Look, the gypsies are coming,' as they arrived.

She hung back at the entrance, not wanting to be the first to go in, until Tess swept her forward, casting a scornful look at the loiterers as she did so. Inside there were people everywhere: on the stairs, more in the combined lounge and dining room, including a bunch sorting through CDs by the stereo, and yet more in the kitchen, shaking packets of crisps into bowls and a tall blonde girl making fruit punch.

'Hi,' she said as they came in, 'I'm Karen. Ian's sister.'

'Hello,' Magda said shyly and Karen smiled at them in a slightly patronizing way. She was older than Ian and Jo guessed she was there to keep an eye on the party even before her next remark.

'No alcohol and no drugs,' she said in a schoolmistressy tone of voice. 'And no trying to go into any of the locked rooms, all right?'

'I'm sixteen,' Tess said, staring Karen down. 'I don't need your permission to drink.'

'But we'll be good,' Magda added quickly and Karen glanced at her after giving Tess a cool look.

'Help yourself to punch, if you like,' she said. 'It's got cranberry juice and ginger ale in it.'

'Mmmm, *delicious*,' Tess sneered and Karen blushed before lifting the bowl of punch and taking it into the dining room.

'You're such a liar – you're not sixteen any more than I am. Why'd you have to be so horrid to her?' Carly objected. 'She was nice.'

'She's a priss,' Tess snapped. 'But don't let me stop you sucking up to her. I'm off for a smoke.'

She crossed to the back of the kitchen, where a half-open door led out into a dim green garden, overshadowed by conifers. Jo could hear people laughing out there and see glowing points of cigarettes. She considered going with her, but instead she said, 'I'm going to look around.'

As Carly and Magda went to get punch, Jo headed upstairs, trying to climb past the people sitting there without giving them a view up her skirt. Upstairs some of the doors were shut, but the last one was open, revealing an untidy bedroom with a desk and a computer. Two guys were wresting with joysticks, playing a beat-'em-up on the computer screen. They didn't look up as she loitered in the doorway.

Ian's room had posters from computer games and current bands on the wall. It was about five times larger than her own room and clothes and school books were piled up in a great heap behind the computer. There was an Arsenal cover on the duvet, which Jo glanced at for a moment. But no Ian.

'Hey, you want a turn?' one of the boys asked, as

178

the screen lit up with a high score. 'We're playing loser stays on.'

'Uh, no, cheers,' Jo said, turning away from the room. 'I'm going to get a drink.'

A couple were snogging on the landing. Jo edged past them and back down the stairs. There was a crush of people in the lounge and she finally caught sight of Ian's spiky hair in the middle of a crowd of his friends, but she didn't fancy fighting her way through to him. She didn't know what she'd say anyway. So she headed out of the kitchen into the garden after all, looking for Tess.

She found her at the far hedge, standing very close to an older-looking guy with blond dreads and a girl with a nose stud and bright pink hair. They all looked up quickly as Jo came near and Tess laughed guiltily.

'It's OK, it's Jo. She's a friend of mine,' she said, passing a hand-rolled cigarette to the guy.

'Hey,' Jo greeted them, adding 'thanks' as the girl fumbled in a bag and offered her a beer.

'Jaycee,' the girl introduced herself. 'So how do you guys know each other?'

'We're gypsies,' Tess said.

'You're Roma?' the guy looked interested and passed the cigarette to Jo.

'I'm part Roma,' Tess said as Jo took a drag from what she realized was a reefer. She coughed a bit, before passing it on to Jaycee.

'I'm not really anything,' she said. 'Just a Traveller.'

'Cool.' Jaycee looked stoned already, her eyelids drooping as she looked vaguely at Jo. 'There's a Traveller girl that works on reception at the centre . . .' she said, her voice tailing off as she inhaled smoke again.

'The sports centre?' Tess said and when Jaycee nodded she went on, 'That's probably Gwen Hughes.'

'You know her?' Jaycee looked briefly surprised and then shrugged as if it didn't matter. 'She's all right. Bit too good-looking for her own good though.'

'What do you mean?' Tess looked suddenly belligerent and Jaycee said quickly, 'Nothing bad, just that our boss is such a letch. He's married, but he hits on all the pretty girls.'

'He's a complete wanker,' a boy said suddenly and all four of them jumped, twisting around to see a figure standing in the shadow of the shed, looking at them.

'Do we know you, mate?' the guy with dreads looked suddenly threatening and the stranger came forward, so they could see he was wearing an expensive-looking black jumper and black jeans.

'I know Jo,' he said, looking at her, and she recognized him finally as the boy from the graveyard.

'Hey. Seb, right?' she said and the others relaxed again, although Jaycee was looking confused.

'You know my boss?' she said.

'Mark Swayland?' Seb nodded. But before he could say any more, Tess spoke up fiercely. 'So you're the gorgio Magda's seeing.' She looked him up and down slowly.

'You must be Tess.' Seb met her eyes levelly. 'Magda talks about you all the time.'

'And do I live up to my legend?' Tess asked, her tone shifting slightly from hostile to flirtatious.

180

'Every bit of it,' Seb laughed, and as Jo looked from him to Tess she realized they both had the same bright blue, challenging eyes.

'So where is Magda?' he asked, turning back to Jo. 'You're the first person I've seen here I recognize. I was wondering if she hadn't come after all.'

'She's here,' Jo said. 'I'll help you look if you like.'

As they re-entered the house, the girls Jo'd seen before turned to look. She could see them eyeing Seb admiringly. She bit back a smile as they went into the lounge – she might just be taking Seb to find Magda, but she didn't mind people seeing her with a good-looking guy and wondering a bit.

'There she is,' she said, spotting Magda's blonde hair, and registering a second later that she was sitting on a couch next to Ian.

'Hey,' Seb said as they arrived, sitting down next to Magda and putting an arm around her shoulders. Magda turned, suddenly seeming to light up as she blushed and smiled. Ian looked across her and met Jo's eyes.

'There you are,' he said. 'Someone told me you were here, but I couldn't find you.'

The party was busier now. More people had arrived in the last half-hour and the room was packed enough that Jo couldn't see where Carly had got to. And people were drinking despite Karen's warning, she noticed, some hiding their cans a bit but most not even bothering. Getting up from the couch, Ian moved round Seb and Magda, who were whispering together, and touched Jo's shoulder.

'Cool top,' he said. 'Hey, you want to go and play some PlayStation or something?'

Jo couldn't resist a glance back as she followed Ian out of the room and she saw Magda's gaze shift away from Seb for long enough to flash her a quick smile.

○

Later, Ian's room was full of people. Jo sat on the bed, leaning against the wall, drinking beer and watching the boys take turns playing computer games. She felt relaxed. The boys had included her as part of their group, but every now and then they seemed to remember that she was a girl and would offer her a drink, or a cigarette, or start a conversation about nothing very much. It was hard to talk anyway, with the music pounding up from down-stairs, and the thumps and yells coming from the console. In another room someone was playing more music, a syrupy sort of classical something that seeped through the walls. But Jo didn't mind not talking much, as long as she wasn't being left out.

She wondered vaguely what had happened to the others, but she wasn't bothered about finding them. Tess would be making herself the centre of attention and Magda would too, whether she intended to or not. But in the end Carly found *her*.

Jo looked away when she saw her in the doorway. Carly shouldn't be at this party in the first place. She was too young, and in her ruffled dress she looked it. But Carly spotted her and squeezed past the game players to reach her.

'Jo . . .' she said. 'It's eleven o'clock.' She was still carrying her bulging bag with her, as if she was scared someone would steal it, and it got in the way as she tried to find space to sit on the bed.

'So what?' Jo shrugged.

'Gwen said I could stay at hers, but her mum gets back at midnight. If I'm not there by then, I won't be able to get in without her seeing me.'

'That's your problem,' Jo told her. 'If you want to go, go.'

'I'm not going on my own,' Carly objected, her voice rising.

'Shh!' Jo glared at her. 'Get Magda to take you back. She's staying there too.'

'I can't!' Carly said. 'I can't find her and Tess is drunk.'

'Oh for God's sake.' Jo swung her legs to the floor and got up. 'If I help you find Magda, will you stop bugging me?'

Carly nodded, looking hurt.

Downstairs, the party had thinned out. There were small groups clustered around the couches and a couple snogging in the kitchen.

'Where's Karen?' Jo asked Carly, who was following her like a lost sheep.

'I think she went to bed,' Carly said. 'She got annoyed about people not listening to her. She was nice though.'

Outside the guy with blond dreads was sitting at the garden table, rolling a cigarette. He glanced up at Jo.

'Hey,' she said, 'have you seen Magda?'

'Is she the one you were with earlier?' the guy said vaguely. 'She's still down the end of the garden, I think.'

Jo shook her head. 'No, that's Tess. But maybe she knows where she is. Cheers.'

Carly trailed after her as she headed down past the shed. 'I've seen Tess already,' she whined. 'I told you, Jo. She's drunk. She told me to . . .' she looked upset again, 'you know . . . *eff off.*'

Tess was at the end of the garden. She was still talking to the girl with pink hair, Jaycee, and Jo could hear them across the dark lawn, see the tips of their cigarettes glowing trails as they waved their hands about.

'I can't believe it.'

'I swear to you . . . he's a right jerkwad.'

'I knew those pool posters were a scam. Bloody Gwen, she's such a liar.'

'Yeah, that's well bitchy, unless she didn't know . . .'

'I still can't believe it . . . what a conniving bastard . . .'

They were sitting together on the grass and when Jo reached them they looked up. Tess looked as stoned as Jaycee had earlier, her eyes lidded as she blew a plume of smoke upwards. Jaycee looked more than half asleep.

'Tess, have you seen Magda?' Jo asked and Tess shook her head.

'I *said* I didn't know where she was.'

'She's got to take Carly home,' Jo tried. 'Come on, Tess, she wouldn't just leave. But she's not in the house, according to Carly.'

'She's probably snogging,' Jaycee said. 'This party's full of couples.'

184

'Magda hasn't got a boyfriend,' Carly said and Jo shook her head in disbelief. What planet was Carly on?

'Yeah, she does.' Jaycee rolled her eyes. 'Maggie's the blonde, right? The one dating the sexy Greek guy.'

'He's not Greek,' Tess said. 'He's, like, Italian or something.'

Jo was getting bored of this. But suddenly Tess got up and stood, swaying a little.

'I bet they've gone round the side,' she said. 'There's a bit of lane or something round that way. I'll show you. I've got something to talk to Magda about anyway.' Her voice was rough with smoke and her face looked hard and mean.

Tess led the way, taking them round the side of the house, along a narrow passage with black bins and bicycles, to the front garden. It was dark now, the sky a deep dusky blue and the only light coming from the splash of street lights. Pointing leftwards round a corner of hedge, Tess said, 'There's a garage and another bit of garden round this way – people went out there earlier when that Karen was yelling at everyone.'

'You're sure she went that way?' Jo thought Tess looked completely out of it and Carly next to her was practically vibrating with worry.

'I'm going to be in so much trouble . . .' she said now. 'It's not fair . . .'

'Oh, shut up.' Tess swung round and glared at her. 'You know, there's more important stuff going on here than you and your whining, all right? That bastard Swayland—'

'Tess.' Magda's voice rang out suddenly from slightly up the road. She emerged into a pool of street light, with Seb beside her. 'What's the matter?' she asked, going in and out of the patches of artificial light as she approached them.

Tess was in no mood to speak quietly, to wait for Magda to reach her side before carrying on. 'That bastard Swayland, Gwen's boss, you'll never guess what he's been up to . . .'

Magda shook her head. 'Tess,' she said again urgently, with a quick concerned look in Seb's direction. His eyes were fixed on Tess, his face pale. 'Tess, be careful what you're saying,' Magda went on. 'Whatever he's done, that's . . . that's Seb's dad you're talking about.'

The sudden look of absolute horror on Tess's face stopped Magda in her tracks. But when she turned to Seb and saw a similar look on his face she almost wailed, 'What? What is it?'

Suddenly Tess was running forwards, her dark hair streaming out like a banner of war behind her, and she was shouting something at Magda, and at Seb. Jo couldn't make it out though, through the party noise, Tess's slurred obscenities – and the sudden sound of a car swerving squealingly and stopping with a loud crunching of gears.

Then a voice shouted out, 'Carly Dixon!'

'Oh no, it's Uncle Alan,' Carly hissed frantically as Jo and Tess jumped and turned to see Alan Hughes and Mike Lakely slamming the car doors shut and advancing on them.

'Shit!' Tess took a step back and looked as if she was about to make a run for it.

'Tess Lovett, you stay right there!' Magda's father caught up with them in a couple of long strides and grabbed her arm. 'I thought you'd be up to your neck in this. Where's Magda?'

Alan had got hold of Carly and was looking at Jo coldly. 'You've been lying to your mum too then, have you? Does she know you're out here boozing and smoking?'

'Get off me!' Tess yelled, shaking Mr Lakely loose and glaring at the men. 'You're not my dad, neither of you. You can't come here telling me what to do.'

'If your dad gave a shit about his kids, he'd do what I'm doing,' Mike Lakely thundered at her. 'Now, where's Magda?' Jo looked around quickly – it seemed Magda and Seb had melted back into the shadows.

'She's not here!' Tess lied and Mr Lakely grabbed both her arms this time and shook her hard.

'She's round that way!' Carly wailed, before breaking into choking sobs, her face blotching with tears.

The door of the house had opened and a group of kids were staring out at them, obviously wondering what all the yelling was about. Jo felt like sinking through the floor as Mr Lakely released Tess to turn in the direction Carly had pointed.

It was then that Magda stepped back into the glow of the street light, a pale figure in white with the darker shadow of Seb behind her. She turned to him and whispered something. He hesitated for a moment then, as

Mike Lakely looked in their direction, he stepped back and was lost in the darkness.

'Da . . .' Magda said softly, as she saw her father's face tighten angrily, 'please don't be mad . . .'

16

CONCRETE WASTELAND

Tess slammed out of the trailer and into the drizzling rain with Reenie still screaming behind her. She'd yelled herself hoarse last night and she'd started in again first thing in the morning.

As if in sympathy, the sky that yesterday had been blue was now a dull washed-out grey and heavy with clouds. Tess turned round and kicked the trailer hard. Then, hearing Reenie heave herself up inside, she turned and ran as the door was thrown open.

Reenie screamed after her, 'You'd better run. Get out of here, I'm not having you back. You're nothing but trouble . . .'

Ducking her head to block out the rain and the stream of abuse, Tess skidded between trailers, sliding on mud and wet grass. But as she drew near to one of the Lakelys' trailers the door opened and Pam Lakely came out quickly, grabbed Tess's arm and hustled her round a corner and towards the hedge.

'Hush now,' she said. 'I want a word with you.'

'Yeah, you and the rest,' Tess snapped back and Pam let her go.

'Mike doesn't want you seeing Magda right now,' she said, her voice low and tense. 'So there's no point coming knocking on the door.'

Tess rubbed angrily at bruises from hard fingers that had bitten into her arms last night and stared Magda's mam in the face. 'Maybe I wasn't anyway. Besides, it wasn't all my fault . . .'

Pam's expression was caught between anger and concern. 'It's not you I'm worried about right now. Who's this boy Magda was with?' Worry won out and her face crumpled like wet newspaper as she tried to look into Tess's eyes. 'Her da's going spare. How long has she been seeing him? What's she been up to?'

'I'm not saying anything.' Tess wrapped her arms around herself, cold in only a T-shirt.

'Theresa, don't make this more difficult than it already is,' Pam said intensely. 'Look, tell us where he lives and then we can talk to his parents. Magda's too young for boyfriends, especially one of those town boys who might take advantage of her . . .'

'I'm saying nothing,' Tess repeated, shivering now.

'Why do you have to be such a pain in the neck?' Pam's voice rose as she glared at Tess. 'Magda won't say anything either and, I'm telling you, Mike's getting more and more worked up . . .' She dropped her voice again abruptly. 'Look, was he just someone she met at the party, was that it? A boy from school?'

'Leave me out of it, all right?' Tess snarled, clenching her hands into fists.

The door of the second Lakely trailer opened and as Pam turned anxiously Tess took off.

'TESS!'

She didn't know if Mike was following so she jumped the stile, landing awkwardly on her right ankle and sprawling against the hedge. Turning to look back, she saw a white face in the window of the trailer before a curtain fell back down across it. She stumbled upright again and limped off down the footpath. It sounded as if Magda had properly caught it and her parents didn't even know the worst of it yet. When they found out who Seb was, surely they'd lose it completely. Just as she had.

Last night Alan Hughes and Mike Lakely had rounded them all up and bundled them into the car, cramming them together in the back seat. It seemed Pam had called Gwen's mum to remind Magda of something and it had set off a chain reaction of parents talking, over the phone and around the site, that had exposed all the lies. Carly had been dropped off at her parents, still sobbing and hiccuping. The remaining three had been marched back in through the site gates, Magda pale and shaking like a leaf and Jo silent and sulking. Tess had tried to break loose three times and each time been pulled back roughly. Bitterly, she hoped that *everyone* had been kept up by Reenie's yelling last night. Mike's voice had been thundering out from the Lakely trailers as well, although Jo seemed to have got off lightly.

At the far end of the footpath Tess came out into

blattering rain and hunched her shoulders miserably as she turned towards the overpass. Normally she'd head out to the dump when she felt like this, but since everyone had heard the row last night she thought the men weren't likely to be sympathetic.

She had kept her dad's campsite secret like he'd asked her to, but now she had to find him again. It sounded as if Reenie was going to chuck her out for good this time and Tess had nowhere to go. But before she reached the bridge she came to a line of cones and a rough tarmac access road veering steeply left down through the scrub. A sign covered in plastic and taped to a metal pole read: 'We apologize for the inconvenience while works connected to the Accleton roundabout are carried out at this site.' Tess kicked over the whole line of cones, booting one clear off the pavement and halfway across the road. A passing car hooted angrily at her and she gave it the finger, then turned and headed down the steep path before the driver could think about stopping and giving her grief.

The tarmac track cut a swathe through the bushes and widened as it turned away from the road. Tess heard the rumble of heavy machinery before she saw the diggings. She hadn't come this way in over a month, never even looked in the direction of the roundabout, and now she stared at the view ahead of her like someone just arrived in a foreign country. Last time she'd been here there were piles of earth and sand and a cleared circle. But now concrete bases had been poured and metal stanchions planted and as the fat wet raindrops splattered down from the dirty sky, yellow bulldozers and earth-movers rumbled forwards and backwards, digging and gouging and tearing into the churned-up earth. Engines roared and clattered, cement mixers rumbled and men in thick jackets yelled at each other across the site. A crane was transporting an iron girder and it swung back and forth above her, a vast black beam sweeping the sky.

A new roar behind her alerted Tess to another bulldozer coming down the access road and she stumbled off the path just as it went by. Her ankle twisted again underneath her and she half limped, half slipped on to the concrete wasteland and came to a halt at the side of a Portakabin.

Her hair was wet, her T-shirt half soaked and her jeans filthy almost up to her knees. Her trainers were completely sodden and she shuddered in the cold damp air. A humming generator was attached to the cabin and she could feel the warmth through the thin walls, and smell tea and tobacco. Trying to get a look in one of the windows, Tess had to jump back when the door opened unexpectedly. She jarred her ankle again.

'What are you doing here, kid? Clear off!' A thickset man with a beard glared at her as he came out of the cabin.

'It's a free country,' she said, glaring back at him as she bent down to rub at her ankle. It felt as if it was starting to swell. She'd turned and begun to limp away when the man's hand caught her shoulder and she whirled, stumbling and swore at him.

'Get your bloody hands off me!'

'Hey, hey! Easy there.' The man backed away with his

hands up and another man, in a grey suit, came to the door of the cabin.

'What's going on?' he asked, looking sharply from the construction worker to Tess.

'I found this kid hanging around,' the guy with the beard said, looking belligerent. 'I was just asking her what . . .'

'All right, Ted.' The man in the suit waved him off. 'I'll handle this.' He looked Tess up and down, unimpressed. 'You're trespassing,' he said coldly.

'Give us a break,' Tess steadied herself on the side of the cabin. 'I've done my ankle in or something. Let me catch my breath a sec.' A squall of rain blew past her and she shivered again.

'Oh, for Christ's sake . . . Get inside.' The man in the suit stood back from the door and held it open for her. 'Whatever you're doing here, you'll have to be escorted off the site.'

It wasn't the warmest welcome ever, but the blast of heated air from inside made up Tess's mind for her and she limped her way into the cabin and sat down on a folding chair. There were a couple of tables inside, one had a kettle on it with steam still rising from the spout. The man in the grey suit had a Styrofoam cup of coffee he picked up and moved as if Tess might steal it.

'Are you homeless?' the suited man asked curtly and Tess flushed with anger.

'I'm a Traveller!' she said. 'You know, one of the people whose homes you're going to be tearing up to build this thing.'

'That's nonsense.' The man frowned at her but Tess could see he hadn't liked that answer one bit.

She was still shivering and he continued to watch her before crossing the room suddenly in annoyance and grabbing an orange Day-Glo jacket from a row of hooks.

'Put that on,' he said, shoving it at her. 'Before you get pneumonia, you stupid girl.'

Tess didn't want to take it, but she was cold and wet so she fumbled into the over-large sleeves while the man went to a walkie-talkie and began to speak into it.

'. . . gypsy kid . . . wandered on to the site . . . no, I don't know . . . Send one of them over to sort it out . . .'

He clicked the thing off again and went back to frowning at her.

'I should call the police,' he began after a moment and Tess sneered at him.

'Don't give me that,' she said. 'Or I'll tell them how your man grabbed me.'

'That's nonsense,' the grey man said again, like a robot. But he hadn't liked that either. Tapping his fingers on the side of the table, he said, 'I'm going to have someone take you back to where the access road starts. If you come on this site again, I'll have you arrested.' After another moment he stood up abruptly and said, 'Don't touch anything!' before leaving the cabin.

Immediately Tess stood up and went to the kettle. It was still warmish and she put a teabag in a mug and poured water on to it, stirring it up with a spoon and lifting it to her mouth all in under a minute. There was a packet of chocolate digestives on the counter and she put it in a pocket of the orange jacket.

She took her tea over to the window and looked out. The man in the grey suit was standing by a stationary digger, gesticulating. It looked as if he was taking his annoyance with her out on someone else, hidden from view. Gulping down the rest of her tea and putting the mug back where she'd found it, she went over to the man's desk. Beside his computer there were a pile of messy papers and a photo of a horsey-faced woman. In the first drawer of the desk she found a jumble of pens and rubber bands, a Dictaphone, a wallet and a mobile phone. Closing the drawer thoughtfully, she opened the second and saw computer disks and stationery and crouched down to look in the third. More stationery, a manual for a fax machine, a computer cable and a plastic folder. Tess was already bored of snooping, but she pulled the folder out and glanced through it, still crouching on the floor, dripping strands of her long hair hanging wetly across her shoulders and getting in the way. The file looked boring, full of technical jargon she didn't understand. But halfway through was a series of pages with loops and swirls of road layouts on them, superimposed over a map Tess recognized.

The map didn't have place names marked, just built-up areas shaded in grey and everywhere else in green, brown or yellow. But Tess knew Accleton like the back of her hand and as she traced the path of one of the slip roads she saw the way it curved across the corner of the temporary side of the Traveller site. She was still staring at it when she heard voices outside.

'. . . not paid to think. Get her out of here and make sure she doesn't come back!'

Tess stood up, glancing quickly towards the window as a blur of grey went past. Too late to put the file back – she crammed it into the other pocket of the orange jacket before stumbling to the chair just as the door opened.

The man in grey stared at her suspiciously but, after the first moment, Tess wasn't looking at him. Dressed in an identical orange jacket, his curly hair covered by a black woollen cap, his blue eyes rounding with shock even as his mouth twisted into the familiar awkward smile, was the construction worker supposed to escort her off the site. Her father.

The man in grey must have sensed something. He frowned from Kieran to Tess. 'You don't know who her people are, do you? Your lot seem to all know each other.'

'Never seen her before in my life, Mr Edwards.' His eyes met Tess's again, with a trapped expression. 'Right you, come on, out of it.'

In shock, Tess limped past the grey man and into the drizzling rain. Her father's hand rested on her shoulder for a second and she shook it off violently. 'Don't touch me,' she spat and the other man sighed.

'Better not, Lovett. She's got a nasty tongue, this one.' He glared at Tess. 'Give Lovett any trouble and we'll have to call the police. If you know what's good for you, you'll leave like a good girl.'

Tess tried not to limp as she stomped in the direction of the access road.

'Make sure she gives that jacket back!' the suited man called as she heard heavy footsteps jogging after her.

Tess made about ten steps before her ankle throbbed and she had to start favouring it again. As she reached the access road she wondered where she was going. Before she'd gone to look at the site she'd been planning to look for her dad. Now he was right here and she wondered why she'd ever believed he would help her.

'It was all lies, wasn't it?' she said, looking straight ahead as she began to walk up the access road. 'You weren't hiding from the police. You were hiding from us. Because of what people would say if they knew you were working on the roundabout.'

'Don't be like that, Tess,' her dad said. 'It's just a job, right? A man's got to eat, hasn't he?'

Tess laughed harshly, the laugh hurting her throat as it came up through clenched muscles.

'It's not just a job though, is it?' she said. 'You're helping the council to ruin our site. What about rights for Travellers, Dad? What about refusing to give up our land or be pushed to the edge . . . Doesn't that matter any more?'

'The site's got no chance anyway,' Kieran said gruffly before turning scornful. 'And what rights? You know the government doesn't care about us.' He launched into the familiar criticisms Tess had heard so many times before. 'They want to kill our way of living, take away our freedoms . . .'

'Yeah, right.' Tess flashed her father a sidelong look. *'They* don't care about us. What about you? You're not doing anything to stop it. At least people like Alan Hughes tried, but you . . . You're working here! Whose side are you on?'

'I'm on my side!' Kieran shook back his head and fixed Tess with a dangerous look, one that warned her not to push it. 'No one's going to help you if you don't help yourself. That's my motto.'

'Like the time you helped yourself to the launderette cash register?' Tess demanded. She was too far gone to listen to the warning in her dad's eyes and suddenly all the stories Reenie had told about the Lovetts coming from bad blood were ringing in her ears. 'Or when you helped yourself to Mum's earrings and sold them for booze . . .'

An orange blur came at her through the rain and Tess threw up her arms to deflect the blow, slipping on a patch of mud as she did. Her right leg went out from under her and she landed hard, scraping her arm and legs against the tarmac and knocking her head. He hadn't hit her, but now he stood looking down at her and didn't offer a hand.

'Shut your mouth,' he said, his face twisted with anger. 'If you go running to Reenie with this, I'll teach you to tell tales. Now go on. Get!'

He stood watching Tess as she sat up. Her face felt sore. Touching her jaw, she brushed away bits of gravel and brought her hand back bloody. Getting her feet underneath her she stood up shakily and opened her mouth to speak as Kieran turned his back on her.

'I said, *get*!' he snarled over his shoulder as he jogged

back down the path and Tess watched him go before closing her mouth. There was nothing left to say anyway.

Limping back up to the ring-road turn-off she felt light-headed. Her eyes weren't focusing properly and she wondered if she'd banged her head badly, until she realized the blur was tears. By the time she reached the main road, the rain had started again.

17

THROUGH THE KEYHOLE DOOR

Wednesday was the last day of term and, although you were allowed to wear your own clothes to school, Carly hadn't bothered to dress up. After the party she didn't feel like dressing up ever again. Instead she'd put on an old pair of jeans, a dark hooded top and Magda's pink duffle coat. She didn't even care if her hair frizzed up in the rain.

It had been raining since Sunday morning. On Monday, word had got around that there'd been some sort of trouble at Ian's party and that 'those gypsy kids' had been at the bottom of it. After all this time, Carly suddenly found herself lumped in with Tess and Magda and Jo. People whispered about her behind her back and watched her when they passed her in the corridors. Meanwhile Jo refused to speak to her, blaming Carly for them getting found out. Magda and Tess hadn't come to school at all.

Tuesday had been worse. Magda had shown up, walked to school by one of her older brothers and looking pale and ill. Carly tried to talk to her, but she and Jo had gone off together and whispered for hours behind the bike sheds, and Jo yelled at Carly when she tried to join them. That evening the police came round to ask her if she knew anything about where Tess might have gone. Apparently Tess hadn't been home in days and Reenie had finally reported her missing. Carly's parents had told her to tell the police whatever she knew, but really she hadn't known anything. She'd said Tess liked to hang out at the dump, but they'd looked there already, and she'd said that she knew all sorts of short cuts and hideouts and they'd looked a bit grim. But in the end they'd said that, since Tess had run off before, she'd probably show up, though if anyone heard from her they'd like to know about it.

Mainly, Carly felt sorry for Magda. At school, after the news came out about Tess being missing, everyone looked at her as if she had two heads. In assembly the head had asked everyone to be specially nice to Carly Dixon, Jo Rowland and Magda Lakely since a friend of theirs was missing. Then Amy and Deborah had tried to whisper to her all through first and second period and Genevieve had grabbed her at lunch and asked if it was true Tess was her cousin. Amy had even asked if she thought that Tess had been kidnapped. Carly had gone to the bathroom after that and thrown up the three mouthfuls she'd eaten of her lunch.

She'd hidden in the library during afternoon break and even then people had stopped her and asked her how she was in a fake way. She'd finally gone to the really skanky girls' bathroom near the science block that everyone avoided and found Magda there, sitting on the floor, writing in an exercise book.

'I've been trying to talk to you for days,' Carly said when she came in and Magda looked up, revealing reddened eyes with purple shadows under them.

'Can you do something for me?' she asked and Carly crouched down next to her.

'Course I will.'

Magda tore a sheet out of her notebook, folded it over and wrote something on the outside. 'Can you get this to Seb?' she asked, creasing the folds with her fingers nervously. 'I didn't know who else to ask – I knew you'd do it for me, you'd . . . understand.'

'To Seb?' Carly blinked. 'Oh, um . . .' she was blushing. 'Where does he live?'

'At the top of Nightingale Hill,' Magda said hurriedly. 'The house with the keyhole door.' She stood up. 'I have to go. I've got maths in five minutes.'

'All right, give it to me then,' Carly said and Magda passed the letter across almost reluctantly. 'Look, Magda, do you know where Tess is?'

'No.' Magda shook her head. 'I saw her run off Sunday morning. But Da wouldn't let me talk to her. He and Mam fought about it all last night.'

'It's not your fault . . .' Carly began.

Magda shook her head again and then looked at the folded paper in Carly's hand.

'It's *all* my fault. Promise you won't tell anyone about that,' she said.

'Cross my heart and hope to die,' Carly said automatically, then when Magda looked upset added quickly, 'It's sort of romantic, isn't it? Like . . . like Romeo and . . .'

Magda was crying. Silently. Huge tears rolled slowly out of her eyes and down her face, Carly could actually see each one appearing like a big round bead.

'She'll be all right,' she said desperately. 'She's run off before, hasn't she?'

But Magda only made a choking noise and ran off herself and Carly put the letter carefully away in her bag.

○

She left school straight after her last lesson. Mum wouldn't be back from work for another couple of hours and she'd have time to get to Seb's house and back by then. Following the directions she'd been given, she headed for Sacred Heart church and then started walking up the hill behind it.

It was steep and her legs were aching long before she was halfway up. It was hot too. The rain had finally stopped and now the clouds were burning away and she had to take her coat off. Bundling it under her arm and hoisting her rucksack up on her back again, she glared at it. It was Magda's old coat, the pink one she'd swapped for her anorak, and looking at it she wondered what she'd been thinking. Pink clashed with her ginger hair and the coat was too short. It had been too short on Magda too but on her it had looked . . . Carly frowned, trying to work out why she'd wanted it in the first place. It had made Magda stand out, but Magda stood out anyway. Even with her hair scraped back and red eyes she was like a glamorous tragic heroine.

'Tess'll be all right,' Carly said out loud. She was sure

of it. You couldn't imagine anything really bad happening to Tess. Consoling herself with that thought, she pushed on. Helping Magda made her feel good as well and when she reached the top of the hill she took out the letter from her bag and studied the address. 'Seb Swayland, Nightingale Hill', Magda had written and Carly surveyed the circle of houses in front of her now, impressed. They were the poshest of the lot, she thought. Seb's family must really be rich.

Each house had something different at the front – pillars or a big porch. Only one had a doorway shaped like a keyhole and Carly went up to it and pushed the bell. Hearing footsteps in the hall, she jumped back and tried to smooth her hair down as the door opened. But it wasn't Seb, it was a woman. She was wearing a cream dress and had a lot of black hair piled up on top of her head. She was holding a mobile phone in one hand.

'Are you selling something?' she demanded. She had a foreign accent and she looked down her nose disapprovingly.

'I'm . . .' Carly swallowed. 'Can I speak to Seb, please?'

'Sebastián?' The woman's thin eyebrows rose up to her hairline and just then there was a tinny sort of noise from the phone. Holding it up to her ear again, the woman opened the door wide with her other hand, revealing long pearl-coloured nails. 'Come in, come in,' she hissed, pressing the phone to her neck for a moment and then bringing it back to her head. 'Yes, Juan, I'm here.'

Carly stepped into the hall and the woman pushed the door shut behind her. Then, with a *flick flick* of her long nails, she beckoned Carly after her. Still talking on the phone, she led the way along a long cream-carpeted corridor, which made Carly nervous of leaving marks, across another room with red leather sofas and a huge fireplace, where a set of suitcases was standing in the middle of the polished wooden floor and into the largest kitchen she'd ever seen.

'Sit down. I will not be long,' the woman said and went off back through the door into the sitting room. Carly put down her bag and jacket and managed to get on to one of the tall kitchen stools. She sat and waited, the letter in her lap. Magda hadn't sealed it and she didn't fancy giving it to Seb's mother. What if she read it?

'Please forgive me.' The woman swept back in through the doors and put the mobile phone down on the counter. 'Sebastián is not here. He does not come back from school for another forty minutes. I am Gabriella, his mother.'

'Oh.' Carly looked at her watch. 'Is it all right if I wait for him? I could wait outside if you like.'

'I will not hear of it,' Gabriella flicked her fingers again, waving away Carly's remarks. 'I am also waiting for him. We shall wait together.'

'Oh.' Carly shifted awkwardly on the stool and Seb's mother stalked past her on high heels.

'Would you like a *refresco*?' Gabriella asked. 'A soft drink?'

'Er, thanks.' Carly's eyes crept back to her watch. She wondered what on earth she was going to say to this woman for over half an hour. 'Um, are you going on a trip?'

'I am going back to Spain to live,' Gabriella announced. 'I have had enough. Sebastián will have to join me later.'

'You're going to *Spain*?' Carly nearly fell off the stool.

Gabriella raised her eyebrows again as she put a frosted glass in front of Carly. The drink, whatever it was, was a greenish creamy yellow.

'I think you are a little young for Sebastián,' she said, looking Carly up and down.

'That's not . . .' Carly struggled for words. 'I'm not dating him, I'm just . . .' She came to an abrupt halt. 'I just need to tell him something.'

'What sort of thing?' Gabriella brought her face closer and peered into Carly's eyes as if she could see right through her head. 'Is it about his father? About Mark?'

'No!' Carly squeaked. 'I don't even know his dad.' She paused, as something clicked in her memory. 'Unless he's Mr Swayland, the swimming-pool man.'

'He is the swimming-pool man.' Gabriella tapped her fingers on the kitchen countertop. It was made of a grey flecked stone and Carly gritted her teeth at the noise. 'He is also the man who is never home before midnight. Which is one of the many reasons why I am leaving him.'

Carly goggled at her. Gabriella seemed satisfied with the look of shock on her face and sat down on another stool, crossing one slim leg over the other and smoothing down her skirt.

'I am going to Spain because my husband is having an affair with a *gitana*,' Gabriella said. 'And it is not the first time.'

Gabriella was beginning to seem a bit like someone in a soap opera; it was hard to take her seriously as Seb's mother. Carly wondered if she ever did the washing, or got the tea, or helped Seb with his homework. 'What does *gitana* mean?' she asked suddenly, surprising herself and blushing. But Gabriella didn't seem surprised at the question.

'A gypsy girl.' Gabriella tossed her head.

Carly looked at the frost condensing on her glass and wondered what to say. After today she didn't feel like making an issue about being a Traveller for the sake of it, but she wasn't sure she wanted Seb's mother to talk that way about them either.

'Seb's friends are gypsies,' she said eventually and Gabriella's eyebrows went the highest yet as they looked at each other across the counter.

'Sebastián is an idealist. Unlike his father.' Gabriella stood up. 'I must finish packing. You can wait here or in the room next door.' She swept out and Carly stared after her and wished Seb would hurry up.

○

After sitting uncomfortably on the stool for another five minutes Carly got up and went quietly back into the hallway to look for a toilet. The doors were all shut and she opened one carefully and saw a smart dining room, then another lounge before she found a pristine bathroom and went in. Before she left it again she looked at herself in the mirror. Slowly she removed the hairband from her plait, unravelled her hair and shook it out. Then she went back into the hallway, stepped out of her shoes and went upstairs. Gabriella was in a big office room, packing up a laptop computer, and she didn't see Carly at first, so concentrated was she on getting it into its bag.

'Is it Tess?' she asked.

'Is what Tess?' Gabriella sat back and frowned at Carly.

'Is it Tess who's having an affair with your husband?' Carly said. 'No one ever tells me anything,' she went on, 'so I just wondered if it was Tess and if she's run off with him or something. Because people are really worried. Magda's worried.'

'I have no idea what you're talking about,' Gabriella stood up. She was still frowning though. 'A girl is missing?'

'Tess is missing.' Carly was almost enjoying herself – at school you never got to talk back to people. But Gabriella wasn't like a teacher and she didn't seem to think Carly was being rude, or perhaps she was so used to saying outrageous things herself she didn't notice that Carly was. 'No one's seen her since Sunday morning.'

Gabriella stared at Carly, then she asked slowly, 'Does Tess have your colouring?' Carly blinked and Gabriella's fingernails flicked out and caught a strand of Carly's hair and shook it. When Carly cringed back she dropped it and rolled her eyes. 'Does Tess have this colour hair, like you, but little, petite?'

'No, she's got dark hair,' Carly said. 'Gwen's the only other one with reddish hair.'

'Then it is not Tess, although it may be the other one,' Gabriella replied.

Carly laughed. 'Not *Gwen*,' she said. 'Gwen's much too sensible to go out with a married man.' She was beginning to think this whole thing was a mistake on Gabriella's part. 'Gwen works at the swimming pool though,' she continued. 'Maybe that's why someone *thought* she was seeing Mr Swayland, but she wouldn't do something like that.'

Gabriella fixed Carly with another of those penetrating looks. 'But you said yourself no one ever tells you anything,' she said coolly. 'How well do you know these people?'

'They're Travellers,' Carly told her. 'I mean we're Travellers, or I was until my parents settled here. I've known them my whole life.'

Gabriella raised her eyebrows again. 'I have known my husband for eighteen years,' she pointed out, 'which is longer than you have been alive, I think. And so I know that he tries to attract any young woman who works for him. And how do you know Sebastián . . . ?'

'I met him at a party.'

'Sebastián went to a party with gypsies?' Gabriella looked suspicious, as if she thought Carly was lying. 'Did he mention the roundabout?'

'What?' Carly was sure her face must look as blank as she felt. 'What about the roundabout?'

'Then he didn't.'

Carly glared at her. 'What about the roundabout?' she said again and as Gabriella opened her mouth to speak her eyes shifted to something behind Carly.

At first Carly had thought that it might be the mysterious Mr Swayland, but it was Seb. Even then, it was alarming enough. He was taller than Carly had realized and very good-looking. Gabriella let loose a stream of Spanish over Carly's head and he gave back as good as he got. But eventually the conversation or argument or whatever it was came to an end.

'Let's talk about it later, Mama,' Seb said suddenly and decisively and to Carly's surprise Gabriella fell quiet.

'I have more packing still to do,' she said. 'But my ticket is booked already. Don't expect me to change my mind.'

'I don't think you should change your mind,' Seb said seriously, touching Gabriella's arm as she swept out of the room. Then finally he turned to Carly and asked, 'You must be a friend of Magda's?'

'I'm Carly,' she told him and fumbled in her pocket for the letter. 'Magda asked me to bring you this.'

'Thank you,' Seb took it quickly, but before he opened it he eyed Carly doubtfully. 'What were you and my mother talking about before?'

Carly blushed. 'She said . . . she said your dad was cheating on her,' she stammered. Then suddenly indignant she added, 'And she as good as said it was with my cousin Gwen. That's ridiculous – Gwen wouldn't have an affair and your dad's much too old for her anyway!'

'You don't need to tell me.' Seb looked angry. 'My dad's a jerk. If he's seeing your cousin I feel sorry for her. But that's not what I meant. What were you saying about the roundabout?'

'She asked *me* about it,' Carly protested. 'She wanted to know how I knew you and everything and then she

211

started talking about the roundabout. I'm sick of that stupid roundabout. It makes everyone act crazy.'

'Not as sick as I am,' Seb said. 'Look, come and sit in my room while I read this. I've been desperate to hear from her.'

She followed him to his room. It was big and very tidy, with another laptop computer lying on a desk. There was a whole wall of bookshelves. The only poster was of a flock or swarm or whatever it was of butterflies.

'Sit down,' he said, whipping a jumper off the back of an armchair. 'Sorry, I've already forgotten your name.'

'Carly,' she said again.

'Sorry.' He shook his head. 'Everything's such a mess right now, it's hard to concentrate.'

'That's all right,' Carly told him. 'I know all about it. Gwen and her mum stayed with us when her parents broke up . . . She said it was really hard to concentrate on homework. I'm sure she wouldn't go out with a married man . . .'

She stopped talking. Seb had unfolded the paper and read it quickly, his eyes flicking left and right as she talked. But now he had fallen still and was looking down at the letter with a suddenly expressionless face, as if the feeling had dropped right out of it.

'What is it?' she asked.

'It's . . . Well, you might as well know. Magda's broken up with me. I can guess why.'

'She hasn't!' Carly stared at him. 'But she really loves you. I'm sure she does.'

'She must have changed her mind,' Seb said sharply,

cutting her off. 'And I can't blame her, if she's heard what my dad's been up to. Probably from Tess – I think that was what she was about to mouth off about at the party.'

'But I'm sure Gwen's not seeing him.' Carly felt like crying. Why would people never listen to her? 'And Magda doesn't know anything about it anyway.'

'Not that,' Seb said. 'Although that's probably enough. But the roundabout.' Carly opened her mouth but this time Seb finally explained. 'My dad's financing it,' he said. 'He did a deal with the council. It's his project.'

18

FALLOUT SHELTER

The sky had been bright blue at eight in the morning when Jo's mum had woken her to help with chores. But by ten it was raining and all the washing she'd pegged out on the line had to be brought in again.

'It'll have to go to the launderette,' her mum said. 'And I don't know when I'll find the time.'

'I can do it,' Jo offered. Since term had ended the previous week her mum hadn't let her go out alone. Even offering to be helpful had been getting her suspicious looks. But it seemed as if her mum was finally giving way.

'I suppose I can't keep you cooped up here forever,' she said reluctantly. 'And lord knows you need something to wear. Those jeans you have on are filthy, your black pair is soaking and your old ones have gone missing, I can't find them anywhere.'

She'd left them in her den, Jo remembered suddenly. She and Tess had never had the chance to go back and she'd been kept in since the party. Suddenly she had another idea. Picking up the laundry bag, she said casually,

'Do you think the Lakelys have washing too? I could ask Magda to walk with me.'

'That's a good idea,' her mum said. 'It'd do her good to get out of herself a bit. She looks so pale and sad nowadays.'

Pam Lakely had come by on Sunday and asked Jo if she knew anything about Magda's boyfriend and Jo had said she didn't. Her dad had looked disapproving, but after Pam had left Jo's mum had shaken her head and said, 'Poor Magda.' She must have been thinking about that as well, because when she handed over a handful of twenty- and fifty-pence pieces for the machines she added 'Joanne . . . ?'

'Yeah?' Jo stopped in the doorway, hefting the bag from hand to hand.

'You know you can tell me anything, don't you, love?' her mum said. 'If you had a boyfriend, for instance . . .'

'I don't,' Jo said quickly. 'Honestly, Mum, I don't. Just boys who're friends – no boyfriends.'

'Well, about anything, just so you know, you can tell me,' her mum said again and Jo nodded awkwardly.

'I'd better go before people bag all the machines,' she said. 'I'll call for Magda on the way.'

If the Lakely kids hadn't been acting up again, Jo didn't reckon she'd have managed it, but Pam plainly hadn't had the strength to say no. 'Go on then,' she had said eventually, turning weary eyes on Magda. 'But for heaven's sake don't go anywhere else. And don't even think of seeing that boy.'

'I've told you, Mam –' Magda seemed just as tired –

'that's over. I promise.' She looked as if she'd made that promise several times before.

They hurried out of the site. 'I've hardly seen you,' Jo said, glancing across at Magda. 'How is it?'

'Da's still furious,' Magda said quietly, hunching her shoulders against the rain. 'And Mam said this morning she didn't know who I was any more.'

'Have you really broken up with Seb?'

'Yes.' Magda was looking straight ahead. 'I had to. I should never have gone to that party.'

'But . . .' Jo tried to think of something to say.

'It wouldn't have worked anyway,' Magda said. 'I got Carly to take him a letter and when she got back she said Seb had told her it's his dad's company that's building the roundabout. That's what Tess was so worked up about at the end of the party, I think. He thought that was why . . .'

'Why you broke up with him?' Jo finished for her and Magda nodded. 'But it wasn't?'

'No, it was just too hard . . .' Magda's voice wobbled as she continued. 'Lying to my parents and getting into trouble and letting people down. I didn't even know about the roundabout connection, but that makes it even worse, of course. He should have told me.'

'You can understand why he didn't though. He said at the party, he hates his father; he said he was a jerk.'

'I know.' Magda bit her lips. 'But I shouldn't have seen him. It's just messed up everything. It's all my fault.'

'You mean Tess going missing?' Jo moved up closer to Magda and touched her arm. 'That's not your fault.'

'I wasn't there for her,' Magda said, sounding tragic. 'I

didn't go to the protest and I saw her run off, but I was grounded because of Seb and couldn't go after her.' Now that she'd started talking about it she didn't seem able to stop. 'And Da blamed it all on Tess, said she'd made me wild. He just wouldn't believe me when I told him it was all me, Tess didn't even know about it. All she's been doing this summer is trying to stop the roundabout. And even then I was dating the enemy . . .'

'You know, she was even working at school for a while. She was really fired up about it,' Jo agreed.

'I let her down,' Magda said. 'And Tess doesn't have anyone. Her dad's not around, her mum ran off years ago. Reenie didn't even seem bothered when Tess went missing. It was two days before she called the police.'

'It's still not your fault she ran off,' Jo insisted. 'And anyway . . . I think I might know where she is.'

Magda stopped walking and stared at her. Jo lowered her voice and said, 'You know I have a place I go to be alone—'

'Hey, Jo!'

They both started and turned as the door of the mini-supermarket slid shut behind Ian, who was hurrying towards them. As he reached them he stopped and looked awkward.

'Hi,' he said and Magda ducked her head, swinging her hair over her face.

'Hi.' Jo looked back at him, holding the bag of washing in front of her like a barrier. 'Are you allowed to leave the till?'

'Not really,' Ian admitted. 'Look, I just wanted to

217

know if you guys were all right.' He paused. 'You're not on the phone, so I couldn't call you. Has Tess shown up yet?'

'Not yet,' Jo said and Magda looked tragic.

'Hey.' Ian's voice was serious. 'I'm sorry you got in trouble for coming to my party. It was really great you came.' Then he looked straight at Jo and added, 'Really.'

'Don't worry about it,' Magda said softly and Jo knew she was dreading Ian saying something about Seb. She looked about two seconds away from tears already.

'Look, we've got to go,' Jo said, sliding her free arm into Magda's as Tess would have done, 'and you should get back to your till. But I'll call you tonight, OK? From the phone box.'

'That would be cool.' Ian grinned at her and then ran back into the mini-market.

'He fancies you,' Magda said, her voice still a bit shaky and Jo shrugged as they headed into the launderette.

'Yeah, he's all right,' she said. 'But look, about Tess . . .'

The launderette was empty, although a couple of the machines were going. Jo and Magda bagged two free ones and began loading clothes in as Jo continued.

'The night we went to the party,' she said, 'I showed Tess this place where I go. It's a sort of a shack, down south in the wasteland. I think maybe that's where she is. If you kept watch over the machines, I could get there and back to check by the time the drying was done.'

'No.' Magda shook her head. 'I want to go with you.'

'But your mum said if you went anywhere but here—' Jo began, but Magda interrupted her.

218

'This isn't about Seb,' she said. 'It's about Tess. I want to come.'

'OK,' Jo said, shaking powder into her machine and then feeding it with twenty-pence pieces, 'but we'd better go quickly.'

Leaving the launderette, they jogged round the back of the shops and into the beginnings of the wasteland. Despite the rain, it was warm. They could see the trailers through the fence at the back of the Traveller site as they skirted round it. As they got closer to the motorway they could hear the sound of the traffic, a distant whooshing noise like a river.

Jo took the lead through the bushes and as Magda followed her there was a ripping noise.

'I've torn my skirt,' she said. 'I wish I had some jeans.'

Jo glanced back and saw the way Magda had to bundle up her skirt to stop it catching. 'You should stand up for yourself.'

'Da says while I live under their roof I'll live by their rules,' Magda told her. 'What would your parents say if you went out with Ian?'

'I don't know.' Jo blushed and was glad Magda couldn't see it. 'But Mum's started asking if there's anyone.'

'Da seems to think I've been running about town with half a dozen boys,' Magda said, sounding suddenly fierce.

'Well, you haven't told him about Seb, have you?' Jo pointed out. 'So he's imagining the worst, I suppose.'

'It's only cos I couldn't bear it if I had to see him and Da argue.'

'Well, if you've broken up with him for good, I guess

you won't have to,' Jo said. 'As long as Carly keeps her mouth shut about who he is – his dad and the round-about.'

'Oh, Jo . . .' Magda sounded tired, 'lay off Carly. She's been trying so hard and you're all always putting her down. She used to be your friend.'

'I grew up and she didn't,' Jo replied defensively. 'And you know how annoying she can be.'

'Everyone grows up, Jo,' Magda said suddenly. 'It's not a competition. Carly's just trying to fit in. She's not tough like you or Tess, but she's a lot less selfish than me – or Gwen, for that matter. All this summer Carly's been try-ing to do the right thing and getting smacked back for it.'

A sudden crack of thunder sounded like a gunshot and they both looked up at once. The sky was streaked and patched with clouds in white and stormy grey, some lit brown or gold by the sun blazing brightly behind them.

'Come *on*, Jo,' Magda said. 'Where is it?'

'This way,' she said and set off at a run for the taller stand of bushes that hid the shack. Magda ran after her and they arrived at the small building together. Jo heaved open the sagging door.

The shack was empty. One quick glance round showed them that and Magda sank down on the ground, looking abruptly exhausted.

'She's not here,' she said flatly.

'But someone has been,' Jo said. She was looking at the bag she'd left here. The zip was open and there were clothes lying next to it. She held up a pair of muddy jeans. The mud had dried and stiffened and they were now more brown than black, but she'd recognize Tess's jeans anywhere; no one else's were so torn and tattered at the bottom. 'And she's nicked mine,' she added, going through her bag.

'Then she has been here.' Magda grabbed for the jeans and looked at them as if they were a holy relic. 'And she's coming back.'

'Probably,' Jo said. 'Since it's Tess, she'd probably have nicked off with the bag and everything in it if she'd gone for good.' Investigating the trash pile, she added. 'It looks as if she's been living on chocolate biscuits and crisps.' Jo stood up. 'So what do we do now? Leave a note?'

Magda looked at her as if she was crazy. 'I'm waiting,' she said. 'Until Tess gets back.'

'But . . .' Jo stared at her. 'We're going to get in trouble,' she warned and it wasn't until Magda shrugged that she realized how much finding Tess mattered to her. She was obviously determined to make up for letting her down in the past, even if it made things worse at home.

○

Sitting inside the wooden shed, Jo stared out through the open doorway to the tangle of bracken. There was no wind and the rain was coming down in long dotted lines, like a kid's painting. A rumbling growl of thunder made her twist her head around to see if she could spot lightning and a few seconds later a bright light flooded the sky to the west. Slowly Jo began to count off seconds, getting to nine before the rattle and bang of the thunder sounded again. On the other side of the shack Magda was sitting patiently in the driest spot.

It was Jo who spotted the figure running through the field. It was dressed in Day-Glo orange and she thought at first it must be one of the construction workers. But as its path slanted over the rise of ground she caught a glimpse of long loose dark hair whipped out like a flag behind the running figure.

'Magda!' she said, standing up and staring through the rain as the blurred orange jacket bobbed behind the scrub of bushes.

'Is it Tess?' Magda came to join her at the entrance and then pushed past her into the rain. She waved an arm wildly just as the orange blur wrestled through the last bushes and a pale face with intense blue eyes looked up through the tangle of wet hair.

'Tessie.' Magda grabbed Tess and clung to her tightly and Jo threw an arm round Tess as well, forcing her forward and into the shelter.

The thunder was still chomping up and down the hills, but by heaving the door shut Jo managed to cut out the worst of it. 'How have you been living here?' she said, managing to catch Tess's eye over Magda's head. 'You should be dead of pneumonia!'

'I haven't been here the whole time,' Tess said. 'I hitch-hiked down the motorway for a bit, looking at round-abouts, junctions, service stations, eating a lot of chips. All in the cause of research, of course. But yes, you're a shitty landlord, Jo. I want my rent back.' She grinned unrepentantly.

But suddenly Magda was gasping for breath in between great gulping sobs.

Tess looked at her with a frown. 'Hey, Magsie, it's all right,' she said. Meeting Jo's eyes again, she asked, 'What's up?'

'I'm not sure.' Jo rummaged in her bag and found a jumper. 'Here, Mags, put this on and sit down.'

'Put your head between your knees,' Tess added. 'You look like you haven't eaten in a week.'

'She probably hasn't,' Jo realized. 'She's been worried about you, Tess Lovett!'

'Don't call me that.' Tess glared at her.

'It's true,' Jo insisted, still thinking about how Magda had been fretting after Tess on their way over. 'She's broken up with Seb over it.' It was only then Jo registered what Tess had just said. 'And don't call you what?'

'You broke up with Seb?' Tess ignored Jo and stared at Magda. They both saw tears slide down her face as she hiccuped for breath. 'Oh, snap out of it, Magsie. It's wet enough out there without you drowning us all in tears too.'

Jo thought that was a bit harsh, but Magda did calm down and get the jumper on as Tess took her orange jacket off.

'Why are you dressed like a construction worker anyway?' Jo asked and Tess sneered suddenly.

'I'm not,' she said. 'It was all I had. It was useful, that's all.' Then she grinned at them both. 'I've been spying on the roundabout,' she said. 'And I've been talking to truckers. I've been all over.'

'What for?' Jo asked, but Tess ignored her again.

'What happened with Seb?' she asked Magda.

'I didn't know Seb's dad was involved in the round-about, I swear,' Magda said. She looked about to dissolve in tears again. 'I wouldn't have kept that from you.'

'Do you think Seb was involved too?' Jo asked, still trying to understand properly why Magda was so miserable. 'Did he keep you away from the protest deliberately?'

'No. That was all me.' Magda shook her head. 'I went to meet him.'

'It's OK, Magsie. I was wrong to freak out about that. Why would Seb need to keep one person away when his dad's free offer had half the Travellers off at the pool?' Tess said, looking scornful. 'Besides, Seb hates his father. Perhaps he's just as against the roundabout as we are. It's not fair to compare him to Swayland – just cos he's his son! It's no reason to break up with him.' Her voice was suddenly savage, and Magda blinked while Jo wondered why Tess was being so emphatic.

'He said Swayland was a letch too,' Tess went on. 'Or Jaycee did and he didn't deny it. Jaycee said he'd put the moves on her and he was pulling the same thing on Gwen. Which might explain why she's on his side.'

'But is she?' Magda asked. 'Maybe she doesn't know about the roundabout either.'

'She made it pretty clear she didn't care,' Tess said judgementally. 'Carly was the only one of you who came to the protest and I was foul to her.'

'I've been trying to tell Jo how much Carly's trying,' Magda said. 'She took a note to Seb for me and I wish I hadn't asked her to now. She came back completely miserable and said Seb's mother was a witch and Seb was moving to Spain because of his dad. And that she didn't understand why I'd broken up with him.'

'I don't really understand that either,' Jo said and Tess nodded.

'Nor me. One moment the two of you are like Romeo and Juliet and the next—'

'Shut up!' Magda all but screamed it. 'That's exactly what Carly said. I hate that stupid play. We've been doing it all summer in English and it makes me want to kill myself. If my parents actually read my school report they'd see I'm failing English because I can't bear to write about it. It's horrible being in love with the wrong person. It's just as well Seb's mother is vile and his father's a bastard and he's moving to Spain. Because I can't live with myself this way.' She was crying again and through the tears she continued passionately, 'I never thought I was good, but now I know I'm bad. I'm a horrible, lying, selfish person. I let my parents down and I let *you* down, Tess. All I could think about was being with Seb, no matter who it hurt. If it wasn't for me, you wouldn't have had such a bad time recently, or got in so much trouble and run away.'

Tess and Jo stared at her and then, as Magda bowed her head, her shoulders heaving, their eyes met. Now Jo understood that Magda blamed herself for everything, even things that weren't even slightly her fault. No wonder she was such a mess.

'Mags,' Tess said, touching Magda's shoulder. For a

moment she was as gentle as Magda could be. 'Your parents just don't want you dating anyone. They don't see you properly. They've seen you as their little nun for too long. You know, you're allowed to be yourself.'

'And there's nothing wrong with wanting a boyfriend,' Jo added. 'You wouldn't have had to tell a heap of lies if your parents just accepted that.'

'And I didn't go all because of you, Mags. You're my best friend. I just needed some time to think,' Tess continued.

'Look,' Jo went on, 'ask yourself what you really want, Magda. What would make you happy.'

'What if I want to live here in Accleton all year round?' Magda asked. 'And stay on at school after sixteen and go to college and get a job? What if I'd like to live on the top of Nightingale Hill in a house with stained-glass windows and a heated swimming pool instead of shivering in a freezing cold caravan full of screaming children?'

Surprised by this stream of confession, Tess looked at a loss for words.

'Well, if you want that you'd better pass English,' Jo said finally and Magda smiled, blushing at her own vehemence.

'It's not wrong to want to change, Magsie,' Tess said after a minute. 'It's how you do it that's important. If you want your parents to see you, you have to tell them how you feel, instead of pretending to yourself and letting them go on believing you're someone you're not.'

'She's right,' Jo said. 'Now, Magda, your mam made you promise you'd go straight to the launderette and back.' She stood up. 'If we run we might get lucky and they won't have spotted we're gone; otherwise we'll be grounded until the end of time.'

Jo opened the door. It was still pretty wet outside, the trees and bushes dripping.

'We're going to have to brave it,' she said. 'Come on, Tess, get your stuff, you're coming with us.'

'Says who?' Tess said, bridling, and Jo rolled her eyes.

'You can't stay here forever,' she said, 'and Magda won't come back without you, and if we don't get back soon her parents will throw her out and she'll have to live with me, and it'll be very cramped in my bedroom.'

'It'll be cramped there anyway,' Tess said, 'since if I come back, I'm not staying with Reenie.'

'Go and stay with Carly then,' Jo suggested, picking up her bag. 'I'd like to see what you'd look like in *her* jeans.'

Tess laughed. 'That's not a bad idea though,' she said as they went out into the dripping field. 'A week in that shack and all Magda's talk about cold caravans make the idea of a house very tempting. For now anyway.' She glanced at Magda. 'But what was all that about stained-glass windows? You always did get moony about that one in the church.'

'It's where I met Seb,' Magda said, slowing down. She still looked a bit shell-shocked, but there was some colour in her cheeks now and at least she wasn't dissolving into tears any more.

'What're you going to do about that?' Jo asked carefully and Magda sighed.

'I don't know,' she said. 'Even if my parents let him see

me I don't know if he'd want to get back together. Not if he thinks I broke up with him because of his father – it's a bit shallow, isn't it? And it's hardly an ideal match anyway. Besides, he might be going to Spain.'

'It'll be all right,' Tess said fiercely. 'Anyway, even if your parents do ground you forever they'll have to let you out for my roundabout protest.'

'You're going to have another?' Jo asked. 'But I thought you said it was useless.'

'Probably.' Tess shrugged. 'But I'm going to try anyway. I've got some new ideas.'

Magda smiled. 'The sun's coming out,' she said. 'Look, there might be a rainbow.'

'We don't have time to gaze at rainbows,' Jo said, hurrying her along.

She could see the parade of shops ahead and remembered suddenly that she had promised Ian she'd call him tonight. Another reason not to get grounded. Not letting go of Magda's arm, she broke into a run and the others ran with her, soaking wet and grinning like idiots.

19

ROOM OF MIRRORS

Gwen had reception to herself on Tuesday morning. Tuesday was often a quiet day, which was why Mark kept it free for answering his emails and going through his mail. Whenever Gwen saw a shadow come down the glass stairs she tried not to jump and glance up. Mostly it was people leaving the gym, but Mark had been down twice that morning since he first came in. Then, he'd taken his post and his hand had touched hers as she handed it over, lingering long enough to make her blush. Later he'd come down with a fax he wanted her to send, and stood behind her watching as she'd sent it, annoyingly clumsy with the buttons. Just half an hour ago he'd come down to get water from the cooler in reception; the one upstairs was broken, he'd said. Then he'd paused at the desk for a moment before his mobile phone started ringing and he'd gone back upstairs to take the call in his office.

It was nearly lunch time now and Gwen wondered if, instead of getting a sandwich from the cafe, she could ask Kelly from the gym to cover for her for an hour while she went to the pub. If Mark left a bit before her, no one would notice. They'd managed it a few times already.

She fiddled with the work on her desk, trying to make up her mind. A few weeks back, when Charmaine had suggested Jaycee might have a room free in her flat when Kelly moved out, they'd all gone to lunch together a couple of times. But there was a barrier somehow between her and the other girls. The last few times Gwen had seen them they'd looked at her oddly as they'd gone up the stairs to the gym.

A girl in an army coat came through the doors and shook herself off, raindrops splattering over the mat and on to the carpet. For a moment Gwen thought it was Tess, but when the girl pulled the hood of the coat down she saw it was Carly. The sight annoyed her. She'd been cross with Carly and Magda ever since they'd decided to make her their alibi for that wretched party. She'd known it was a bad idea and she'd never exactly said she'd lie for them. When Mark had called that night and said he was free, she'd forgotten their parents might phone the flat and had gone out.

'Gwen –' Carly crossed the atrium and came up to the desk, dripping everywhere – 'I need to talk to you.'

'This isn't a good time,' Gwen said. 'Do you want a swim pass?'

'No.' Carly shook her head furiously. 'And there's no one here anyway.'

'I'm working,' Gwen snapped.

'This is important,' Carly said. 'Look, Tess is back . . .'

'Back from where?' Gwen said. 'Isn't that her jacket you're wearing?'

'No, it's mine.' Carly tossed her hair. 'She went with me to buy it though. She's staying with us now.'

'Tess? Is staying with you?' Gwen raised her eyebrows. 'Is this one of your stories, Carly?'

'Oh, just shut up and listen,' Carly said; her cheeks were flushed. 'I came to talk to you about something important.'

'All right, but keep your voice down,' Gwen said, casting a nervous glance upwards.

Carly started taking off her jacket. 'It's really hot in here,' she said. 'Is that why you're wearing just that little top?'

Gwen blushed and resisted the urge to cross her arms across her chest. 'What's this important thing you have to tell me?' she said brusquely.

'Tess went missing,' Carly said. 'Which everyone else knew because the police were looking for her. She had a big fight with Reenie and she asked if she could come stay with me. And Magda stayed at Jo's one night but now she's back at home. And we all went shopping in the market and I got this jacket and Magda found me this top and everyone got jeans, all different ones, even Magda.' Gwen waited pointedly and Carly added hurriedly, 'Anyway, Tess said she was going to hold another protest about the roundabout, a better one, on the site this time. We went to see Mrs Mills and she's going to contact newspapers for us, so they'll cover it properly, and help Magda pass English.'

'I don't see why Mrs Mills helping Magda pass English is of importance to me,' Gwen said impatiently and Carly burst into speech again noisily.

'It's the protest that's important. None of the others were going to tell you because they all think you're on his side. But I told them you didn't know anything about it.'

'Know anything about what?' Gwen was getting angry now.

'Your boss,' Carly lowered her voice to a conspiratorial hiss that seemed shockingly loud. 'Mister Mark Swayland. He's the one behind the roundabout.'

'That's not true,' Gwen said immediately.

'But it is. Seb said it was true and so did Gabriella.'

'Who?' Gwen felt bewildered by this sudden flood of information.

'Seb's his son – he was going out with Magda, but he isn't now – and Gabriella's his wife.'

'Magda doesn't have a boyfriend and Mark doesn't have a wife.'

'He does. I've met her,' Carly said. 'While I was waiting for Seb after school last week. She . . .' She stopped and looked at Gwen. 'She thinks you're having an affair with Mr Swayland and she's going back to Spain.'

'She doesn't!' Gwen went scarlet to the roots of her hair. 'I'm not!'

'That's what I said,' Carly said. 'I told the others that too.'

'You told who?' Gwen grabbed Carly's arm over the counter. 'What have you been saying to people?'

'I told them you weren't,' Carly said, pulling her arm

back, 'and that when you found out about the roundabout you'd quit. So come on.'

'What? Don't be ridiculous. This is my job. I work here full-time now.' Gwen subsided back into her chair. 'Don't be ridiculous,' she said again. 'And *stop* talking about me to other people!'

Carly hung over the edge of the desk and looked down at her. Her expression was angry and suddenly despising. It seemed she'd picked up some of Tess's mannerisms as well as her clothes.

'All right then, be like that. But I tried to tell you. It's not my fault if you won't listen.' Her voice broke suddenly and her next words were faltering. 'I told them I didn't b-believe it. But it has to be *true*, d-doesn't it? Or you'd c-care . . .' And suddenly she was gone. The doors swung open and shut again behind her, letting in a cool blast of air and a hiss of rain.

Gwen stared at the shredded tissue she found in her hands. She tried to sort out what Carly had been saying, but it had been such a jumble of things – about Magda's boyfriend and Jo's jeans combined with the news that . . . that Mark was married.

She got up from her desk, switching her phone across to the gym office line as she did so. She felt dizzy as she walked up the glass stairs, looking out and seeing the drop down to the car park and the road beyond. In the distance was a dot that looked like Carly and she turned away and saw herself reflected in the walls of Mark's office, her thin summer top almost see-through when backlit by the sunshine. If he was in there he could see her – she tried not to smooth her hair back in the mirror and knocked on the door instead. But there was no answer.

Heading along the corridor, she went to look in the gym. She threaded her way past the customers and their islands of gym machinery on purple carpet, separated by pathways of wooden flooring. It was all one room. The far wall was glass but the nearer ones were mirrors and Gwen saw distorted reflections of herself coming and going as she approached the gym office.

She spotted Kelly before she saw Mark and wondered what she was looking at. She was standing by a piece of gym equipment and her face was contorted in a grimace of disgust. Nearby, on another carpeted island, was a machine for stretching the muscles in your thighs. A girl Gwen recognized vaguely as a sixth-former from school was using the machine, her long blonde hair knotted up on top of her head, her crop top exposing her flat stomach and her long tanned legs in cycling shorts slowly and carefully lifting weights. Beyond the machine was the desk which watched over the entrance to the changing rooms and Mark stood there, leaning over it as if he'd been talking to Kelly, but looking at the girl exercising, staring.

Gwen felt suddenly sick. But Kelly had seen her now, she couldn't turn away. She crossed the room towards Mark, feeling as if everyone in the gym was watching her. 'Hi,' she said as she reached the desk. 'I was just looking for Mark actually.' She looked at him and he straightened up from the desk and smiled at her, showing his even white teeth.

'And you found him,' he said. 'What can I do for the lovely Gwendolen?'

Gwen blushed. She was sure Kelly was watching, for all that she was suddenly pretending to be busy.

'Um, could I have a word with you in your office?' she asked. She saw Kelly hide a smirk and Mark suddenly frowned.

'Well, if it's something that can't wait. But it'll have to be quick,' he said. 'I've got a lunch engagement.'

When they reached the office he opened the door and went in ahead of her, turning when he reached the desk and sitting on it.

Gwen stopped, seeing herself reflected in the mirror glass walls and feeling as pale and watery as her mirror self.

'I wanted to ask you . . .' she said, trying to find words. 'Is it true your wife's left you? Because of—'

'Where did you hear that? No, it's not true. Gabriella's mother is ill and she's gone back to Spain to look after her. Who've you been talking to?' Mark's face looked cold and hard.

'I'm sorry,' she said. 'I . . . I just wondered . . . you never said you . . .'

'Is that all?' Mark asked, cutting her off. So it was all true, Gwen realized. He was married, and he didn't even care if she knew it. And if that was true . . .

'Remember when we talked about my Traveller background?' Gwen asked, feeling shaky as she remembered how he'd said it – she already knew the answer. 'You know there's a Traveller site next to where this new roundabout's being built, don't you?'

'The development doesn't come within a hundred metres of the legally protected area,' he said sharply. 'Has someone been asking about it? Was it the press?'

'No,' Gwen said, 'I'm asking. I want to know, are you involved with the roundabout?'

'You make it sound as if I'm having an affair,' Mark said, laughing suddenly, and Gwen hugged her arms across her chest and stared blankly out from his office, towards the main reception desk. The view Mark had of her every day. 'What are you looking at?' Mark demanded and Gwen was about to say 'nothing', when she realized she was, in fact, looking at someone climbing the stairs. It was a man in a long dark coat. Mark seemed to stiffen as the visitor reached the top of the stairs and approached the door. Then for a moment she thought she'd made a mistake and it was Mark's reflection she'd seen, before the door opened and he came in. He was a teenager, not an adult.

'Sebastián.' Mark stepped away from Gwen suddenly and the boy looked from him to her.

'Am I interrupting something?' he asked, his voice a cold echo of Mark's, and she realized this must be the boy Carly had mentioned.

'Miss Hughes was just leaving,' Mark said quickly and the boy turned blue eyes on her, a much brighter blue than Mark's. Without even looking at her Mark said, 'Will you give us a minute?'

'Of course,' she managed to reply. She almost ran out of the office.

When she got down to the atrium she went into the

bathroom and threw up her morning cup of coffee. Washing her mouth, out she wiped off her lipstick and then splashed water on her face and took off the rest of her make-up too. Back at her desk, she sat down in her chair and stared at the keyboard, trying to remember what she was supposed to be doing. She didn't know how long she'd been sitting there when a shadow came down the glass stairs and she glanced up. It wasn't Mark. It was the boy, his son, Seb. She tensed as he came over to the desk and looked down at her.

'You're Gwen,' he said eventually.

'Yes,' she said faintly, wishing herself invisible. The expression on his face was almost frightening. Mark's blue eyes had always seemed to strip her naked, but his seemed to see right through her.

'Do you know if they've found Tess?'

'What? Why?' Gwen felt as if she was in a madhouse, nothing was making sense. But the boy was still staring at her and she managed to gather together her receptionist's manner and tell him, 'I think my cousin Carly said Tess Lovett was staying with her, if that's who you mean.'

'Yes, that's who I mean,' he said softly. 'I'm Seb. My father didn't introduce us.'

Gwen nodded. 'Carly said you were Magda's boyfriend.'

'Then you can't have been listening to her,' he snapped, 'since she knows very well I'm nothing of the kind.'

'I *was* listening.' Gwen felt her lips beginning to shake and she covered her mouth with her hands.

'Listen to this then.' He leaned forward over the desk

and said very quietly, much more softly than Carly's whisper, 'My father is not a very nice person and from now onwards I intend to spend as little time as possible in his company.' He paused and his eyes looked at her searchingly for a long time.

'Why are you telling me this?' she managed to say, regaining her nerve. In another moment she would be able to get angry but he didn't give her time.

'Because . . .' he said, and then he stepped back, raising his eyes to something above him. 'Because I would be ashamed to work for him,' he said. 'Especially if I were you.'

'SEBASTIÁN!' The voice thundered from above and Gwen hunched her shoulders as Mark came running down the glass stairs.

'Goodbye,' Seb said as he walked across the atrium. Mark reached the bottom of the stairs and caught at his arm, but Seb shook his hand off and stalked out. Turning his back on her, Mark went back up the stairs as fast as he had come down them.

Only then did Gwen feel the anger finally arrive and with it a sense of colossal stupidity. He'd acted as if he wasn't married and she'd believed it because she wanted to – even though people had tried to tell her otherwise. His own wife and son despised him. And he was funding the roundabout, whatever he said about 'the wonderful richness of gypsy culture'. You'd have to be an idiot to work for someone like that. An idiot or a stupid teenager with a crush. Gwen clenched her firsts under her desk, hating herself and then hating Mark harder. She remembered him looking at Magda's legs and his expression up in the gym earlier. She'd thought she was so grown up for attracting his attention and all the time Charmaine had been right. He *was* a sad old letch – coming on to younger girls because they were the only ones naive enough to fall for his charms. He may not ever have actually done anything, but she would have been willing to had he tried, and he knew it. She must have been so *obvious*.

She would walk out right now. What would he care? He'd hire the next pretty fifth-former who thought she was a grown-up. She reached under her desk for her bag. But then she stopped. Tess was having a protest, Carly had said. A protest against the roundabout. She remembered Tess phoning up about the outside pool offer on the day of the other protest and realized how deep Mark's plans had gone. Well, two could play at that game. Gwen smiled a hard bright smile, the smile of the receptionist, and finally logged back into her computer. It was a pity she didn't know how to trash the entire system, but that would be illegal. However, there was nothing illegal about telling people the truth.

20

BEYOND THE BARRIERS

Tess had woken at six that morning, too keyed up to sleep. Carly was still face down in the pillow with the blankets over her head. Tess had got dressed in the bathroom and scrawled a note reminding everyone what time they were meeting later, before letting herself out of the flat.

This early in the morning the estate was quiet and the sky was a serene blue, letting Tess hope the day would continue fine. Passing the parade of shops she grinned at the multicoloured posters in the window of each one. On blue, yellow, pink and green the black capitals announced:

Accleton shopkeepers say no to the roundabout.
Sign the petition here!
Protest on the Traveller site
Friday 1 August

The Castle shopping mall in town had been useless, but at least half the shops on the ring road had agreed to display the notice. It had been Carly's idea that not all the shopkeepers would be keen to have the traffic load around the town increased, especially those on a main road. Car fumes would get worse and traffic jams would make it harder for local people to get to them.

Carly had gone round the shops the day before, taking Amy, Deborah and Genevieve with her. The three girls had probably come over to Carly's because they were curious about *her*, Tess realized, and hadn't intended to stay. But Tess had convinced them otherwise. They weren't interested in the protest at first, but as Tess had talked they'd become more enthusiastic. They'd promised to come back today too, though Tess thought she knew another reason why; town kids were fascinated by the Traveller site: even when they pretended to look down on it.

Tess was carrying a large shopping bag stuffed with posters and as she reached the chain-link fence around the Traveller site she stopped walking and took them out, resting her other bundle on the ground. The posters were covered in plastic to stop them getting wet and one by one she began to fix them to the fence, exactly as the swimming-pool adverts had been months ago. She made sure each one was at a different eye height so the words could be read by people walking or driving by:

'Make the council listen – speak up for Traveller rights'
'No to more traffic in Accleton'
'Our site, our say!'
'Boycott Bluewater Sports Centre'

They'd decided yesterday that Carly would put up a similar set around the council estate and to Tess's surprise the local girls had said they'd flypost the north end of town and Nightingale Hill.

When she reached the site entrance Tess put down the carrier bag and began to unroll the other bundle, a large sheet wrapped round two tall poles. 'Protest Against the Roundabout – here today!' it read and Tess set it up so it overhung the gate. The poles had to be tied to the fence and Tess was still knotting twine when she heard an angry yell and Peggy came rushing up to the gate, her face red and annoyed.

'Tess Lovett,' she said, 'take that rubbish down at once. You can't put things up here.'

'Yes, I can,' Tess met the site supervisor's eyes. 'People are always putting signs up. Mr Swayland, for example. You didn't tell him to take the swimming-pool adverts down.'

Peggy's face got redder; she'd read the banner by now and was glaring at it. 'No one's said anything to me about a protest,' she growled. 'What makes you think you can just hold an event any time you like?'

'It's a free country,' Tess said, tossing her head. 'And there's no rule that says we have to get your permission.' She waved at the set of rules stuck up on the wall of the site office. 'This is our home, and you can't stop us doing anything that's legal.'

'It's not your home,' Peggy snapped. 'I've heard Reenie's come to her senses and finally thrown you back in the gutter.' She sneered. 'Why am I bothering, anyway? It'll probably be just as pitiful as your last protest.'

Tess bit her tongue as Peggy whirled round and headed back to the office. She continued along the rest of the fence, but her cheerful mood had faded. What if no one came?

When she'd finished she went back in through the entrance, and headed over to the Lakely pitch. In the back of her mind she'd been worrying about Magda, who was still inclined to dissolve into tears suddenly. She'd really been trying these past few days to talk to her parents – but was finding it difficult. However, when Tess reached the trailers she grinned. Magda was already up and she'd got the little kids sat around an old sheet colouring in big letters with felt pens:

Petrol fumes and engine smoke are bad for kids and animals. Don't make us live on a ROUNDABOUT!

The kids had already drawn brown smoke on the top half above grey loops and swirls of roadway. Now they were adding flowers and butterflies to the bottom of the sheet.

Magda looked up from a heap of real flowers. She seemed to have most of a field of daisies soaking in buckets of water, as well as a pile of poppies and a heap of dandelions. Her clothes were covered in pollen and loose petals as her hands worked, twining string around little posies.

'Hey, Tessie,' she said, smiling. 'What do you think of the banner?'

'It's great.' Tess grinned. 'What are you doing though?'

'I thought we could give people posies at the gates,' Magda said. 'You know, when Jo and I last went out that way I noticed how many flowers there are near the construction site. I thought it might make people think about that.'

'It's a nice idea,' Tess said. She looked at Magda, actually seeming happy again, her blonde hair newly washed and hanging loose around her glowing face. 'I don't see how anyone'll be able to resist you,' she said teasingly, and Magda laughed.

The posies were obviously going to take a while, but Magda said she didn't need any help.

'The kids'll help me when they're done colouring in,' she said. 'And Mam'll lend a hand as well. She's inside making pastry now. She said people will need to eat and lots of people are making things so we can sell them to raise money for the fund.'

'What fund?' Tess was surprised. She'd been the one to go all over the site knocking on doors and persuading people they needed to have another protest. They'd been grumpy at first, but Tess hadn't given up. She'd stayed calm and she'd talked, and kept talking, about their rights, about Mr Swayland and how he'd spoilt the earlier protest, and how he was behind the roundabout plan.

'Against the roundabout. It was Alan Hughes's idea,' Magda said. 'Everyone was talking last night and someone pointed out that Carly's folks paid for the posters and they're not exactly rich. Besides, that way people who want to support us can donate to the cause. We're going to

244

ask for the same amount as entry to the swimming pool, that seems fair – since Mr Swayland used it against us.' Her face got hard suddenly and Tess changed the subject.

'So your parents are helping out?' she said and Magda smiled again.

'Mam's doing pies and Da's gone with the men to get tables,' she replied. 'Go on and say hello, everyone's been asking after you.' She paused and looked awkward for a moment before meeting Tess's eyes and saying more softly, 'I talked to Mam at last.'

'Good for you,' Tess said, hugging her impulsively.

'She listened – properly listened,' Magda told her. 'It's a start anyway.' Then she laughed suddenly. 'You know she gave Reenie a piece of her mind for kicking you out. Mam said if she couldn't be bothered to look after you she didn't have any right to tell you how to behave.' She met Tess's eyes again and said seriously, 'Lots of people agreed with her.'

'That's . . .' Tess shifted uncomfortably. It was strange to hear people standing up for her. 'Well, I should go and find out about this fund. Maybe I can get Alan to pay me a wage for organizing the protest!' She grinned to show she was joking and Magda giggled.

○

People were getting up by now and as Tess passed a lot of them called out to her or waved. By the time she reached the central grassed area by the pump, where the kids normally played, she was almost feeling popular. She'd have liked to have been a fly on the wall when Pam Lakely was laying into Reenie.

Trestle tables had been put up on the grass and a group of men was unloading kegs of beer from a van. One of them stopped her as she went by and pointed out a tower of bottles of water.

'Look, Tess, remember when you brought us water at the dump?' he said. 'We thought you'd better have some for your protest.'

Going on past the van, she saw Jo. Like Magda she was surrounded by piles of stuff, but in her case it seemed to be old clothes rather than flowers. Joining her, Tess saw what she was doing. On her own T-shirt she'd drawn the Highway Code sign for a roundabout and then crossed it out with a thick black line. Now she was doing the same thing to each of the ones in the pile.

'Hey, Jo, you're an artist,' Tess said, impressed.

'They look good, don't they? When I heard about Magda's flower idea I thought I should do something.' Glancing up, she added, 'Besides, what else am I going to do? You realize we'll probably never get to go swimming again. Bluewater's the only sports centre in Accleton.'

'No, there's a posh one in the north of town,' Tess corrected her. 'This girl Genevieve was talking about it. They don't have a pool though – it's tennis and riding and that. But she said it's really popular among the townie crowd. Maybe we should all check it out.'

Sitting down next to Jo, Tess started looking through the pile of T-shirts and Jo cocked her head at her.

'Leave those, Tess,' she said. 'Everyone donated their

own in this lot, so they can have one to wear. Ian's got the ones we're going to sell. He's just gone to get more fabric pens.'

'He has, has he?' Tess narrowed her eyes. 'Sounds like you two are getting on pretty well.'

'He's just being a friend,' Jo said quickly, but she ducked her head forward so that her hair swung down to hide her face.

By the time the T-shirts were finished, Magda and the children had shown up with the baskets of posies and they walked together to the main gate. Tess was already there, with Alan Hughes, talking to some people who had stopped to look at the notices. Carly and her parents were there as well and Carly was pouring handmade badges into a big bucket. The kids raced off to offer the first posies.

'It's really all happening,' Carly said, looking flushed and excited. She was carrying the banner she'd brought on the last protest. 'When are we going to march?'

'Not until midday,' Tess told her. 'We need the crowd to build up a bit. Besides, it won't take as long to get to the sports centre as it did to get to the town hall. If we go now it'll all be over too quickly.'

'I wonder how Gwen will feel,' Magda said softly, 'seeing us out there.'

'Forget her,' Carly said, her face looking suddenly pinched and tight. Tess looked at her curiously. 'She's made her choice,' Carly went on. 'It's not our fault.'

'Carly's right,' Tess agreed. 'We don't need any traitors.'

247

◯

By eleven o'clock the site was more like a country fair. Peggy sat inside her office and fumed as more and more people stopped outside the fence to look at the posters, then took a badge or a posy of flowers. Kids from school swarmed in through the gate and a football game was going on at the back of the site. The food stalls were doing a roaring trade – money was building up nicely in the donation tubs. Other Travellers had taken advantage of the situation to advertise building or gardening work or to sell some of the home-made things they'd normally take to the Saturday market.

As she wandered around the site, Tess overheard snatches of conversation between Travellers and townies. It really seemed as if people from town wanted to help. Once Tess passed by a group of people she didn't recognize and heard one say quietly, 'It's nothing like I imagined.'

'Makes you think about those leaflets that come through the door, saying that Travellers are a nuisance,' another replied. 'This site's been here ten years and I've never heard about any trouble.'

'Ten years of fighting just to keep your home,' said a woman holding a toddler. 'Makes you tired just to hear it. No one should have to worry that long.'

Over near the tables of food one woman had draped the door of her trailer with a velvet curtain and set up inside with a pack of tarot cards and a crystal ball. Carly came out of it looking a bit shamefaced and confided to

248

Magda, 'She really did say I'd meet a tall, dark stranger. I thought that was a joke!'

Sitting with the others in a patch of shade, Tess kept looking around the site, counting. '. . . say sixty here, and twenty-two playing football and another ten . . .'

'There'll be enough people, Tess,' Jo said, suddenly coming up behind her. 'Stop worrying. Here.' She tossed a bundle of blue fabric at Tess. 'I made it for you.'

Tess grinned and opened it out, before looking for somewhere to change.

'You can use our trailer,' Magda suggested.

'But you'd better hurry,' Carly added. She'd already unfurled her banner and was practically bouncing on the spot. 'It won't be long now.'

'We can't go without Tess regardless,' Jo said. 'She's the star of this show.'

'And don't you forget it,' Tess told them.

Hurrying back towards the Lakelys' trailers, she passed Reenie standing by a tea table talking to one of her friends. As Tess raced by Reenie looked uncomfortable. Tess held her head high and ran on.

She changed T-shirts in Magda's room. Jo had got better at drawing since the morning, she decided, looking in the mirror at the crossed-out roundabout sign. Leaving her old shirt on Magda's bed, she turned to go but stopped for a second. Magda used to have a mobile of butterflies on strings over her bed. But now it was gone and the butterflies themselves were all over the room, attached to the walls, to corners of furniture and to the window; they glittered and sparkled. Tess smiled at them and then let herself out, beginning to run when she saw the football game had stopped and there was almost no one left between the trailers.

Back on the central bit of grass Alan Hughes was calling through a megaphone, herding people up from the site entrance in rows of three or four. Already the line of the march was snaking around the improvised stalls and trailers and running out of space. Tess ran alongside until she spotted Carly's banner near the front. Carly and Jo were holding either side of it and Magda was stood next to them, tilting her head to check it could be seen above the line of people. Tess squirmed through the crowd to join them.

The Lakely kids were at the very front. Tess could see only the back of their colourful banner, but the felt pens had bled through the sheet so the bright flowers and the grey and brown swirls of roundabout and smoke were clearly visible. There were two police cars pulled up on the pavement and Tess felt a stab of nerves, but the officers were just standing watching. There was also a photographer snapping pictures. In fact there was more than one and as the line began to press forward Tess saw Ian's sister scribbling in a notebook as she talked to one of the Traveller men.

'What's she doing here?' she said.

'She's studying journalism at college,' Jo said casually.

Carly added, 'She interviewed me earlier – she's going to send her article to a national paper. She says she wants to get a photo of all of us.'

Alan Hughes's voice boomed out suddenly from the

megaphone and everyone quietened down as he announced that they were about to leave. Then they were moving forward, people from behind pushing them on as the wave of marchers surged out of the gates and along the pavement of the ring road. Tess turned to see if people in the passing cars were watching and realized that they were stationary. Probably a traffic jam up ahead, she thought. But a lot of placards said things like: 'No more traffic in Accleton' and some of the drivers hooted their car horns in agreement as they passed. The noise mingled with sounds from behind and in front of her. The Lakely kids were shouting the words on their banner like a chant and Ian and his friends, along with Genevieve and *her* friends, were belting out a chorus of 'We Shall Overcome' as if they were at the Cup Final. From further back Tess caught a snatch of a folk song from some of the older people still coming out of the site.

It really was a march; people's feet were falling into step as they came along the road. Tess felt a shout break out of her.

'We don't want a roundabout!' she yelled and then like a drum beat she heard voices echo her words back from behind her:

'WE DON'T WANT A ROUNDABOUT!'

'We don't WANT a roundabout,' Tess deliberately lifted her voice above the noise of the crowd now. 'Make the council sort it OUT!'

'WE DON'T WANT A ROUNDABOUT! MAKE THE COUNCIL SORT IT OUT!'

This time the echo was louder and as Tess raised her voice for the third time more people joined in. It was like a Mexican wave, she thought. Her voice cracked halfway through but the shout continued. Suddenly Alan Hughes was pushing his megaphone into her hands. Tess took it and, as the march came up to the overpass turn-off she found herself leading a chant that shifted and changed as she thought of new words.

'We don't want a roundabout!'

'MAKE THE COUNCIL SORT IT OUT!'

'Listen to the people shout . . .'

'WE DON'T WANT A ROUNDABOUT!'

'What's this protest all about?'

'WE DON'T WANT A ROUNDABOUT!'

She was panting for breath by the time they reached the turn and she shoved the megaphone into Carly's hands as Magda passed her a bottle of water. Carly just managed the next line of the shout in time.

'Carly's even louder than you are,' Magda said as Tess gulped water down. 'You shouldn't smoke, Tess. It's bad for your voice. You could be a singer, you know.'

Tess smiled. 'Shouting's more my line.'

Up ahead was a blur of yellow and Tess suddenly saw what had been slowing all the traffic. A yellow digger seemed to have broken down on the road to the overpass, near the site turn-off. With a recovery truck and police car next to it, traffic was only able to use the one remaining lane. The marchers shook their fists at the digger and doubled their noise as they passed.

'That's a bit of luck though, really,' Tess was saying, when suddenly Magda stiffened next to her.

'That's Seb's dad's car,' she said, pointing. Breaking away from the line of the march, she ran a few metres down the road and Tess followed her, seeing now what Magda had spotted. The digger hadn't broken down. It simply couldn't get on to the works road. A burned-out car blocked the entrance, a red Lexus, now with its soft top charred and the paint peeling away.

A policewoman was arguing with the man in the grey suit whom Tess had met that day on the construction site. A couple of men in orange jackets stood nearby, watching the march as it passed the end of the road.

'Your people will have to go round by the motorway,' the policewoman was saying. 'You can't block traffic like this.'

'I'm making a formal complaint,' the man in the suit insisted. 'This is sabotage. Those Travellers did this.'

'You've no proof of that, sir,' the policewoman said. She turned to look back in the direction of the march and glanced at Tess and Magda. 'You'll have to move this vehicle. We don't want any trouble.'

'They're the ones causing trouble!' The suited man recognized Tess suddenly, his eyes narrowing to an angry glare. 'That girl there's a vandal. She broke into our site a few weeks ago.'

Tess opened her mouth to defend herself but she was interrupted by an adult voice behind her.

'You don't know what you're talking about, mate.' It was Michael Lakely. He had followed them when they left the march and now he put a hand on Tess's shoulder and the other on Magda's. 'None of our kids did this,' he said, meeting the policewoman's eyes. 'They don't steal or damage cars.'

'I'm sure they didn't, sir,' the policewoman said, suddenly much politer than she had been to the suited man. 'Besides, this car wasn't stolen. The owner isn't going to be pressing charges.'

'Mr Swayland certainly will be,' the suited man took a mobile phone out. 'If you'd like to speak to him directly—'

'We've already contacted the owner,' the policewoman interrupted him, 'and since the culprit was his own son he's not interested in going to court. We're giving the boy an official caution. Now, you're going to have to move this vehicle or you'll be arrested for breach of the peace.'

The suited man looked apoplectic. Tess met his venomous glare with a smirk. Then Mike turned her and Magda around.

'Come on, girls,' he said. Tess could hear the chant continuing as he herded them back to the group. 'Don't get mixed up in that,' he added. 'We don't want people thinking Traveller kids are to blame. But shows you what sort of man he is if his own son hates him that much, doesn't it?' He missed the glance Tess and Magda shared briefly. Suddenly he reached out a hand and tousled Magda's hair. 'You're a good girl,' he said, before looking at Tess. 'Both of you are.'

'I am?' Tess said and Mike looked at her steadily.

'You are, Tess, and I've told Reenie that as well. She needs to stop thinking about Kieran when she looks at you. I know you'll not thank me for saying this, Tess, but you're better than that.'

'You're wrong,' Tess said quickly. And then she explained: 'I will thank you for it.' She met his eyes seriously. 'I don't want people thinking I'm like my dad any more.'

Mike looked surprised, but he touched her shoulder again lightly before looking back at Magda.

'I was wrong about Tess,' he said, 'and wrong about you too. It's done you good to have some of her fire.' He laughed suddenly as he added, 'It's just going to take a while not to see you as a little girl dressed up in a wimple! Now, let's get on with this protest.'

Tess and Magda pushed their way forward again through the march. The sports centre was coming up ahead and people were shouting extra loudly as they went past the tall glass office building.

'Tess . . .' Magda said, her voice uncertain. 'Why do you think Seb did that? Wrecked his dad's car?'

'Well, since his dad's a complete bastard it could be for almost any reason,' Tess began. Then she rolled her eyes. 'Oh, come on, Magsie. He did it for you. He's still as crazy about you as you are about him.'

'But I can't be, and how can *he* be if he's going to Spain?' Magda said, sounding desperate. 'I just can't be,' she said again sadly.

'Magda –' Tess turned and met her best friend's eyes – 'you *are*.'

Magda blushed, but she didn't look away. It was Tess who turned, registering that the march had slowed to a shuffle although the chanting was as strong as ever. People were waving their placards and banners at the sport centre's offices. Windows had opened as people looked out of the building at the marchers, but they were too far away for Tess to tell if any of them was Swayland.

There were a couple of police cars in the car park and a short row of uniformed officers near the front steps. The plan for the march had been to come here and leave their banners and signs. But no one had really thought about what they'd do afterwards, except go back. Then Tess saw the TV cameras. There were three of them, each with a journalist stood in front of it with a microphone. Mrs Mills had promised she'd try to contact the news for them and she'd obviously come through. Carly pushed to the front of the crowd to reach the cameras and started talking nineteen to the dozen as she pulled photocopied pieces of paper out of her bag – copies of the plans Tess had found, in case they wanted to use them in their reports. Notes that Tess had written up – from her research into other such builds around the country, the repercussions these'd had.

'Quick!' Tess said, turning to Magda. 'Go and find the little kids and make sure they get in front of a camera.' She didn't wait for a reply but ducked and dived through the crowd until she found Alan Hughes's megaphone. Turning to face the crowd, she shouted:

'Tell Swayland what it's all about!'

People's mouths opened and banners waved as the crowd shouted back:

'WE DON'T WANT A ROUNDABOUT!'

Magda had brought the kids to the front and Tess could see the cameras turning to focus on her. Jo and Ian were holding Carly's banner and they shook it wildly. Jumping up on to the low wall of the car park, Tess urged the crowd on, her dark hair flying wildly. Suddenly the group of policemen seemed more nervous.

The glass doors at the front of the building opened and the chant faltered for a moment as people looked over and saw a petite girl with long red hair coming outside.

'Isn't that Alan's niece?'

Tess spun round to see Gwen coming down the steps of the building. She was walking slowly and deliberately and behind her were about ten other people. Tess recognized Jaycee from the party and some of the others as life-guards. The police and the cameras both turned to watch the group and then suddenly the crowd cheered as Gwen broke into a run and came flying across the car park and into the march. The other staff came with her and turned to join the crowd and face the sports centre, linking arms with the people already standing there.

'What's going on?' Tess said, lowering the megaphone.

Gwen looked up at her. 'It's a sympathy strike,' she said. 'At least, these guys are on strike. I've resigned.'

'I knew it!' Carly grabbed Gwen's arm. 'I knew you would really.'

'I thought it might help if we waited until now to come

out,' Gwen said, putting her arm round Carly. 'But we've been sending people to the Traveller site all day.'

'Let's not waste the moment then,' Tess said, lifting the megaphone again. 'WHAT'S THIS PROTEST ALL ABOUT . . . ?'

21

AROUND AND ABOUT

The campaign went on for most of the summer. It got pretty noisy around the Traveller site for a while. Half the cars that passed would hoot their horns in support. But any noise from the diggers and earth-movers at the western edge of the site had stopped. In a statement to the press, staff problems were blamed. A group of construction workers had left the day after the protest and it was difficult to hire replacements.

Bluewater sports centre cut prices twice and laid off staff as well. The lay-off brought Swayland even worse publicity, since the local newspapers claimed staff had been punished for supporting the protest. In a storm of accusations and counter-accusations the campaign was mentioned several times in the national news and almost daily in the local papers. Anti-roundabout badges and T-shirts were everywhere and even people who were in favour of it got tired of the endless debates in pubs and shops and started saying that even if a roundabout was a good idea, it had been a bad one to try and build it slap bang next to the Traveller site.

Tess was interviewed three times on the news and she half suspected the reason Reenie suggested she move back into the trailer was because her aunt wanted to be seen on TV. But she did go back, because living in a flat just didn't feel right. Besides, on the site she could be where the action was.

The third night after she came back she and Reenie had another screaming match. But she was used to that. What was a lot stranger was when Peggy came round the next morning to complain.

'You Lovetts are always trouble,' she sneered. 'Do you think everyone wants to hear you yelling half the night, Tess? You've got a voice like a bullhorn.'

'She gets it from me,' Reenie said, staring the site supervisor down. 'Has anyone actually complained or are you just poking your nose in where it doesn't belong?'

Peggy gaped at her and Tess grinned suddenly.

'You're as bad as each other!' Peggy spat before storming off.

○

Jo spent a week making T-shirts before announcing she'd go crazy if she drew another roundabout sign. Besides, there was plenty of money in the fund already, so much so that people were talking about using it to lease the temporary side of the site from the council and pull down the barrier in between the two parts.

'If we rent it ourselves, like a cooperative,' Jo's mum

said, 'we can get rid of that awful Peggy and appoint our own supervisor. Alan perhaps or Pam Lakely. Or hire one from the town.'

'Like Pam has time,' Dan pointed out. 'With all those kids.'

'She's got Magda to help,' Jo's dad said, but Jo shook her head.

'Magda's only helping out some of the time now,' she said. 'She's having extra tutoring. You know she was failing half her subjects in her last report.'

'It's about time Pam realized that girl's been doing too much,' her mum said a little indignantly. 'Those kids had worn her down to skin and bone this term. And all that fuss when you girls went to that party . . . If you ask me, Mike Lakely blew it out of proportion. As if Magda's the sort to do something silly. She's such a sweetheart.'

Jo said nothing. She was sewing up the side of a top she was making out of a greeny gold fabric she'd bought at the market. She was actually starting to get good at making her own clothes, and Jenny Hughes had offered to let her sell things from her stall if she'd come and work there on Saturdays.

'Did Magda even have a boyfriend?' Dan asked.

'Ask her yourself if you want to know,' Jo answered.

'She doesn't have to say.' Jo's mum looked at her affectionately. 'You and Magda and Tess are all thick as thieves nowadays, Joanne.' She beamed. 'I knew it'd be good for you to have more girl friends. You're becoming quite a lady.'

'She is?' Dan looked incredulous and Jo aimed a punch at him.

'So anyway, Mum, can I go out tonight?'

'With the girls?' her dad asked and Jo shrugged.

'If they're allowed. And some of the boys from school. We're going down the cinema.'

'If it's a big group,' her mum said carefully, 'then yes. But you're to be back by eleven.'

O

Carly was learning to play tennis. She'd asked her parents if they would pay half the cost of a season pass for the posh sports club that Genevieve went to, if she paid the rest out of her pocket money. To her surprise they'd agreed to pay for the whole thing. She and Genevieve went almost every day, playing doubles against Amy and Deborah. Carly wasn't the best at it, but she was getting better. All four of them played in the anti-roundabout T-shirts Jo had made, and they weren't the only ones.

'Your friend's selling tops to everyone,' Amy said one day as they took a break between sets, sitting together at the side of the courts. 'I saw her selling stuff in the market last weekend.'

'I know,' Carly replied. 'I want her to make me about a million things, but I can't afford it all. Maybe I'll get a job.'

'Maybe we could do babysitting or something,' Genevieve said slowly. 'I'd really like a top like that white one she made for Magda Lakely.'

A boy passing by stopped and looked at them as

Genevieve spoke. Carly realized she knew him just as he said her name.

'Carly, isn't it?'

'I thought you went to Spain,' Carly said. The girls were watching them curiously and Carly blushed a little. She'd forgotten how good-looking he was.

'I did. For a couple of weeks,' Seb said. 'But I came back. My mother decided she wanted to keep the house, so she hired a lawyer, who told her she'd better be living there when the court date comes around.'

'What about your dad?' Carly asked. 'I heard what you did to his car.'

Seb laughed bitterly. 'He's got a Jaguar now,' he said. 'He's living in a flat in town. I haven't seen him since my mother threw his clothes out in the street.'

He was looking at Carly intently and she felt Magda's name on her lips and bit it back. No one mentioned Seb around Magda. But there was something else she felt she wanted to clear up.

'It wasn't true about Gwen, you know,' she said, stepping away so the other girls wouldn't hear. 'She said she went to the pub with him a couple of times but she didn't . . .' Carly trailed off and Seb nodded.

'Though if nothing happened, I bet it's not because he didn't try it on, or plan to,' he added.

'Well, he'd better not try it again,' Carly said. 'Gwen's seeing this guy called Craig now and he is really really muscled. He'd take anyone to pieces if they looked at her wrong.'

'That's . . . good.' Seb gave a twisted smile. 'I almost hope Dad does. I'd like to see that.'

They laughed together a bit awkwardly and Carly glanced back at her friends. 'I should go,' she said. 'We're halfway through a doubles match.'

'Sure. See you around, I suppose.'

The others were eyeing her with interest as they walked back on to the court. Deborah said enviously, 'He's gorgeous . . .'

'He's still looking at you, Carly,' Genevieve whispered, glancing over Carly's shoulder. 'So who is he? Your tall, dark stranger?'

'He's not my tall, dark anything.' Carly grinned at them. 'But . . . wait just one minute, you guys, there's something I forgot to tell him.'

She ran back across the court. 'Look,' she said, 'I know I'm a blabbermouth and I shouldn't say anything. But just in case . . .'

'Yes?'

Carly fiddled nervously with a loose strand of her hair. 'Well, I just thought you should know that Magda's parents are letting her wear jeans now.'

Seb looked completely confused and Carly rattled on quickly, 'And not just that, they're letting her go out with Jo and Tess and these lads from school.'

'What lads?' Seb's voice was tight and Carly sighed.

'No one, no one important. I'm just saying. Things have changed a bit. And . . .' she met Seb's eyes: 'And she misses you. That's all.'

She didn't wait for his reply. She ran back on to the

court, grateful for the cool breeze on her flushed cheeks, and picked up her racket. The others looked at her curiously, but Carly ignored them. It was her turn to serve and she placed her feet carefully, throwing the ball high in the air and getting ready to hit it hard.

○

When Gwen went back to school on the day of her results Mrs Mills stopped her in the hall to congratulate her and to ask once more if she'd reconsider coming back. For months she'd been saying no, but this time she said, 'Maybe.'

'That's wonderful.' The librarian beamed at her. 'I certainly hope you do decide to come back. You've been a real inspiration to some of the other Traveller children, Gwen. I've had a whole group of them come in over the summer and ask to use the library. That's your influence.'

'It isn't,' Gwen shook her head. 'Really.'

Walking back from school into town, she read through her results again. She'd passed everything. Nine passes, two of them As, three A stars. But it seemed as if it they belonged to someone else. She couldn't even remember now doing all that revision. It was the same with Mark; looking back, she felt like an idiot when she remembered the way those gentle hand presses had made her feel. In fact, she blushed to think about it. Even now she wasn't sure how many people knew she'd almost had an affair with him. She'd gone for coffee a couple of times with Jaycee and Kelly and although neither of them had said anything directly, they'd both told stories about Mark hitting on girls in the gym, in a pointed sort of way, before trying to persuade her to apply for a job at the tennis club.

'I don't know.' Gwen sipped her coffee. 'I might go back to school.'

'But aren't you seeing Craig?' Jaycee asked. 'He's working there too now.'

'Well, I don't have to work with him to see him, do I?' Gwen said.

To be honest, she wasn't sure why she was seeing Craig. But the day they'd walked out of Bluewater he'd told her she was a firecracker and he'd called her two nights later to ask if she'd like to come for a drink. In the pub she'd felt nervous, remembering going there with a different man. Craig hadn't been alone, some of his mates were there, although he'd left them when she arrived. Then his mates had joined them later and, although she hadn't said she was going out with him, she'd sort of let them assume it. Craig had offered to walk her back at the end of the evening and she'd said no. But when he'd asked her out again she'd found herself saying yes.

○

Magda stood next to Marianna, holding the hymn book as they sang together. It was hot outside, but in the vast vault of the church it was cool, the stained-glass windows patterning the floor with a patchwork of colour.

As the last verse came to a ringing crescendo Magda put the hymn book down and followed her family out of the pew. They hadn't made it to church together very often this summer, so that morning Mam had said it was time they all went as a family.

There was a queue of people passing the stoup to cross themselves and as the Lakelys moved to say goodbye to the priest an elegantly dressed woman stopped them, putting out a hand with long fingernails.

'Excuse me, you are Miguel . . . that is, Michael Lakely?'

Magda's da stopped and her mam turned to look at the woman rather doubtfully. She was tall and very made up, her eyebrows thin arches and her black hair piled in an elaborate knot on top of her head.

'That's me,' her da said.

'I am Gabriella Delgado,' she went on. 'I wish to donate money to your campaign, against the roundabout. Much money.'

'That's very generous of you, Mrs Delgado.' Magda saw her da trying not to smile.

'*Ms* Delgado,' Gabriella said firmly. 'You see, I have a great interest in your campaign succeeding.' Her eyes passed over from Magda's da to her mam. 'You are Mrs Lakely? I am very pleased to meet you. Are these all your children?'

'That's right.' Pam nodded, always willing to show them off. As she named them in turn, the elegant-looking woman made some polite comment to each of them.

Magda's attention drifted and it was with surprise that she realized everyone was looking at her.

'I'm sorry,' she said, colouring.

Gabriella spoke, eyeing her with a piercing look. 'I

said, you have the face of an angel; I should like to paint you some time.'

'Oh.' Magda looked away. 'I don't think—'

'That's a lovely idea,' her mam spoke across her. 'Are you a painter then, Ms Delgado?'

'I have painted,' Gabriella said. 'I have painted *gitano* boys in España. I would like to paint your children. I have seen some interesting faces among you.' Her eyes narrowed briefly and Magda thought she looked rather alarming. But her mam was beaming and her da looked pleased too.

'Yes, plenty of good-looking kids on our site,' he said. 'Tess is a real Romany. I bet she'd love to be painted.'

'But Tess wouldn't stand still for five minutes,' Magda's mam broke in quickly. 'Would you like to come . . . ' She paused suddenly and Magda guessed what she was thinking. This elegant woman with a foreign accent wasn't exactly the kind of person you invited back to tea.

'I should very much like to see your home,' Gabriella said. 'I have a great interest in your protest and we will also discuss a fee for your daughter. If I am to take up her time, I should pay her for it.'

'That's very—' Magda's da began, but she cut him off again.

'First I must find my son. He will have to drive the car back if I am coming with you.'

Gabriella swept off and they looked after her in silence for a moment before they reached the doorway and the kids ran ahead, out into the sunshine.

'Well, she gives her orders, doesn't she?' Magda's mam looked rather red-faced.

'You get all sorts,' Magda's da was smiling.

'I don't think I want to be painted,' Magda said uncertainly and her mother patted her shoulder.

'Well, if she's no good it hardly matters, but there's no need to make up your mind yet. It would be lovely to have a proper painting of you and if she's willing to pay you for it she must think it'd be worth her while.'

They shook hands with the priest and Magda blinked as they came out into the sunshine. Suddenly there was the clicking of high heels and a black blur appeared to the left.

'Ah, Mr and Mrs Lakely,' Gabriella said and Magda felt herself freeze in the shaft of bright sunshine as she looked past a flash of long fingernails and met dark blue eyes. 'This is my son, Sebastián.'

'Pleased to meet you.' Magda could see her parents talking and she saw Seb's mouth move, but her heart was hammering so hard in her ears she couldn't make out a word.

'. . . Magda? She's off in another dream. Magda . . .' Her mother put a hand on her shoulder and from a long way away she heard the clipped foreign accents of Gabriella Delgado say, 'This sun is too hot for such fair skin; she looks as if she is about to faint. Sebastián! Help her into the shade.'

There was a hand on her other arm and all Magda could see was blue eyes watching her, not moving from her face, as the sunlight faded and she found herself leaning against the cool grey stone of the church wall.

'Shall I get you some water, love?' her mother was asking, feeling her forehead.

Her father appeared again and pushed a slightly warm plastic bottle into her hand before turning to Seb. 'I hope you don't mind, son, but your mother's volunteered you to drive Magda and her mam back to the site.' He ruffled Magda's hair absent-mindedly before adding, 'Go on, Pam. She's been overdoing it on all that schoolwork. We'll catch up to you.'

'Will your mother be all right walking in those high heels?' Magda's mother said and Seb showed white teeth in a sudden grin.

'Gabriella always does what she wants. I'd be honoured to escort you home.' Suddenly warm brown fingers closed around Magda's hand and he bowed over it.

'How about it, fair lady?' he said.

Magda swallowed and pushed herself upright, out of the shade and into the light.

'Thank you,' she said, still feeling light-headed. All summer long she'd felt trapped in a script leading towards a tragic ending but now, suddenly, she was off the page and in another story entirely. Gabriella was an unlikely sort of fairy godmother, but Seb . . . Seb was every inch the prince. And they'd swept in from nowhere, saying all the right things to her parents. Bridged the divide effortlessly, without her having to lift a finger. Perhaps it had never been as big as she'd imagined.

Her mam was still fussing around her as Seb led them to a green Escort.

'Would your daughter like to go in the front? The air-conditioning's a bit better there?' Seb said and they both turned to look at her at once.

Seb was trying to seem serious, but his eyes were shining like stained glass. Her mam appeared thoughtful suddenly, looking from Magda to Seb and back again.

'Yes, I think she'd better,' she said finally. She was already climbing into the back seat. 'So you're Catholic, then, Sebastian?'

'Not a very good one.' Seb's hand slid over Magda's arm as he helped her into the car. 'But I'm trying to be,' he added.

'Well, going to church is a step in the right direction,' her mother said firmly as Seb started the engine. 'Don't you agree, Magsie?'

Her eyes met Seb's and she took a deep breath. 'Yes,' she said softly. 'I do.'

EPILOGUE

From the grey ribbon of the M1, passing motorists can see the sprawling construction site. Metal girders jut out of the churned ground, but the piles of earth, gravel and sand are almost gone, battered down to nothing by wind and rain.

In December the ground is frozen and the scrubby bushes, hacked back to make space for the construction site, provide little cover. The bulldozers and earth-movers are long gone. But pieces of paper and plastic bags are strewn about, collected into piles by the wind. A piece of newspaper flaps wildly as a gust assists its flight. Snagging on a concrete post, the newspaper page flutters like a flag. The words of the headline appear and disappear as the paper struggles to escape: Travellers Win Stay on Development Plan. *Beneath it, a photograph of five girls staring defiantly into the camera, with newsprint-shadowed eyes and blurred ripples of long hair. At first there's no obvious similarity between the subjects of the photograph and the five figures coming sideways along the slope, forcing their way against the gusts of wind. The tallest of the five is the first to stop, brown hair whipping into her face, shading her eyes to look back in the direction of town.*

She's dressed in a dark blue jacket that fits as if it's been made for her, despite the fact she's grown another inch already this month.

'You know,' she says out loud, 'they may build it after all. Once the fuss has died down.'

'I doubt it.' The smallest of the group has come up beside her. Her red hair is ruffled this way and that by the breeze. It's not short, reaching to her shoulders, but it's not long either since she chopped off a good two feet of it with a pair of kitchen scissors. 'A bunch of people at the pub were saying they should move the roundabout north to where the dump is and relocate that.'

'Seb says his dad is thinking of selling Bluewater,' the third girl says slowly. Her face is pink with cold, framed with loose waves of blonde hair from which the sun-streaks have long since faded. A butterfly hairclip holds it away from her face. 'It's had so much bad publicity – a lot of people are still boycotting it.'

The fourth girl jumps up to stand on a large concrete block. Of all of them she's the least warmly dressed, wearing a red jumper instead of a jacket, but she doesn't seem cold. Her expression is calmly confident and her blue eyes snap with determination.

'Maybe the roundabout will get built somewhere,' she says clearly, 'but we know about it now and if the council wants to build it here they've got a fight on their hands.'

'That's right,' the youngest member of the group agrees, nodding so vigorously that the hood of her new army coat

falls back, spilling thick ginger waves of hair down her back. She looks at the concrete block. 'Give me a hand up?'

The girl on the block reaches down to pull her up. Then she turns, in the rapidly shrinking space, to offer a hand to the next.

'Why is it whatever we do always ends up in climbing something?' the girl with shorter hair asks. But once all four of her friends are standing on the concrete block and reaching their hands down for her, she gives in and lets them help her up.

Now they're standing together it's easier to see the resemblance to the newspaper photograph. But the wind has finally torn that piece of paper from its temporary flagpole and sent it flapping across the site. The girls too are balancing precariously, clinging on to each other, half supporting and half threatening to push. Another sharp gust surges and the girl in the red jumper leaps out, landing with a scrunch on the ground below. The others follow almost at once, jumping or dropping down to join her and then following as she runs down the slope.

'I borrowed a twenty from Dan,' she calls back, long dark hair whipping about her face, 'and got us some Coke and crisps. They're back at the den if you want some.'

'That's my *den,' the girl in the handmade jacket points out, 'and* my *brother.' But she's laughing and the girl in red grins back at her.*

'He must be sweet on you if he keeps lending you money,' the youngest says shrewdly. 'Surely he knows you're not going to pay it back.'

'She'll pay it back,' the girl with the butterfly hairclip says, smiling as she adds, 'eventually.'

'If you need cash, there's that job going at the country club,' the girl with shorter hair reminds them. 'I was tempted, but I've decided I'm going back to do A levels.'

There's a chorus of refusals, but the girl in red looks thoughtful. Glancing up the hill to the distant town she says, 'Well . . . maybe. I can see me at a tennis club.'

The others laugh at the idea and she joins in, but as they slip and slide down the hill, pushing through the under-growth along the motorway verge, she's back to looking thoughtful again. Her fingers itch for a cigarette but she's cut down to three a day, so that's not surprising. On either side arms are linked through hers and the five girls hunch together into the wind.

As they push on through the wasteland the driver of a haulage truck glances away from the road for long enough to see them silhouetted against the hillside. It's not often you see anyone on the motorway verges. He's been doing this route for just over a year and he's only seen people up there once before. Travelling the long roads, you did get a glimpse of the people living beside the grey ribbons of the motorways, once in a while.

ACKNOWLEDGMENTS

This novel was inspired by a photograph of a group of Traveller girls taken by Jo McGuire.

During my research of the gypsy and Traveller lifestyle I found the following books especially helpful: *Traveller Children* by Cathy Kiddle, *Moving On* by Donald Kenrick and Colin Clark and *The Traveller-Gypsies* by Judith Okely. Any mistakes are, of course, my own.

Also by

RHIANNON LASSITER

WAKING DREAM

When Bethany's father dies she feels her life is over. Forced to spend the summer with her awful cousin Poppy, she escapes into her daydreams.

Poppy is always the centre of attention. Pretty and popular, she uses black magic to keep it that way. But secretly she'd like to leave it all behind.

When Rivalaun, a beautiful, strange boy, arrives out of nowhere to claim he's their cousin, all three start to doubt that what they've been told about themselves is true. Unable to resist the chance to find out who they are, they follow the truth that calls from their dreams. But, as sleep closes in, can they be sure they will ever wake again?

'Gripping and terrifying'
Bookseller

A selected list of titles available from Young Picador and Macmillan Children's Books

The prices shown below are correct at the time of going to press.
However, Macmillan Publishers reserves the right to show new retail prices
on covers, which may differ from those previously advertised.

Rhiannon Lassiter

| Waking Dream | ISBN-13: 978-0-330-39701-8 | £4.99 |
| | ISBN-10: 0-330-39701-X | |

Julia Bell

| Massive | ISBN-13: 978-0-330-41561-3 | £4.99 |
| | ISBN-10: 0-330-41561-1 | |

Julie Bertagna

The Opposite of Chocolate	ISBN-13: 978-0-330-39746-9	£4.99
	ISBN-10: 0-330-39746-X	
Exodus	ISBN-13: 978-0-330-39908-1	£5.99
	ISBN-10: 0-330-39908-X	

Julie-Burchill

| Sugar Rush | ISBN-13: 978-0-330-41583-2 | £5.99 |
| | ISBN-10: 0-330-41583-5 | |

All Pan Macmillan titles can be ordered from our website,
www.panmacmillan.com, or from your local bookshop
and are also available by post from:

Bookpost, PO Box 29, Douglas, Isle of Man IM99 1BQ
Credit cards accepted. For details:
Telephone: 01624 677237
Fax: 01624 670923
Email: bookshop@enterprise.net
www.bookpost.co.uk

Free postage and packing in the United Kingdom